CANARY ISLAND

Center Point
Large Print

Also by Robin Jones Gunn
and available from Center Point Large Print:

Under a Maui Moon

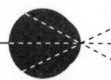

**This Large Print Book carries the
Seal of Approval of N.A.V.H.**

CANARY ISLAND Song

ROBIN JONES GUNN

CENTER POINT PUBLISHING
THORNDIKE, MAINE

This Center Point Large Print edition is published in the year 2011 by arrangement with Howard Books, a division of Simon & Schuster, Inc.

This book is a work of fiction. Names, characters, places, and incidents either are products of the author's imagination or are used fictitiously. Any resemblance to actual events or locales or persons, living or dead, is entirely coincidental. Scripture quotations marked MSG are from *The Message*. Copyright © 1993, 1994, 1995, 1996, 2000, 2001, 2002. Used by permission of NavPress Publishing Group. Scripture quotations marked NLT are from the New Living Translation, copyright 1996, 2004. Used by permission of Tyndale House Publishers, Inc., Wheaton, Illinois 60189. All rights reserved.

The text of this Large Print edition is unabridged. In other aspects, this book may vary from the original edition. Printed in the United States of America on permanent paper. Set in 16-point Times New Roman type.

ISBN: 978-1-61173-159-0

Library of Congress Cataloging-in-Publication Data

Gunn, Robin Jones, 1955–
Canary island song / Robin Jones Gunn.
p. cm.
ISBN 978-1-61173-159-0 (library binding : alk. paper)
1. Weddings—Fiction. 2. Chick lit. 3. Large type books. I. Title.
PS3557.U4866C36 2011b
813'.54—dc22

2011012181

For *mis niñas*
Anne, who invited me to her Canary Island
hideaway where we sat together in
the sun and wrote our hearts out.
Christiana, who signed us up for
flamenco lessons.
Lydia, who taught the three of us to
dance "from the stomach up."

Don't let your heart wander off.
Stay vigilant as long as you live.
Teach what you've seen and heard
to your children and grandchildren.
—Deuteronomy 4:9, MSG

The Spanish language is rich with sage
sayings called *refranes*. These adages reflect
the insights of the one who speaks them
and are considered to be given either as a
blessing or as a warning to the listener.

1

"Dime con quién andas y te diré quién eres."
"Tell me with whom you walk,
and I will tell you who you are."

THE WEDDING COORDINATOR calmly placed her hand on Carolyn's back and whispered, "Not yet. Wait for your song."

Carolyn lowered her chin and listened. All the planning, all the stress, all the tiffs with her twin sister fell away. She drew in a grateful breath and listened. This was it. The long-awaited moment had arrived.

Self-consciously fingering the nape of her neck, Carolyn checked to make sure her coffee-colored hair still complied with the hairpins holding her French twist in place. All was as it should be. She was ready—more than ready—for this day and all the changes it would bring.

The airy-fairy harp music that had subdued the guests as they were being seated came to a resonating pause. From the balcony the first decisive notes of "Air" from Handel's *Water Music* flitted about the cavernous space of the beautiful, landmark San Francisco church.

"Okay, this is it." The wedding coordinator nudged Carolyn forward. "This is your song."

Carolyn squared her bare shoulders. Inwardly

she corrected the wedding coordinator. *No, this is not my song. This is my sister's song.*

Leading with her left foot, Carolyn trekked down the white runner, keeping pace with the song Marilyn had insisted be used as the processional music. The seventy-five guests, who were gathered in the first twelve rows, turned their heads. Carolyn was aware of their gaze as she made her way forward in her tight-fitting satin dress.

Larry, the perspiring groom, stood by the altar with his hands firmly clasped and his quivering smile fixed in place. Carolyn gave her soon-to-be brother-in-law a confidence-boosting grin, and he responded with a nod of acknowledgment.

From the end of the second row, Carolyn's twenty-three-year-old daughter, Tikki, leaned out into the aisle with her camera ready. She gave her mom a wink and snapped a picture. Carolyn smiled back and noticed that Tikki's boyfriend wasn't with her. *Where's Matthew? Why isn't he here?*

A familiar ache and longing came over Carolyn as she thought of Jeff. He should be here today too. But he was gone. The weighted memories of Jeff's death threatened to take Carolyn into a deep, dark place. She refused to go there. Not today.

Casting aside all thoughts except the ones essential for the moment, Carolyn took the next few steps slowly and reverently. She found her masking tape mark on the burgundy carpet. She pivoted toward the congregation just in time to see Marilyn's two teenage daughters making their way down the aisle in their bubble-gum pink bridesmaid's dresses. Once again Carolyn was aware that her forty-five-year-old figure didn't pull off the ensemble the way her nieces' adolescent bodies did. But this was Marilyn's day, and all the choices were hers, as they should be.

The *Water Music* faded. The organist took her cue and played the familiar bridal march as Marilyn came into view. Her sequined wedding gown caught the light and shimmered. Marilyn promenaded down the aisle, every inch the stunning bride she had worked so hard to be.

The congregation came to their feet and turned toward the bride. With a full-lipped smile, Marilyn came forward beaming. She placed her hand in Larry's and proceeded to the altar.

As the vows were recited, Carolyn bit the inside of her cheek. She couldn't stop thinking about Jeff. During the exchange of rings, she curled and uncurled her toes. When the soloist sang out from the balcony in clear soprano notes that pierced the air, Carolyn blinked back the tears and swallowed several times in quick succession. Larry and Marilyn kissed, and the organist played the recessional march, going

11

after the keys and foot pedals with gusto as the newlyweds stepped forward into their life together.

Carolyn took the arm of her assigned groomsman and proceeded down the aisle with the broadest smile she could muster. Her heart was pounding fiercely, and her throat was tightening. She pushed against the intense feelings with well-disciplined determination and reminded herself that this was a celebration.

Marilyn and Larry had stepped to the side, where they posed for the photographer. Carolyn wanted to slip away to the hidden refuge of the restroom so she could give way to the tears that kept rising up in her with such a bittersweet persistence. But she wasn't allowed the luxury. The photographer's assistant directed Carolyn to take her place beside her sister, lean in close, and lift her bouquet up to her chin.

With a resolve that had grown in her spirit over the past seven years, Carolyn folded her private grief the way her mother used to fold her valued linen tablecloth. All the corners matched neatly. All the wrinkles were smoothed away. Then, in the same way that her mother would place the tablecloth into her bottom dresser drawer, Carolyn tucked her personal pain back inside where no one would see it. She smiled for the photos and whispered to her sister, "I'm so happy for you. You look radiant, Marilyn."

Marilyn turned to her and lowered her chin. "How's my eye makeup? Did I smear it?"

"No. You look good."

"Are you sure?"

"Yes, I'm sure."

"Would you mind clearing out things from the bridal room before you leave for the reception? And bring my purse, will you? We're going to dash for the limo now before everyone comes out."

"Sure." Carolyn trotted down the hall in her not-so-comfortable shoes, ready to dutifully fulfill another errand for her twin. This was good. As long as she was busy, she felt balanced. Using a trash bag as a catchall, Carolyn cleared their belongings from the bridal room. She was just gathering up the last sweater and a pair of her niece's flip-flops when Tikki appeared.

"I thought I'd find you here." Slim, vivacious Tikki looked around the room. "Do you need help with anything?"

"No, I'm done. I just need to put this in my car and head for the reception. Remind me to take Marilyn's purse in with me when we reach the restaurant."

Tikki took the trash bag from her mom. "Just think, you won't be cleaning up after the little princesses anymore."

"Tikki, be kind. They're your cousins."

"I know. I'm just saying that, when Aunt

Marilyn returns from her honeymoon, they'll all move into Larry's town house, and you'll have your home to yourself finally after . . . how many years?"

"They moved in about six years ago."

Tikki opened her hazel eyes wide in response to her mother's reply. "Has it been that long?"

Carolyn noticed the way the thin February sunlight coming through the thick-paned window rested a moment on Tikki's face, touching her eyes with flecks of amber. Years ago, on a golden beach far away, Carolyn had been told that her hazel eyes did the same thing—they captured the sunlight and "were sprinkled with gold dust."

With a gathering boldness in her voice, Carolyn said, "We are Women of the Canaries. And Women of the Canaries stick together."

Tikki laughed. "Now you sound like your mom or Aunt Frieda."

"Well, it's true. I was there for Marilyn when she needed me, and one day, if I ever need her assistance and support, she'll be there for me."

Tikki gave her mom a skeptical glance and flipped her long brown hair over her shoulder. She gripped the trash bag and linked her arm through Carolyn's. "I wish your mom could have come today. I know it's a long way from the Canary Islands, but it felt as if someone were missing without her here. When it was time for Aunt Marilyn to come down the aisle, it didn't feel right seeing Aunt Frieda stand instead of Abuela Teresa."

Carolyn was glad Tikki felt that way. She was also glad that Tikki still referred to her grandmother by her Spanish title of "Abuela Teresa," complete with the proper accents. It had been more than three years since Abuela's last visit to California. She had planned to come to the wedding up until a week ago, when a virus got the best of her and settled in her ears. Her trusted doctor in the Canary Islands advised her not to fly because her eardrums might burst.

"I wish she had been able to come too. I really miss her." Carolyn tried to make a smooth transition to her next comment. "What about Matthew? I was looking forward to seeing him today too."

Tikki pulled her arm out of her mother's and put a significant amount of muscle into opening the door that led to the church parking lot. "He had to work. He tried to get off, but it turned into a mess. I told him I understood, but now I'm not feeling quite so understanding. I wish he were here."

As they drove across the Golden Gate Bridge on their way to the reception in Sausalito, Carolyn found it difficult not to ask questions about Matthew. Tikki's relationship with Matthew had seemed strong for so long. Carolyn adored the twenty-five-year-old self-starter and had thought, from their first date more than two years ago, that he was an ideal match for her only daughter. Tikki chatted about her job the whole way. Thoughts of Matthew and Jeff were neatly put aside. This was a good thing.

Carolyn turned into the parking lot of Sadie's Garden Restaurant and walked toward the awning-covered front door. Tikki asked, "Has this been hard for you, Mom, watching your sister get married?"

"No, of course not. I'm happy for Marilyn. Why? Am I coming across differently?"

"No, you're coming across as your normal gracious self. It's just that she's married now, and I know you're a strong woman, like Aunt Frieda always says. But I wondered if it was hard on you, or if you're eager to move on. Because it seems to me you're in the perfect place to make a fresh start. With Marilyn and the girls out of your house, you can focus on your own life and future instead of theirs."

Carolyn felt her defenses rise. She would be the first to admit she had spent the past few years conveniently hiding behind her twin sister's slightly chaotic life. It was a large enough life to hide behind. But Carolyn could admit that truthful fault only to herself. She didn't want to discuss it with Tikki or anyone else.

They were almost to the restaurant's door when Tikki stopped and placed her hand on Carolyn's arm. "Mom, I hope you're not taking any of this

16

the wrong way. All I'm saying is that it's time for you to get a life. Your own life."

Tikki opened the door and entered the restaurant, leaving Carolyn alone with the uncomfortable implications of her daughter's brashly delivered insight. Keeping her expression fixed, Carolyn entered Sadie's Garden and made her way to the reception being held in the expansive, covered, back patio area. The walk through the restaurant allowed her time to regain her composure after Tikki's pointed comments. She knew her daughter's motivation was born of kindness, even if her tact was a bit undeveloped.

The wedding reception was in full swing as the two of them entered the area reserved for their private party. Carolyn smiled when she saw the beautifully decorated patio. Everything had turned out even lovelier than she had imagined. Marilyn had left all the details of the reception to Carolyn, explaining to anyone who asked that parties weren't her thing and that her sister had much better instincts when it came to decorating.

Carolyn had enjoyed the assignment. She had assembled a binder, complete with garden party pictures from magazines and oodles of printed-out ideas she had found online. The patio was garnished with enormous hanging baskets of white flowers. Cutout white lanterns hung from every pillar, sending out firefly twinkles as the sun set. Space heaters warmed the enclosed area on this cool February afternoon, and the cushioned chairs around the elegantly set tables invited guests to sit, relax, and enjoy.

"Wow! This is beautiful," Tikki said. "You did this, didn't you, Mom? You helped Aunt Marilyn pull this together."

"I did. It was fun to work on. Marilyn wanted an enchanting 'fireflies and fairy-tale' reception. So what do you think? Did I capture it?"

"I think you captured it perfectly. You could do this for a living, Mom. You're a natural."

"Thanks." All her earlier frustrations toward Tikki and her "get a life" comment dissolved.

Joining other guests in the buffet line, Carolyn and Tikki leisurely helped themselves to the assortment of appetizers artistically arranged on fluted seashell serving platters. Happy conversations started up as Marilyn flitted from table to table with her much more relaxed groom in tow.

Spotting Carolyn and Tikki, Marilyn made a beeline for them. Carolyn anticipated hearing her sister rave about the decorations and how everything had turned out. Instead, Marilyn said, "I'm having a lipstick crisis here. My lips are so dry they're cracking. And I need a breath mint something terrible. Where's my purse? You didn't forget it, I hope."

"No. It's in the car. I'll get it."

"I'll go, Mom." Tikki gave Marilyn a smile

before dashing off. "Don't you think my mom did a great job with the decorations?"

"Of course she did a great job. She always does." A tinge of adolescent envy clung to Marilyn's words. Turning to Carolyn, her expression softened and she added, "It's exactly what I wanted. Thanks."

"You're welcome."

"Can you do one more favor for me?"

"Sure. What do you need?"

"When Tikki comes back, would you put my purse over by the cake table? We're going to have our first dance and then cut the cake. They're ready for us to cut the cake now, but I don't want another picture taken until after I reapply my lipstick."

Marilyn became the center of attention as she and Larry hit the dance floor. This was their debut performance after an eight-lesson crash course in ballroom dancing. The guests gathered around as the newlyweds swayed to their song, "Let It Be Me." Carolyn knew that Larry wanted to go with the original version recorded by the Everly Brothers, but Marilyn's preference prevailed. And here they were, dancing to David Hasselhoff crooning the lyrics.

The song concluded, and Marilyn led Larry by the hand to the cake table. Carolyn had everything ready—the purse, the lipstick, the breath mints. Tikki stood beside her, snapping pictures as the couple linked arms to sip their toast and politely offer each other their first bite of wedding cake.

The DJ turned up the volume, and the bass tones caused tiny ripples in the water in the crystal goblets around the table. Marilyn raised both arms in the air like an Olympic champion and pointed. Her gesture seemed to be a universally understood indication that the dance floor was now open for everyone to join in the fun.

Tikki was among the first to take Marilyn up on the invitation. Carolyn returned to her place at a table where she unstrapped the narrow band on her high heels and tucked her bare feet under the long white tablecloth. It felt good to wiggle her toes and stretch her arches. Her days of traipsing around in stylish but agonizing shoes had come to an end. Her duties for her sister were about to come to an end too. Carolyn drew in a deep breath.

Aunt Frieda came toward her carrying a piece of cake. Before taking her seat, she tilted her head at Carolyn and said, "I don't know if anyone else has mentioned this to you, *Carolina,* but you should know that that shade of pink you're wearing is not your best color."

"I would agree, Aunt Frieda. It's not my best color."

"You look like you're wearing undergarments."

"I am wearing undergarments."

"No, I mean the dress looks like an undergarment. If you didn't have such nice legs, that outfit would be a complete disaster."

"Thank you, Aunt Frieda. I'll take that as a compliment." Carolyn had a special place in her heart for her orange-haired aunt. Frieda insisted her stylist had done her a favor years ago by "coaxing out her inner redhead." She refused to believe the shade was more on the orange side than the red side of the color spectrum. She also refused to believe that the quips that came out of her mouth were often more on the offensive side than the helpful side. Aunt Frieda was always herself and Carolyn liked her. Very much.

"Aunt Frieda, I'm surprised you're not out there dancing your little heart out with Tikki and Marilyn's girls."

"I'm waiting for them to play the real music. Then I will show you what real dancing looks like." Frieda lifted her arms over her head and snapped her fingers as if she were clacking a pair of castanets.

"I don't think Marilyn requested that the DJ play any flamenco music."

"No? Such a pity. You know, if it were not for the obvious fact that the two of you are identical twins, I would think Marilyn was your sister from another mister. You have the heart of a Woman of the Canaries, but Marilyn . . ." Frieda gave her wrist a dismissive flip in the air.

"She's not been there yet. She didn't have the same advantage I did."

"That was her choice. You know she could have gone with you and your mother the summer you were eighteen, but she refused. Refused! What teenage daughter would refuse the gift of such a trip? There is nothing of the Canaries in her spirit. But you! You are the favorite. You always have been."

Carolyn never enjoyed being compared with Marilyn, even if she was the one coming out ahead. Even so, she offered a faint smile of appreciation for the compliment.

"Now, *dígame,* tell me," Frieda said. "What do you have to say of your romantic interests?" She leaned back, poised to receive all the pertinent details, her eyes fixed. She reminded Carolyn of a cat sitting in front of a fishbowl, swishing its tail, waiting for just the right moment to make its move.

2

"A palabras necias, oídos sordos."
"Take no notice of the stupid things people say."

I'M AFRAID I have nothing to report in that area." Carolyn noted that it had taken her aunt longer than usual to bring up the question of Carolyn's love life. She had her sister to thank for that, since Marilyn had been the focus of Aunt Frieda's love life questions for the past six months. Now the spotlight was back on Carolyn.

Aunt Frieda lifted her right hand and pointed at Carolyn, with her large amethyst ring dominating her index finger. *"Perro que no camina, no encuentra hueso."*

As a child Carolyn had picked up bits of Spanish here and there from her mother's side of the family, who had come to the United States from the Canary Islands in the late 1950s. Three of Carolyn's aunts had returned to the Canary Islands and had convinced her mother to join them almost fifteen years ago, when Carolyn's father passed away. Since then, Aunt Frieda was the only Spanish-speaking relative who lived nearby. She took seriously her responsibility of keeping touches of their shared heritage alive, and Carolyn appreciated her efforts. But she didn't remember enough Spanish to translate her aunt's quote.

"You know what that means, don't you?" Frieda asked.

"No, I don't."

"Of course you do. It means, 'The dog that doesn't walk doesn't find a bone.' And you know who the dog is, don't you?"

"I suppose that would be me."

"Exactly. If you don't get out there and look, Carolyn, you're not going to find anything. *Nada.*

How can you stay warm in your bed at night with *nada?* Look at your sister. Look how happy she is. That could be you. But not unless you start to look."

Carolyn was having a hard time keeping a straight face. Her aunt appeared so serious and intent, just like Tikki had with her admonition about getting a life. With Tikki, the advice stung. With Aunt Frieda, the presentation humored Carolyn.

"You aren't listening to me, are you? Of all people, you should know that each of us must do what we must do." Frieda pointed to her nose and tapped it as her object lesson for this conversation.

Carolyn should have known this oft-repeated topic would be Frieda's next line of attack. Frieda was born with an unusually large nose. When Carolyn was eleven, she and Marilyn came up with a brilliant idea. They took a close-up, side view photo of their aunt and sent it to the *Guinness Book of World Records.* A month later an official reply letter arrived requesting measurements, and the twins were disciplined with the worst restriction of their lives.

The extended family had rallied to Frieda's side now that the elephant in the room had been spoken out into the open. They all pitched in to start a reconstructive surgery fund, and within nine months the necessary amount was raised.

Frieda emerged from the week of bandages and ice packs with the long, slender, Meryl Streep nose she had ordered. In the end, all the relatives gave Carolyn and Marilyn credit for the transformation, and Aunt Frieda insisted that her new nose resulted in her acquisition of a fine husband when she was forty-one.

Carolyn knew the moral of this object lesson and braced herself for Frieda's pronouncement.

"Make opportunities for yourself. That's all I'm saying. You need to help God work out his divine plan for you in this world."

Carolyn quickly retorted, "I don't think God needs any assistance from me. He seems to do whatever he wants."

Frieda tilted her head, examining Carolyn's expression. "Your mother and me, we worry about your heart sometimes, Carolyn. You have always had a heart of pure gold, *un corazón de oro,* just like your mother. But then you say something, and I see in your face such sadness. I taste the vinegar in your words. You cannot live like this. You must move on, *mi niña.* If your mother were here, she would be saying these same words to you. You need her. Call her. Tell her everything we talked about. She knows the sorrow you still sleep with."

Part of Carolyn wanted to protest and part of her wanted to cry. But before she could do either, Tikki bounded up to the table, her skin glistening from dancing. She reached for a glass of water and took a long drink. A lightness returned, and Carolyn silently thanked Tikki for showing up at just the right moment. Scrunching her feet back into her shoes under the table, Carolyn saw this interruption as a good opportunity to make an exit.

But Frieda leaned back and clapped her hands in a private jubilation. "I have it! Yes! *¡Perfecto!*" She laced her ring-laden fingers as if congratulating herself. "You must go see her. The two of you. Carolyn, it will be just like the summer you were eighteen."

Tikki looked at Frieda and back at her mom. "What are you two talking about?"

Frieda grabbed Tikki by the arm. "We are talking about your opportunity to reconnect with *su sangre,* your blood."

Tikki pulled back her arm and cast a wary glance at both women. "Seriously, Mom, what are you two talking about?"

"I think Aunt Frieda is suggesting that you and I go to the Canary Islands to see my mother."

"*Sí!* Abuela Teresa and all the rest of your relatives. Carolyn, you have not been there since you were eighteen! *Cuando toca, toca.* You know what that means, don't you?"

"I have no idea," Tikki said.

"Of course you have no idea. You have not kept up with what little Spanish you did hear as a

26

child." Frieda shot a disagreeable glance at Carolyn, presumably for her mothering skills, and translated the quote. "It means, 'When it's your time, it's your time.' And now is your time. For both of you. You must go."

Tikki didn't protest.

Frieda looked pleased. With a sly grin, she leaned closer to Tikki. "And who knows, Teresa Katharine, maybe it will be your turn to fall in love the way your mother did."

Tikki's eyes opened wide. "The way my mother fell in love? Is that true?"

Carolyn felt her face and neck redden. She knew she would have to be nimble with her responses, or Aunt Frieda would embellish the little she did know of that summer when Carolyn was eighteen.

Tikki pulled out a chair and leaned forward. "Did you fall in love, Mom? How come I've never heard this story?"

"Because there's nothing to tell," Carolyn said quickly.

"Nothing to tell?" Frieda made an unattractive scoffing sound. "Your mother fell in love with a ruffian."

"It wasn't love," Carolyn heard herself say.

"Oh, it was love," Frieda countered, piercing the remainder of her cake with her fork as if it were an arrow sent from Cupid's bow. "It was teenage love. The worst kind."

Now Tikki was fully engaged. "So, where is he now?"

"I have no idea." Carolyn bent down and adjusted her shoes, ready to make her escape from this table and this topic.

"What's his name? We can look him up on the Internet. Maybe he has a social media page. This could be fun, Mom. You obviously really liked him. It's all over your face."

Carolyn felt trapped. She looked down at her fingers and folded her napkin, matching the corners just right, pressing the sides so the lines would stay neatly in place.

"I am surprised at you, Carolyn. Why is it you have never told your daughter about Bryan Spencer?"

Carolyn couldn't believe Frieda remembered his name. But then, Frieda was gifted in such matters.

Frieda jumped in again. "This young man was a wild one. Those broad shoulders and that hair! Crazy beach hair, kissed by the Canary sun. He was so good looking. His stepmother lived next door to my mother, and Bryan used every excuse he could think of to come over to our house, didn't he, Carolyn?"

In an effort to give Tikki enough to satisfy her piqued curiosity and at the same time keep Aunt Frieda from providing any more details, Carolyn took command of the untold tale. "Bryan and I were about the same age. We were two American teens who ended up spending the summer with our families in Las Palmas. That's it. The beginning and the end with nothing worthy of spinning into a fairy tale."

"That's not what you said the day you rode the camels," Frieda argued. "You were smitten. All of us saw it on both of your faces when you returned with Tío Jorge. We accused him of not doing his job chaperoning the two of you. He said you were holding hands. And kissing! He saw you kissing under the canopy of bougainvillea."

Tikki's mouth opened in amazement. "I can't believe I never heard any of this before. I especially can't believe you rode a camel. I didn't know they had camels on the Canary Islands."

Frieda held out her hands to Carolyn, palms up in a position of supplication. "Do you see this? This is why you need to take your daughter to the Canaries. She knows nothing of the islands."

"Yes, I do," Tikki protested. "I know that Christopher Columbus set out from Las Palmas in 1492 when he sailed the ocean blue."

"Everyone knows that. But do you know where the Canary Islands are located?"

"Of course I do. They're off the coast of West Africa. See? I know where my blood is from—*mi sangre*."

"Well, then, you must go. You will love the beaches. And the food! Such delicious fresh fish!

And at night, you will see so many stars you won't be able to count them all."

"Sounds incredible."

Aunt Frieda clapped her hands to mark another epiphany that seemed to have rushed over her. "I have it! We'll all go! I'll go with you! This summer. A return visit. Oh, your mother will be so happy to see us. And when we go, you can take Tikki to the sand dunes at Maspalomas. Then one day she can tell her daughter that she rode a camel just like you did."

As Frieda had been talking, Carolyn picked up her plate, ready to slip away from the table and the conversation. "The only return visit I'm making at the moment is to the buffet. Does anyone want anything?"

"You can't leave the table now," Frieda said. "We have plans to make."

"I'm not ready to make plans. I need time to think about all this," Carolyn said firmly. "It's a big decision. A big trip. I'll give it some thought and talk it over with Tikki. We'll get back to you."

"I would love to go sometime," Tikki said. "But this summer is probably too soon for me. I don't have a lot of vacation time saved up yet at work."

Frieda looked undaunted. "It will work out. You'll see. We must have faith and stick together. We are the Women of the Canaries. The two of you need to be reminded of what that means."

Tikki stood and gave Aunt Frieda a quick hug and a kiss on the cheek. *"Yo te amo, mi tía."*

Looking pleasantly surprised at Tikki's use of Spanish to express her "I love you" words, Frieda replied, *"Yo te amo a tí, también, mi niña."*

Tikki scooted off with Carolyn and linked her arm in her mother's. "So? Did you notice how I shifted the attention from your summer love to the fascinating camels?"

"Thank you."

"Anytime. I've got your back, Mom." With a playful grin Tikki added, "But that doesn't get you off the hook with me. I still want to hear all about bad boy Bryan."

Carolyn felt her face flush once again. From the moment Aunt Frieda brought up Bryan's name, the memories had come at her fast and vibrant. She remembered the camel ride as well as the sun-drenched afternoons on the beach at Las Canteras, the shimmering sea and the first time Bryan held her hand. For a glimmer of a second, Carolyn could see it all: the star-filled sky overhead, the rough side of the overturned green fishing boat, and Bryan waiting for her . . .

"We'll see," Carolyn said cautiously. "Some stories are better off left buried in the past."

Tikki unlinked their arms. "I can't believe you just said that. You're the one who taught me to get things out in the open and use the past as the springboard to my future."

Carolyn wasn't sure what to say. Tikki was right. Those exact words had been given to Carolyn by a counselor soon after Jeff's death. She used the phrase as a tool to help sixteen-year-old Tikki come to terms with the sudden and tragic loss of her father. But this . . . this was different. This was her past. Her long-buried memory. This story wouldn't be a springboard into the future for Carolyn or for anyone else. Especially not for Tikki.

Tikki said, "You're not going to tell me about bad boy Bryan, are you?"

Carolyn pressed her lips together and offered only a slight smile.

"I'll pry it out of you later. For now, I think you and I have some dancing to do. Come on, join me out on the dance floor."

"No, Tikki, really, I can't."

"Of course you can. You just need to let down your guard and take a few risks."

"It's not that. It's these shoes. I've rubbed a blister, and my toe is killing me."

Tikki didn't press any further. She gave her mom a grin. "One of these days you'll dance with me for real. I'm confident that if you can ride a camel, you can dance with me."

Carolyn smiled back. The relationship she had with Tikki was so similar to the closeness she had experienced with her mother during her teens and twenties. She missed not having that face-to-face closeness with her mother now. Marilyn, who never had connected with their mother at a deeply tender level, had spent most of her adult life expressing her bitterness over that lack and had used it as the primary reason she wasn't as close with her two daughters as Carolyn was with Tikki.

"One of these days I'll dance with you," Carolyn promised.

"I'll hold you to that."

Tikki returned to where the action was while Carolyn returned to where she hoped the asparagus was. Unfortunately, the asparagus was gone. So were the mushrooms. Carolyn settled for some leftover pita chips and hummus.

A tall man in a dark gray suit came over and stood next to Carolyn, also examining the picked-over offerings. "I was hoping they had some of those mushroom caps left," he said. "They were exceptional."

"Yes, and the asparagus was good too." Carolyn looked at the middle-aged man and was struck by his athleticism.

"You don't remember me, do you?"

Carolyn's expression must have made it clear that she didn't because he connected the dots for her. "I'm Larry's neighbor, Ellis."

"Oh, right. You helped us when Marilyn moved in some of her things last week. You look different. All dressed up. I mean, in a suit instead of in running shorts." She made herself stop before any even more awkward thoughts popped out of her mouth.

Ellis smiled. "You look nice. That's a stunning color on you."

Carolyn tried not to laugh at his word choice of "stunning." It was quite an improvement over Aunt Frieda's earlier comments on the dress. "Thank you."

"I should clarify that I'm actually Larry's former neighbor. I moved out this week."

"Oh, that's too bad." She didn't know why she said that.

"Actually, a place opened up closer to work, and it seemed like the right time to make the move."

"I see. Well, that's good then."

"Yes."

The awkwardness was growing worse. She was never good at small talk. Carolyn knew she could walk away. She could excuse herself and return to the comfort of the family table. But something in her told her to stay and prove to her aunt as well as to her daughter that she wasn't as socially pathetic as they seemed to think.

Ignoring her screaming toe, Carolyn adjusted her position and quietly hoped that Tikki and Frieda would notice that she was chatting with a nice-looking man. She attempted to restart their conversation by commenting on the wedding ceremony. Ellis replied that the music was nice, and they went on to discuss the weather, that Marilyn had recently become a blonde at Larry's request, and the insufficient parking places at most restaurants, but not this one. When her pita bread was gone, Carolyn made another comment on how delicious the stuffed mushroom caps were.

There, now, when I go back to the table, Aunt Frieda won't be able to say that I'm the dog that doesn't get out much or whatever her pithy saying was.

Ellis cleared his throat. "I was wondering if you, if you . . . might be available."

"Available?"

"For coffee sometime. Or tea, if you don't drink coffee."

He's asking me out! Carolyn never expected this. She had no idea how to reply. "I . . . uh . . ."

"Or maybe you prefer mushroom caps instead of coffee. Or asparagus. You said you liked the asparagus, right?"

It somehow helped that he appeared just as nervous and out of his element as she felt.

"Yes, the asparagus was very good."

"It was. I doubt there's any place in the Bay Area that serves better appetizers than this restaurant."

"I would definitely agree with you there."

Another awkward pause broke the flow of conversation but not their eye contact.

"If you would like," Ellis said cautiously, "we could come here sometime. For appetizers."

Carolyn felt her head nod agreeably even though she hadn't anticipated saying yes.

"How about two weeks from today? We could meet here at, say, four o'clock?"

Carolyn hesitated.

"Would another day be better, or . . . ?"

"No."

"So two weeks from today works for you?"

Her thoughts swirled with bits of all the advice that had been delivered to her that day. *Get a life. Get out there and start looking. Let down your guard. Take a few risks.* Once again, Carolyn felt herself nod in agreement in spite of the way her heart pounded nervously.

Ellis smiled back. "Good. I'll see you here two weeks from today—four o'clock." He turned and left Carolyn alone at the sparse buffet table.

What did I just do?

Her feet seemed to suddenly reattach themselves to the rest of her body and piped up with the blaring distress signals they had been trying to send her for the past fifteen minutes.

I have a date. Why did I say yes? I meant to say no. This is crazy.

Then she realized she didn't even know Ellis's last name.

No, this isn't going to work. It doesn't matter what his last name is. I'm not going to meet him for appetizers or anything else.

Slipping out of her annoying shoes, Carolyn toddled around the reception area barefooted in search of Ellis so she could tell him she was sorry, but she had changed her mind and wasn't able to go out with him. Unfortunately, she couldn't find him.

Ellis had left the building.

3

"A río revuelto, ganancia de pescadores."
"There's good fishing in troubled waters."

THE WEEK THAT followed Marilyn and Larry's wedding was one of the worst Carolyn had experienced in many years. As soon as the newlyweds were on their way to Mexico for their honeymoon, Marilyn's daughters made it clear that during their final week under Carolyn's roof they were going to behave any way they wanted. She carried out the duties of a warden, a bouncer, and an extremely patient and concerned aunt.

When she delivered the two teens along with a full report to Marilyn and Larry, her twin said, "I'm sure you and I were just as much of a handful when we were their age."

Carolyn disagreed, but Marilyn was unfazed.

By the time Carolyn had helped to carry the last box out of her house, placed it in the rental truck, and waved good-bye, she was exhausted. Beyond exhausted. Then she remembered that she was blissfully alone at last.

For a moment it didn't matter that her house was a mess. A complete disaster zone. The girls had carved a huge dent in the wall that led to the kitchen when they were arguing while moving their dresser. The wood floor was pitted with dents and scrapes. But she had her house back, and as soon as she got some good sleep, she would be ready to start the needed repairs and renovations.

Carolyn retrieved a pad of paper from the small antique desk that had belonged to Jeff's grandmother. With pen in hand, she assessed the damage, noting the marks on the six carpeted steps that led to the upper level of her fifty-year-old home. Of the three bedrooms on that upper level, two were now empty. And filthy. She already had scheduled the carpet cleaner to come on Tuesday. If she had the energy later in the week, she decided she would wash the walls and start to paint on Saturday.

Saturday. That's when I'm supposed to meet Ellis. How am I going to contact him to tell him I'm not going to meet up with him?

Carolyn had asked herself that question at least

38

twenty times over the past week. The logical answer was to obtain Ellis's phone number from Larry, but she couldn't bring herself to do that.

What is my problem? Do I want to open myself up to a new relationship or not? I'm attracted to Ellis. I think. I don't know. Why am I so skittish about taking this small risk? He seems like a nice person.

She didn't want to evaluate herself anymore. All she wanted was to close out this Sunday evening with a long bath and a good night's sleep. With that objective in mind, Carolyn opened a can of minestrone soup, heated it up, and carried the steaming bowl up to the bathroom, where she ran the bathwater.

The phone rang just as she was kicking off her shoes. Her first thought was to let it ring, but then she recognized the customized ring as the one she had programmed as Tikki's. She couldn't turn down a chance to talk to Tikki.

"I'm going to scream," Tikki announced as soon as Carolyn said hello.

"Why?" Carolyn turned off the bathwater and sat on the tub's edge. "What happened?"

"Nothing. That's the problem. Nothing is happening with Matt. He seems content for everything to keep going the way it has been, but I think we should be moving along a little faster, you know? I'm not saying to rush things but at least to talk about our future. He's taking his sweet time about everything, and I'm ready to look to the future and start a little dream together. What's with him? Are all men this s-l-o-w?"

Carolyn knew that her go-getter girl wasn't given to fits of drama, which made Carolyn take this meltdown seriously. "I take it you two had another DTR recently."

"You know what DTRs are?"

"Of course. Define The Relationship talks. You told me what they were after the first one you had with Matt."

"Well, not much has changed since that first one."

"Did you express to him everything you were thinking and feeling?"

"Oh, yes. Definitely. That's never been a problem. I process aloud. You know that. Matt knows it too. But he's a slow, internal processor. Typical for a guy, right? We're such close friends, but that's part of the problem because I think he's comfortable staying where we are for another ten years. I want to get on with our lives. I want to have children when I'm young. Careerwise and financially, we could get married in a year or even in six months. But you know, it's not exactly up to me to put all the wheels in motion. I don't see him making any effort to even move forward."

"All you can do is give yourselves more time."

"I know. I just hate that that's the best solution."

Tikki sighed. "I want to come home and just be with you for the rest of the weekend. I don't want to be here and wait around for him to decide if we should go do something or rent a movie or whatever. I just want to be gone."

"Are you saying you want to stay here this weekend? This Saturday?"

"Yes. Is that okay? Or do you have a big hot date or something?" Tikki teased.

When Carolyn didn't protest immediately, Tikki said, "Mom, seriously? Do you have a date for Saturday night?"

"Not exactly. Well, sort of. Appetizers at four o'clock. It's not dinner." Carolyn carried her cooled bowl of soup into her bedroom and settled onto her bed as she confided in Tikki about meeting Ellis at the wedding and the invitation to meet him at Sadie's Garden.

"So what do you know about this guy, Mom? Aside from his passion for mushrooms."

"Not much. But I told you, I'm going to cancel. I don't feel right about meeting with him."

"Maybe you shouldn't be so hasty. I mean, you do know there are wedding trawlers out there who prey on single women at receptions. But nice, respectable men also go to weddings hoping to meet someone equally respectable. It's convenient when they are already friends with your friends and relatives. Did you ask Larry about him?"

41

"No. And I don't want to. So please don't say anything either."

"Okay. But, you know, you could always turn it into a double date with Larry and Marilyn. That would be nice and safe."

"I don't think so." Carolyn was pretty sure Tikki was teasing, but talking about dating was new conversational territory for them so she wondered just what Tikki meant.

"If you don't want Marilyn and Larry to go, then I'll go with you. I'll be your chaperone the way you had to have one when you were in the Canary Islands."

"Thanks for the offer, Tikki, but no. Definitely not." Carolyn could tell her daughter was enjoying that Carolyn was far out of her comfort zone.

"To be completely serious, though, Mom, I think you should go on Saturday and meet this guy. If he turns out to be a jerk, you can just get back in your own car and drive home. No harm done. And since I'll be here when you return, you can tell me all about it, and I'll laugh with you over the funny parts. It'll be fun."

In spite of all her gut-level hesitancies, Carolyn promised Tikki that she would keep the date.

"I'll pray for you on Saturday, Mom, and you can pray for me. I really want to follow God's leading with Matt. In my heart I know he's the one for me. But he has to come to that same confident conclusion about me before we can get this party started. You know what I'm saying?"

"I do. And, Tikki, you know that lasting relationships take time."

"I know. But seriously, Mom, don't you think that a year and a half would be enough time for us to know if we want to spend the rest of our lives together? We've become more like best friends than boyfriend and girlfriend. I said that to Matthew last week, and he said the friendship has taken over because we're not sleeping together."

Carolyn was caught off guard by Tikki's comment. She knew that Tikki and Matthew had started out their relationship with a strong commitment to purity. Both of them had come from families as well as church youth groups that provided them with a foundation for making decisions for abstinence. However, Tikki hadn't talked about it much over the past year or so, and Carolyn had assumed that due to the longevity of their relationship, they had made adjustments along the way to their idealistic commitment. Apparently they were still on track.

Now I know for sure that I will never tell Tikki about Bryan and that summer in the Canary Islands.

Tikki confided in her mom about how limiting it had been in her relationship with Matthew for the two of them to be together all this time and still draw the line at kissing. Carolyn pulled the comforter at the end of her bed up over her bare feet while Tikki candidly described how the absence of full expression of their affection had prompted their relationship to fall into a lull. She said the lull was a bigger frustration to her than the sexual tension they had struggled with earlier in the relationship.

For the next twenty minutes, Carolyn listened, adding only a few comments. She let Tikki know how much she admired her strength and sense of discernment. All those character traits that Carolyn and Jeff had labeled as stubbornness when Tikki was a child were now paying off. Tikki had grown into a young woman who knew who she was and wasn't willing to compromise for anything or anyone. She definitely had her father's no-nonsense gene.

"I need to get going. Thanks for letting me moan and groan about this with you, Mom."

"Anytime, honey. I love you. I'll see you Saturday."

When Carolyn finally climbed into bed that night, she fell asleep remembering what her life was like when she was Tikki's age. As she slept, she dreamed of Jeff. They were sailing. He loved to sail in the brisk San Francisco Bay with the wind in his face and the burn in his muscles as he pulled the ropes and hoisted the anchor. Jeff had a joy-infused sort of laugh that he employed only when he was skimming across the water. Carolyn had heard that distinctive laughter from him a handful of times in all their years together.

In her dream that night, she heard it.

They were in the East Bay, in sight of Angel Island, on a cloudy autumn afternoon, bundled up and sitting close on the top deck. The north wind caught itself in a freshly raised sail and made a blustery attempt to escape. But it couldn't let go; it belonged to them. With gusto the captured wind propelled the ready craft forward. Suddenly Carolyn was clinging to Jeff, and they were flying across the feisty whitecaps, kicking spray in every direction.

That's when she heard it. The euphoric laughter of heaven, tumbling from his chest and covering her with the sweetness of their best memories.

The comfort born of that dream clung to Carolyn's spirit for the rest of the day. Small, pleasant echoes of the wind-whipped laughter trailed in and out of her thoughts all week long. It was the best memory and image of Jeff that had come to her since his death, and the freshness of it filled her heart with new breath.

As the week went on, Carolyn spent a lot of time thinking about Jeff and about her future. Seven years was a long time to go without having someone in her life that fulfilled the role of husband, lover, confidant, spiritual adviser, and closest friend. She knew it wasn't possible for anyone to replace Jeff. But she also knew she needed to let herself at least be open to the possibility of a new relationship. Not only for what that person would bring to her life, but also for what she had to offer that other person.

Carolyn kept her thoughts and feelings about her date concealed from friends at work as Saturday drew closer. When the morning dawned, she chose a pair of jeans with a favorite ivory sweater and set them out for later. She thought her wardrobe selection would make it clear that she viewed this as a casual date.

Then she went to work, washing the walls in the two vacant bedrooms, spackling the many holes in the walls, and taping around the floorboards and windows so she would be ready to paint. The physical work invigorated her and burned off any nervous energy she had been storing up. Memories of when she and Jeff last painted these rooms kept her company. She had done most of the work, which was typical and the basis for many of their arguments, including the last argument they had had.

But she didn't want to open her thoughts to that memory. She wanted the sweet memories to stay with her. Carolyn reminded herself that Jeff always was more interested in people than in projects while she preferred the opposite. Tasks energized her, and today was no exception, as she swiftly went at the taping around the doors. She wanted to be done by the time Tikki arrived just in case her daughter entered in a puddle of woe and needed Carolyn's full attention. It surprised her when the door opened at a little past one o'clock, and Tikki's voice called out cheerfully, "Anybody home?"

Carolyn trotted down the stairs and met Tikki with what could barely be called a hug. "I'm really dirty and sweaty."

"What are you doing?"

"You'll have to come upstairs to see."

"First let me get something cold to drink. Do you have anything good in here?" Tikki shuffled the refrigerator's contents around on the nearly vacant shelves and settled for a can of Italian lemonade tucked in the door behind the ketchup. "Looks like you might be running a bit low on a few things." The sarcasm in her voice was evident.

"It's a big change stocking food for only one person. My grocery bill definitely is dropping."

"How about if I go to the store to buy us some snacks while you finish up whatever it is you're doing? Then I'll come ooh and ahh over your masterpiece."

"I would love it. Could you be sure to buy some eggs and milk? There's money in my purse."

"I can cover it, Mom. I'm hoping for a significant raise within the next month. Did I tell you? I applied for the loan officer position and made it past the first interview. The manager in that department told me I pretty much have the position, if I want to take it."

Tikki had worked at the same credit union for the past three years. In that time she had risen from teller to assistant loan processor, and now she was being considered as an assistant officer in the loan department.

"Tikki, that's fantastic! Good for you. We'll have to celebrate tonight."

"We will. After you return from your big date."

Carolyn checked the clock on the stove. "I'm running out of time! I just remembered I'm supposed to be there at four o'clock."

"You better get ready then. I'll run out to buy groceries."

Dashing into the shower, Carolyn realized how odd it was to be in this role reversal with her daughter. Wasn't it just a few years ago that Carolyn was the one making runs to the store, and Tikki was the one preparing for school dances and proms? Carolyn felt grateful for the timing of Tikki's big relationship conversation. If things had been status quo between Matthew and Tikki, she wouldn't have come for the weekend. Coming home to an empty house after her first sort-of date in decades would have been depressing.

As she brushed out her hair, using the hair dryer on the highest setting, Carolyn tried to calculate the time it would take her to reach Sausalito.

Even without the weekday traffic, she had a feeling she was going to be late. Not a good way to start the date. She thought of how some of her longtime neighbors in Fremont took the Bay Area Rapid Transit system, "BART," into the city every day for work. She didn't know how they could stand the commute.

Tikki was gone when Carolyn jumped in her car and backed down the driveway. Three blocks from the house, she passed Mill Creek Elementary and glanced at the school as she habitually did. Tikki had attended kindergarten at Mill Creek, and that's when Carolyn began to volunteer in the front office. The volunteer position turned into part-time, and when Tikki was in fifth grade, Carolyn stepped into a full-time job in the front office.

She loved what she did and loved walking to work every day. She never grew tired of checking the students in and out after dental appointments or helping teachers hunt down missing release forms before a field trip. Jeff used to say she was the bubble that kept that little elementary school on the level.

Carolyn let out a long, anxiety-releasing breath. Memories of Jeff felt out of place in her thoughts when she was on her way to meet another man. Yet, as they had all week, the memories of Jeff calmed and comforted her.

For the hour-and-twenty-minute drive to

Sadie's Garden, Carolyn played out the scenarios of how this date might go and what her escape plan would be. She entered the restaurant with a wobbly expression that immediately fell when she realized Ellis wasn't there. It was four o'clock. She forced herself to slide past the hostess and have a quick look around the bar area. Carolyn hoped he wasn't there. Meeting a man for a date in a bar seemed so out of the range of anything she ever had expected to do. He was late, or perhaps he wasn't coming. Either way, Carolyn was ready to jump ship, drive home, and have a good laugh with Tikki over the rise and fall of Carolyn's dating career, all in one day.

She decided to give him ten minutes. If she were running late, she would want the courtesy of ten minutes. If he wasn't here by then, she would be on her way. The sweater Carolyn had selected felt itchy and seemed far too casual for the way others were dressed as they entered the restaurant.

Checking her watch again and seeing that the time was now 4:12, she let her thoughts flit on to how she was going to feel about all this if, in fact, she had been stood up.

Just then her cell phone rang. It was Marilyn.

"Carolyn, where are you?"

"I'm at a restaurant." She could feel her heart beat faster, as if she had done something wrong. She always felt that sensation when Marilyn used a certain tone in her voice. For being a total of nineteen minutes older, Marilyn knew how to lord it over Carolyn and had exercised her abilities since the cradle.

"Where are the girls?"

"What do you mean?"

"They told me they were going to see you this morning. I just called your house, and Tikki answered. She said she hadn't seen them."

"I haven't seen them either. They didn't come to my house today."

"Okay, that does it. Those two are in so much trouble. Call me right away if you hear anything from them."

"I will."

Just then Ellis entered the restaurant lobby. He smiled when he spotted Carolyn. She put her cell phone back in her purse and nervously greeted him.

"Traffic was heavier than I expected. Sorry to keep you waiting."

"That's okay." Carolyn noticed he was wearing a collared dress shirt and a sport coat. She felt conspicuously underdressed, as the hostess led them to a small table at the front far corner of the restaurant. Carolyn appreciated that the table was out of the main pathway of both waiters and guests, yet she couldn't help but wonder if this was the corner where they put the lower-class clientele.

"I realized," Ellis said as he fumbled to pull out

Carolyn's chair for her, "we didn't exchange phone numbers. If we had, I would have called to let you know I was running late."

If we had exchanged numbers, I would have called you two weeks ago and canceled!

"I've been looking forward to this," he said.

Carolyn pretended she had been too. Then she pretended to still be adjusting her chair, since she wasn't ready to engage in conversation. Her phone rang again, and she reached for her purse to silence the ring. She hesitated when she saw the call was from Marilyn.

"Please feel free to get that if you need to." Ellis politely placed the cloth napkin in his lap.

Carolyn leaned toward the window and partially covered the mouthpiece with her cupped hand. "Is everything okay?"

"I wanted you to know I just reached the girls. They were shopping. I thought they said they were going to your house, but they said they told me they were going to the mall up by your house. So they're fine. They're going to a movie now."

Carolyn doubted the girls were "fine." She knew the sort of friends they had hung out with when they lived at her house. Marilyn was being gullible and indulgent once again, but that was another conversation for another time.

"I'm glad you know where they are. Listen, can I call you back later tonight?"

"I have a better idea. Where are you right now?

What restaurant? We don't have a thing in the house for dinner, so I told Larry we should meet up with you."

Carolyn's heart sped up again. "Actually, ah, it would be better if we tried to do that another time. It won't work for me tonight."

"Why not? We can leave right now. I wanted to tell you all about Mexico and where we stayed and everything."

"I want to hear all about it but just not tonight. Can we meet tomorrow night instead?"

The silent response made it clear that Marilyn was ticked. "Okay. Fine. Call me later, and we'll figure it out."

"I will. And thanks for understanding, Marilyn." Carolyn had to add that, even though she knew her sister didn't understand. She hung up and silenced her phone.

With a sheepish grin at Ellis she said, "Sorry."

"No problem. Is everything all right?"

"Yes." She stared at the menu, finding she wasn't able to focus on the selection.

Why do I feel as if I have to hide from Marilyn that I'm here with Ellis? What am I afraid of? This whole thing feels unbalanced. I can't do this. I'm not ready. I have to get out of here.

Closing her menu and trying her best to appear calm, Carolyn summoned all the courage she could find. "I'm really sorry, but I can't do this. I need to leave."

4

"Caras vemos, corazones no sabemos."
"Faces we can see, hearts we can't know."

Ellis appeared confused and disappointed at Carolyn's sudden declaration. "Are you sure you can't stay?"

Carolyn tried to give him a logical reason for her skittishness. She at least owed him that. "You know, at the wedding you asked if I was 'available,' and I have to be honest and tell you that I'm not. Not really. Not yet."

Ellis seemed to look relieved. He pulled on his earlobe. "Well, to be perfectly honest with you, I'm not sure I'm exactly available yet either."

Carolyn felt a funny sense of relief at his words and the shy way he delivered them. Apparently this midlife dating experience was new and uncomfortable for him. "Besides, I'm not sure I'm ready for this."

"I understand. I'm not sure I'm ready either." Ellis's calm response along with his shared discomfort and hesitation had a settling affect on Carolyn. She wasn't as nervous all of a sudden.

"You know," he said, "if you want, you could just order something to go. I mean, we did come here because of the mushrooms."

"And the asparagus." She mustered a small smile.

"You would hate to go home without those." Ellis smiled at her. His teeth looked exceptionally white. She didn't remember his having such white teeth two weeks ago. Perhaps he had made the effort to have them whitened just to look good for their date. Whether that was the case, the possibility softened Carolyn's case of nerves. The near panic attack was diminishing. She wondered if she later would regret pulling out so abruptly.

Ellis seemed to read her fluctuating emotions and eased into a redirection. "Or, if you would like, we could just eat a little something and then be on our way."

Carolyn took a moment to release a long breath. "That's probably a good idea. It's a long drive home. Some food would help."

"Why don't we do that then? We'll just have a quick appetizer and then go."

"Okay, sure. Let's do that." She felt like apologizing for her indecisiveness but thought it better to let it go and put some food in her mouth so she wouldn't fumble and say anything else she would regret.

Ellis ordered for them as soon as the waiter appeared, and their date was off to a start at last. Their conversation meandered through a maze of impersonal topics. Ellis led with a story about a seagull that had perched on his car when he pulled into the parking lot. That prompted

Carolyn to comment on an article she had read recently about the seagull population at Pier 39. Their conversation fumbled along, and at just the right moment, the scrumptious appetizers were delivered. As they ate, the conversation as well as Carolyn's outlook seemed to improve.

Both of them hesitated when the waiter came to clear the plates and asked if they would like anything else. Carolyn didn't want to be the first to call for the check.

"I understand the chicken dishes here come highly recommended," Ellis said.

"I saw that the special this evening is parmesan-crusted chicken breast with some kind of chutney. It's not always easy to find a place that knows how to serve it. Maybe we should give the chicken and chutney a try."

"Sounds good." Carolyn was surprised at how relaxed she felt.

Dinner provided more space for them to settle in, find interesting topics, and compare their shared interest in certain programs on the History Channel and the Travel Channel.

For dessert they both ordered crème brûlée. Ellis told her he worked in sales for a shipping company in Silicon Valley. Even though he didn't give details, she got the impression he had done well because he talked about his world travels and had a funny story of nearly falling off an elephant when he was in India on business.

She considered mentioning that her mother lived in the Canary Islands but didn't feel ready to divulge that sort of personal information.

Ellis talked about a place called San Remy and how that was where he would like to live one day. Carolyn knew where San Ramon was and San Rafael, but she never had heard of San Remy. "Is that near Palo Alto?"

Ellis seemed to hide a grin. "No, it's outside of Paris. To the northeast. I don't know exactly why, but I'm taken with the area."

Carolyn felt as if she were out of her league and yet that made her feel even more flattered that he still was showing interest in her.

Ellis pulled out his credit card to pay the check, and Carolyn reached for her purse. "Let's split the check."

"No, please, I want to cover it. I insist."

Carolyn protested, but he persuaded her to do him the honor of accepting this small kindness in exchange for her delightful presence. Once again she was flattered as well as intrigued. She was mesmerized talking with Ellis once they had moved past the bumpy first few topics.

As they returned to the parking lot, Carolyn thanked him again for the meal, and he thanked her again for her company. She decided that he had a nice-looking face. He wasn't handsome, in her estimation. His ears were large for his oval-shaped face, and his chin was too narrow for the soul patch of beard he seemed to be attempting to grow.

She decided part of her interest in him was due to the way he salvaged the conversation and talked about interesting topics in places outside of Northern California. She hoped he would suggest another get-together. When he didn't ask, she felt disappointed and wondered self-consciously if he didn't find her as interesting as she found him.

They did agree to exchange cell phone numbers, and that renewed Carolyn's sense of hope. Their parting was as unrelaxed as their greeting, and Carolyn felt relieved finally to be back in her car. Driving home, she felt the nervous conglomeration of emotions and hesitations tangling her thoughts once again. She didn't know enough about Ellis. Why had he said he wasn't exactly "available" either? Had Ellis lost his wife, or was he divorced? He didn't mention any children. He didn't say much about anything outside of his job and travels. But then, this meeting was supposed to be light and breezy. No interrogating needed. She certainly didn't want to reveal personal information about her life.

She did, however, try to convince herself that it was okay to enjoy this unexpected attention. Ellis's noticing her and seeking her out was flattering. Once she was home and in the safe setting of her own living room, Carolyn tried to express her feelings in a noncommittal way when she summarized her evening for Tikki.

"Do you think he was waiting for you to suggest a second date?" Tikki asked.

"I don't know. I'm going to let everything settle and just see what happens."

"You can always call or text him in a few days to see how he responds."

Carolyn took a sip of the tea Tikki had prepared for them and shook her head. "It's such a different world: texting and messaging."

Tikki grinned.

"What? Are you laughing because I'm so technologically challenged?"

"No, I would never tease you about that."

"Yeah, right."

The two exchanged the happy look of best friends, and Carolyn was glad Tikki was there for her tonight.

"Are you ready for a surprise?" Tikki asked.

"I don't know. What kind of surprise?"

"Come with me. You'll see." Tikki sprang to her feet and led Carolyn upstairs to the first vacant bedroom. She switched on the light and called out, "Ta-da!"

"You painted the whole room, Tikki!"

"It's not a very big room. You had everything ready to go. All I did was pour the paint and pick up the roller. What do you think?"

"It's beautiful!"

"You picked a great color. It has only one coat, but since this shade is so light it'll need another coat. I think you have enough paint."

"You did such a great job, Tikki. I love it. Thank you." Carolyn felt choked up, thinking about how many times she had wanted to freshen up this room. It was the room Marilyn had occupied for the past six years, and neither Marilyn nor her daughters shared Carolyn's interest or enthusiasm in redecorating.

Carolyn wrapped her arms around Tikki and gave her a long hug.

"I'll help you paint my old room too, if you want."

Carolyn felt silly-giddy over the prospect of having someone she loved joining her side by side in a project. They went together to check out Tikki's old room and have a look at the paint Carolyn had picked out. It was a pale spring-green shade called "Dragonfly."

"Can we roll out a swatch of it on the wall? I want to see how it's going to look." Tikki already was opening the paint can.

Then, because it was so invigorating to see a patch of the fresh color on the traumatized walls and because Tikki was Carolyn's daughter and they both were eager to start, the two of them gleefully went to work. They had the whole room painted well before midnight and stood back to admire their handiwork.

"The first time your dad and I painted this room was before you were born. We painted it pale yellow with a border of fluffy little lambs."

"I remember those lambs. They were in a border that ran across the middle of the wall."

"That's right, and one day you took a knife from the kitchen and tried to lift the border off the wall. Do you remember that? You were seven."

Tikki grinned. She had a streak of pale green paint on her cheek, and her hair was piled up on top of her head in a floppy bun. Her countenance reflected her impish, seven-year-old self once again. "I wanted princesses on my wall, didn't I?"

"Yes. You insisted we do away with the baby stuff and give you a purple room."

"I remember its being more of a lavender shade."

"It was. That's because I wouldn't let you pick the final color."

"What a mean mom you were!"

Carolyn laughed. "Someday I'll show you the eggplant shade you were stuck on. Trust me, on the paint chip it might have looked like your pretty little princess doll's dress, but on the walls it would have closed in this room and sent you into a deep depression before your eighth birthday."

"Then I'm glad you intervened. You have great taste, Mom. What are you going to do with these two rooms now?"

"I'm still deciding. One of them will be a guest room. Which one do you think it should be?"

As they discussed options, Tikki stopped and said, "I almost forgot. Aunt Frieda called while you were gone tonight. She said to tell you that she can't go to the Canary Islands this summer because she's going to have surgery on her knee. She said you shouldn't worry about the surgery because it's not a complicated procedure. But then she said this means we really have to go with her this fall because the hope that will come from looking forward to our trip will be the sunshine that waits for her behind the storm clouds. Or something like that. The sunshine and cloud part was one of her Spanish sayings, so I might not have gotten it right."

"I'll call her this week and get the update."

"So, what do you think?"

"About the room? I think it looks fantastic."

"No, I mean about going to the Canary Islands."

"I'd love to go," Carolyn said. "It's easier for me to go in the summer while I'm off work. Although I have so much vacation and personal days saved up right now, I could probably go for a week or more just about anytime. What about you? Is this your time to go?"

"I don't know. A lot is going to depend on what happens between Matthew and me. I was dreaming a little about the future while I was painting the other room, and I was thinking what it would be like if he and I do end up getting married. What if we had our honeymoon in the Canary Islands. I know that probably sounds silly, but those are my grown-up princess dreams now. It just seems so exotic, you know?"

"Those are sweet dreams." Carolyn stroked Tikki's face. "You hold on to those sweet dreams."

Carolyn held on to a few sweet dreams of her own as the week progressed. Ellis and the prospect of seeing him again was a small dream on the back burner. Her bigger dream was to at long last follow through with some of the decorating renovations she had been eager to work on now that she had her house back.

She started with both bathrooms by purchasing new shower curtains, fluffy white towels, and plush rugs. She replaced the light fixture over her bathroom sink and splurged on matching pump bottles for each sink that she filled with almond-scented soap and lotion.

After work on Wednesday she went shopping for new dishes and a fun assortment of throw pillows for the sofa, since the old ones smelled like hair product and acne medicine. Her spring-cleaning campaign was pure fun in her new solo state. No one was there to offer a second option. No one tried to steer her in an alternate direction. She was the queen of her domain.

Her Thursday evening project was re-covering

an old lamp shade with fabric that went with one of the new throw pillows. She had found just the right woven edging to put around the bottom and was delighted with how it was turning out.

In the middle of her project her cell phone rang. It was Ellis.

"How are you doing?" she asked buoyantly.

"I'm good. How about you?"

"I'm doing great."

"You sound like it."

Carolyn wanted to tell him about the transformation taking place in her home, but when she realized she still hardly knew this man, the self-consciousness returned to her voice.

Ellis cleared his throat. "I don't know if it's too soon to ask this, but I was wondering if you might be interested in meeting up for dinner again sometime. I read a review this week on a new Chinese restaurant in Milpitas. I wanted to try it out. I thought you might want to join me. But if it's not a good time or too soon for me to ask, I understand."

"No, I think it's fine. Sure. When?"

"Would this Saturday work for you? Four o'clock again? We can beat the dinner rush that way."

"Okay. Sure."

"Great. I'm really looking forward to seeing you again, Carolyn. I'll text you the name and address of the restaurant, and we'll meet there at four."

As soon as she hung up, Carolyn remembered she had agreed to go over to Larry and Marilyn's on Saturday to look at wedding photos and hear about their honeymoon.

A few phone calls later she managed to move the invitation from Marilyn and Larry to Friday. But going to their home on Friday meant that she ended up sitting on the freeway in rush hour traffic for nearly an hour. Her windshield wipers kept time, dismissing the early March drizzle that had settled in on the Bay Area for the weekend. She felt her shoulders tensing as she coached herself to be on her guard and not to reveal anything about Ellis to Marilyn. She didn't want to bring her sister into this. Not yet.

When Carolyn finally arrived at the townhome and sat down to eat pepperoni pizza with the newly formed family of four, she noted that Larry was making heroic attempts to win the loyalty of the three women under his roof. He had showered the girls with new cell phones and lots of freedom. The minute they finished eating, they left the table, picked up Larry's car keys, and exited without saying where they were going.

"I think you guys need to keep a close eye on those two. Do you think they're telling you the truth about where they're going and who they're with?"

Larry looked at Marilyn and back at Carolyn

with an expression that made it clear he never had thought otherwise.

"I told you how they were pushing all the limits at my house while you were on your honeymoon. I think it would help if—"

"That's because they're adjusting," Marilyn said with an edge to her voice. "We're all trying to adjust here. You have no idea how difficult this is."

Carolyn backed down and didn't continue with the advice she wanted to deliver to her sister.

"Larry and I are determined to make it work. Are we going to make mistakes? Sure. Will we need your helpful opinions along the way? Yes. Of course we will. But until we ask for your advice, I don't think you're in a place to tell us what to do."

Carolyn pulled back and kept her opinions to herself the rest of the evening. She didn't want her sister's opinions on her newly sprouting dating life, and Marilyn didn't want Carolyn's opinions on how to raise her daughters. Fair enough.

Marilyn pulled out her brand-new laptop, another gift from Larry, and clicked through the photos of their honeymoon with lots of details about each one. The three of them moved to the couch to be more comfortable, and as the evening wore on, Marilyn and Larry grew cuddlier and exchanged a few too many knowing smiles and winks for Carolyn to feel comfortable. Larry had his arm around Marilyn, playing with her hair, rubbing her shoulders. When he kissed Marilyn's neck, Carolyn said, "I need to get going."

"Are you sure?" Marilyn's tone reflected no disappointment over her sister's departure.

"Yes. I have a lot of projects going at the house. Next time you're over my way, be sure to stop by. I'd love for you to see what I did with the bedrooms and bathrooms."

Larry asked, "Did you get the wall fixed yet? The one that was damaged by the dresser?"

"Not yet. I have a repairman coming next week."

"Send me the bill. I want to take care of that for you."

"Thanks, Larry, but you don't have to do that."

"Yes he does," Marilyn said, getting up and heading for the door as Carolyn followed her. "I told him it happened after we were married, so that makes it our responsibility to fix."

"How about if we figure it out later?" Carolyn gave her sister a hug good-bye and was overwhelmed by an unexpected fragrance. It was Larry's aftershave, an odd mix of evergreens and licorice. The scent clung to Marilyn, and now its faint trail followed Carolyn home.

She wondered if Ellis had a particular scent he always wore. She hadn't been close enough to him to notice if he did. With a little flutter of her stomach, Carolyn remembered she was going to see him at four o'clock the next day.

This time she put more attention into selecting her outfit and spent Saturday morning trying on five combinations before settling on what seemed just right. The black dress pants and heels looked sophisticated, but she hoped the jeans jacket and print shirt would balance out the overall outfit and give her a more approachable and not-so-nervous look.

Her hair cooperated and hung smoothly just past her shoulders with its usual thick bounce. Great hair was one of the best traits shared by all the Women of the Canaries. Even Aunt Frieda's hair had looked beautiful at the wedding.

Ellis was waiting for her just inside the front door of the restaurant. He greeted her with the same happy and approving smile he had given her at Sadie's Garden. This time his gaze seemed to take her in more deliberately. Carolyn could tell by his demeanor that he liked what he saw.

With her confidence boosted, Carolyn followed the hostess to their table and slid into her seat. A server brought tall glasses of water and an Asian-style teapot with cups.

"I've heard the spring rolls here are especially good." Ellis looked over the top of the menu at Carolyn. "That is, if you're interested in appetizers only."

"I'm pretty hungry. This kung pao chicken caught my eye."

Ellis ordered for both of them and then poured the steaming green tea into the tiny cup in front of Carolyn. She held the small cup snuggly in the palms of her enclosed hands and drew in the warmth.

He leaned back and tilted his head. "I don't think there's an accepted way to ask this so I'll just come right out with it. You're not divorced, are you?"

Carolyn felt suddenly chilled and cupped the warm teacup closer. "No, I'm not divorced."

Ellis looked relieved or intrigued or maybe both. "I thought that was the case." He nodded at the band she still wore on her finger. "I just wanted to clarify because, you see, I'm in the same situation."

Carolyn's heart went out to him. She offered a small smile of mutual support. At the same time, she hoped the whole dinner didn't become a group therapy session over coping with loss and grief. She had been looking forward to a nice dinner with an upbeat conversation like their last time together.

To her surprise, Ellis didn't ask any details about Jeff's death, nor did he offer any further information on his situation. She appreciated that immensely. He took a sip of his tea and then asked Carolyn how her week had been. She told him about her recent home improvements and kept the conversation light and cheery all the way through the spring rolls. By the time the broccoli beef, mandarin duck, and kung pao chicken arrived at the table, the topic focused on food.

"It all smells delicious." Carolyn helped herself to the heaping bowl of white rice.

Ellis reached across the table to take the serving spoon for the rice, and as he did, their hands brushed. Ellis caught Carolyn's eye and smiled. Clearly he had felt the tingle she had experienced when they touched.

"I was really looking forward to being with you again."

Carolyn felt herself blush at his words.

"You are a very exciting person to be with. Did anyone ever tell you that before?"

It had been a long time since Carolyn had received any sort of personal compliment. She thought he was overdoing the "exciting" part, but she thanked him and tried to think of something complimentary to say back to him.

"You're a very intriguing person."

"Intriguing. I like that." He tilted his head. "Would you by any chance be interested in a little more?"

Carolyn thought he meant the kung pao chicken that he was spooning onto his plate. "Yes, I would."

Oddly, instead of serving her, he put down the spoon and began eating. Carolyn took his actions to mean that he was allowing her to select her own serving amount.

When he caught her eye again he asked, "Do you like Italian food?"

"Yes, very much." Carolyn added a self-deprecating smile. "As you might have noticed, I like food. All kinds of food."

"I'm glad to hear you say that because so do I. What would you say to us meeting up at the Wellsby Towers?"

"I don't know where that is."

"It's in downtown San Francisco. They have an exceptional Italian restaurant. What do you think? Would you be interested?"

Since her mouth was full, Carolyn nodded her agreement, and he looked pleased. When they had finished eating, she offered to pay the check this time, but he insisted, saying again how much he enjoyed the pleasure of her company.

They strolled to their cars but didn't linger to chat because of the chilling wind and sporadic raindrops. Carolyn thanked him and got in her car. Ellis waited by her door with his collar pulled up against the rain. She started the engine and rolled down the window.

"So what do you think? When would it work out for us to meet up again?"

"I don't know. Next week?"

"It's up to you, but what do you think about meeting for lunch tomorrow?" Ellis shifted his weight, waiting for an answer.

"I'm not sure." She had expected him to

suggest they meet next weekend, not as soon as lunch the next day.

"Okay. That's okay. I don't want to rush you. Do you want to think about it?"

"Sure. Why don't you call me later tonight?"

"Good. I want you to feel comfortable about all this."

"I do. I'm open to meeting up at the place you mentioned downtown. I just . . ."

"I know. This is a pretty daring step for both of us."

Carolyn appreciated that he recognized that.

"You're a stunning woman, Carolyn. I feel as if part of me is starting to come back to life when I'm around you." He reached inside the car and placed his large hand on the curve of her cheek. He held it there a moment, looking at her admiringly. "I want you to know how much I'm looking forward to being with you."

The gesture, the warmth of his hand, and the unexpectedness of his flattering words had an overwhelming effect on Carolyn. He seemed to realize how vulnerable she was. Leaning toward her out of the cold, he made it clear that he was about to kiss her. Carolyn wasn't prepared for his advance and quickly turned her head so that the kiss landed on the side of her cheek.

"I understand," he said, pulling back. Instead of saying good night and going to his car, Ellis lingered in the chill beside her car. Carolyn didn't know what to do or say.

He tugged on his ear, and in a defeated-sounding voice he asked, "Are you sure we can't meet up tomorrow?"

With her heart pounding and all her defenses down, Carolyn said, "Okay."

"Okay?" His countenance brightened. "That's a yes?"

She nodded.

"How about if we meet there at noon? I'll text you the address."

She nodded again, inwardly wishing she had given herself the space to think about it. They exchanged smiles. Carolyn rolled up her window and backed out of the parking area as Ellis strode to his car.

During the fifty minutes it took her to drive home, she thought about his hand on her cheek and the unexpected impression of his quick kiss. Her emotions struggled with thoughts of how it would feel to once again be caressed by a man, to be loved by someone who thought she was "stunning." The longing that his touch ignited inside her was frightening, but it also was intoxicating.

When Carolyn arrived home, she noticed Marilyn's car in the driveway. Her first thought was that something was wrong. Hurrying through the front door, Carolyn found her sister in the kitchen area with a can of diet soda in her hand.

"Where have you been?" Marilyn demanded. "Do you not answer your cell anymore?"

"I was out. Why are you here? Is everything okay?"

"Yes, everything's fine. Don't look so rattled. I just came by to see the decorating changes you were talking about last night. You told me to come by, so here I am. I didn't expect you to be out."

Instead of taking the bait of Marilyn's weighted fishing line of "didn't expect you to be out" and give an explanation, Carolyn asked, "Did you go upstairs and see the new paint?"

"I did. It looks really nice. You did a great job, as usual."

"Thank you." Carolyn put her purse down on the kitchen counter and tried to look relaxed. Inside she was still feeling slightly off balance with thoughts of Ellis and the lingering impression of his touch.

"The other reason I came by was to drop this off. Larry and I wanted you to have it right away."

Carolyn took the paper Marilyn held out to her. It was a check for a thousand dollars. "What's this for?"

"The hole in the wall, the paint, and everything you had to buy to fix up things after we moved out."

"I can't take this." She handed the check back to Marilyn.

"Don't be stubborn. Take it, Carolyn." She slapped the check on the kitchen counter. "I owe you a hundred times that for the expenses you covered for me all these years. Besides, giving to other people is what Larry likes to do. It makes him happy." A sly grin traced itself across Marilyn's face. "Although that's not the only thing that makes him happy lately."

Carolyn really hoped her twin would stop there. The room suddenly seemed warm, so she slipped out of her jacket and draped it over the back of a kitchen chair.

Thankfully, Marilyn changed topics and focused on Carolyn's outfit. "Hey, that's really cute. I haven't seen that top before."

"Yes you have. You've even borrowed it from me."

"Are you sure? I don't remember it. I might have to borrow it again. And what was with the clothes all over your bed? It looked as if you had a fashion crisis. What were you dressing up for?"

Carolyn hesitated.

Marilyn put her hand on her hip. "You know you've never had a good poker face, right? All I have to do is ask questions, and your face tells me when I hit on the right answer. Did you go to a weight loss group meeting? No. A political rally?"

"I had a date."

Marilyn's eyes widened. "A date?"

"I went out with a man I met at your wedding."

Marilyn's jaw dropped. "You can't be serious. Why didn't you tell me? Who is it?"

"Ellis."

"Ellis?" Marilyn looked confused.

"He's Larry's old neighbor."

Marilyn placed the soda can on the counter and gave Carolyn a hard look. "Are you telling me you just went out with Ellis Savone?"

"Yes. It was a second date, actually."

Instead of showing any happiness for her sister, Marilyn's expression caved in. "Carolyn, you can't be serious."

In a quick effort to convince Marilyn of his attributes, Carolyn confidently started in on a list of his credits. "He's a fascinating man. He's brilliant and considerate, and he's traveled all over the world."

"Carolyn, he obviously left out one extremely important detail."

"What's that?"

"He's married."

5

"Al desdichado hace consuelo
tener compañía en su suerte y duelo."
"Two in distress makes sorrow less."

Carolyn refused to believe her sister's shocking statement. "No, he isn't married. He's a widower. Like me."

"Is that what he told you?"

Carolyn tried to remember exactly what he had said. When she pieced together the wording he had used, she realized all he really had asked was if she was divorced. When she said no, he said he was in the same situation. When she said she wasn't ready yet, he said he wasn't exactly "available" yet either.

"Oh, dear. Oh, dear. Oh, dear." Carolyn stumbled over to the nearest counter stool and sat down.

Marilyn came to her side and wrapped her arms around her. "He lied to you, Carolyn. He definitely is married. Trust me."

Carolyn pulled back. "But he said he moved out a few weeks ago."

"That's true. He did because their new place was available early. I just talked to his wife two days ago. She said that since the new owner of their town house isn't moving in until the middle of April, she and their son are staying and taking their time to move."

"Their son?"

Marilyn raised her eyebrows. "Ellis didn't tell you about him either, did he? They have a teenage son. He's handicapped. Ellis's sweet wife cares for him at home."

Now Carolyn had both hands over her face. She couldn't speak.

"It's not your fault, Carolyn. He lied to you. My guess is that he's had affairs before, but his wife puts up with it because of their son."

"I think I'm going to be sick."

Marilyn went to the refrigerator and pulled out another can of soda and popped the top. "Here, drink this. The carbonation will help."

"No it won't."

"Yes it will."

"I don't want anything, Marilyn. I just want to be alone."

"Being alone would be the worst thing in the world for you right now. You need to talk about this and get your feelings out."

Carolyn didn't respond. She didn't speak or move. Her thoughts flooded with all the slight innuendos she had brushed off at dinner: his questions about her "being ready for more" and looking forward to them "getting together." A small alarm inside her had asked if she should be reading something into his expressions and words at the time, but she hadn't allowed herself to think that he had anything but the most noble intentions in mind. *Was he actually checking to see if I was interested in an affair with him?*

Marilyn put her arm around Carolyn. "Listen to me. You didn't do anything wrong. You trusted the wrong man, that's all. A lot of weasels are out there. This one took advantage of your vulnerability and tried to get you to fall for him even though he's married. I think you should call him right now and let him have it."

Carolyn moved to the couch in the living room. She wanted to think. It didn't make sense to her that Ellis would be so open about pursuing her when he knew Carolyn was likely to find out about his wife and son.

Did he honestly think that wouldn't matter to me?

Marilyn followed Carolyn into the living room. "You know, I really wish you would have told me right away when he asked you out because I could have saved you all this pain. Now, where's your phone? You need to call him like I said. Right now."

As sick to her stomach as Carolyn was over the situation, she was even sicker of the way Marilyn delighted in telling her what to do. For the past few weeks in the blissful silence and sanity under her roof, Carolyn had seen clearly all the ways her sister had taken the upper hand for far too long.

"Marilyn, this isn't your problem. It's mine. I can take care of it."

"I know you can take care of it. But the fact is, Larry was the one who invited him to the wedding. If Larry hadn't invited him, none of this would have happened. I'm sure Larry would agree that we're at least partially responsible, just like we were for the hole in your wall."

"This isn't at all like the hole in my wall. It's not your problem, Marilyn." Carolyn's voice rose. "Stop trying to make it your problem. I can take care of this myself. Now, just leave me alone. Please go!"

"Fine."

Marilyn stood up, reached for her purse, and strode to the front door. She jerked it open and paused before exiting, letting the night chill race into the house and cause the heater to kick on. Marilyn seemed to be waiting for Carolyn to apologize and ask her to come back and sit down. That's exactly what Carolyn would have done in the past to keep the fragile peace in her home. But Marilyn didn't live here anymore, and Carolyn didn't have to pacify her sister any longer.

"Are you thinking of continuing the relationship? Is that it? Because if you are, that would be the biggest mistake of your life, you know."

"I'm not thinking of doing that, and you know it." Carolyn tried to soften her voice. She wasn't used to being the one who brought the drama into this house. But she did want the serenity of the past few weeks to return. "All I'm saying is that I can handle this myself."

"Fine. Have it your way. I just want to remind you that, if you had told me what was going on right away, this whole mess could have been avoided." Marilyn slammed the door on her way out, causing the small framed photo by the front door to rattle and fall in her wake. The glass in the frame broke when it hit the floor.

Carolyn reached for one of the new pillows on the sofa and threw it at the closed door. She grabbed another pillow and clutched it to her churning stomach. She left the broken glass and the picture frame where they were. They remained on the floor in shatters while she sat on the couch in equally fragmented pieces.

Her cell phone buzzed from its muted mode in her purse, but she ignored it. A minute later her home phone rang. She let it ring. Her cell buzzed again. Realizing it could be Tikki trying to reach her, Carolyn checked her cell. She saw a text from Marilyn.

SORRY I SLAMMED THE DOOR. CALL ME WHEN YOU'RE READY.

Carolyn hated when her sister sent messages in all caps. It was like she was yelling at her. It made it even easier to ignore Marilyn's text. Then, since the phone was still in her hand, Carolyn drew up her courage and placed a call to Ellis. She hadn't planned what she was going to say, but she knew she wanted to confront him before her hurt and anger had a chance to dissipate.

Ellis answered on the second ring. His greeting came across sounding familiar and affectionate. "I just called the hotel and found out we can check in at eleven thirty tomorrow instead of noon."

Hotel? Check in . . . he is assuming I was agreeing to a whole lot more than pasta for lunch. How did I miss that?

"Does eleven thirty work for you?"

"No, it doesn't work for me. None of this works for me, Ellis. Why didn't you tell me you were married?"

"I did. I said I wasn't divorced, and you said you weren't divorced either."

Carolyn clenched her teeth before forcing out the words, "That's because my husband died seven years ago."

Ellis paused. She could hear him letting out a slow breath. "I'm very sorry to hear that, Carolyn."

Silence lingered between them as Carolyn tried to think of what to say.

"Let me explain my situation, will you?"

Carolyn listened as Ellis did a lot of circular

talking about being ready to make changes in his life and how beautiful she was and how she had fascinated him from the moment they talked at the wedding. "I'm ready to make a fresh start, and I want you to be part of that new beginning. You make me feel alive again."

Instead of being flattered, all Carolyn could think about was his wife and son. She felt sorry for them. She also felt sorry for Ellis. His life was in a tangle. Becoming involved with her or any other woman wasn't going to release the knots she guessed he must have inside. Continuing this conversation wasn't doing her any good.

"Carolyn, listen, I know this isn't making a lot of sense the way it's coming out. Would you just meet with me one more time? To talk. That's all. I want to explain all this more clearly. You deserve that."

"No, I can't meet with you again."

"But I don't think you understand. I—"

"I'm sure you're right; I'm sure I don't understand. But I can't meet with you. I won't. Please don't call me or contact me again."

Carolyn's heart pounded fiercely. She hung up without allowing him an opportunity to say anything else. Striding from one end of the kitchen to the other and then in circles around the living room, Carolyn felt cold tears stinging her warm cheeks. She picked up one of her new pillows and threw it at the door.

Her cell buzzed. She stomped back to the kitchen counter and read Ellis's text:

Please let me explain. Give me a chance to show you how I feel about you.

Carolyn deleted his message and turned off her phone. She felt like throwing up. Retreating to the bathroom, she washed her face and stared at her reflection in the mirror. Too stunned and upset to cry anymore, all she could do was stare.

Outside the wind was blowing up a storm. She could hear the rain pelting against the windows. Putting on her most comforting pajamas, she slipped into bed, curled up in a tightly tucked position, and waited for emotional exhaustion to overtake her.

Carolyn stayed inside all day Sunday and didn't answer her phone. She didn't place her usual call to her mother. This was a personal sick day, the first one she had allowed herself to take in many years.

On Monday, Carolyn went to work as if nothing had happened. Being back in her familiar routine always had been the best way to camouflage her deepest aches. It was like hiding in plain sight. No one would ask how she was doing; they could see she was fine—great even. She was performing at her usual level, paying close attention to other people and their needs and concerns.

By Tuesday, Carolyn still hadn't responded to her sister's many voice messages, e-mails, and texts. Ellis had left a phone message that she deleted without listening. When she arrived home from work at her usual time that afternoon, she saw Marilyn's car parked in the driveway. Her perturbed-looking twin stood leaning against the car's trunk with her arms folded.

"Did you forget your key?" Carolyn asked without making eye contact.

"No, I still have a key. I didn't want to go inside until I knew I was welcome."

Carolyn unlocked the front door and made an exaggerated sweeping gesture for Marilyn to come on in. Taking off her sweater, Carolyn picked up the mail that had been delivered through the slot in the front door. Then, turning her back on Marilyn, she went to the sofa, where she sifted through the bills just as she would have done when Marilyn lived with her.

Much to Carolyn's exasperation, Marilyn seemed to fall into the same old routine as well. She went into the kitchen and turned on the kettle. Carolyn could hear her rattling the dishes in the cupboard. When Marilyn came and sat in the chair across from Carolyn a few minutes later, she brought two mugs of tea. On a plate she had placed a rather soft apple cut into uneven slices alongside a handful of broken Wheat Thins. Carolyn kept her focus on the mail and resisted giving her sister any acknowledgment for her efforts. She hadn't asked her sister to come over, nor had she asked for anything to eat or drink.

"You need groceries." Marilyn delivered her statement with the preciseness of a straight pin into a balloon.

Carolyn popped. "Yes, I do. Is that what you came here to tell me? You drove across town to tell me I need groceries?"

"Well, that's better. At least you're looking at me now. Why have you ignored my calls? I'm not the one who lied to you. You're taking out your anger at Ellis on me. That's not fair, Carolyn. I'm your only sister. I'm here for you. I've always been here for you."

"I told you Saturday night: I want to be alone."

Marilyn dismissed Carolyn's comment. "You're a twin. You're never going to be alone unless I die first."

Carolyn wasn't sure she wanted to believe that. It was probably true, but she didn't want it to be. She reluctantly reached for a cup of tea and noticed that Marilyn had made her favorite afternoon blend of jasmine loose tea. Marilyn had also added just the right amount of honey. It was becoming difficult to remain irritated at Marilyn, since she was trying in her own way to be there for Carolyn and to offer support.

"Thanks for making the tea." She felt herself softening.

"Sure." Marilyn leaned back. "So, I take it you called him."

"Yes."

"And?"

"And that's it. I won't be seeing him again." Carolyn relaxed her tightened shoulders and sipped her tea. If she would be honest with her sister, she would come right out and say that at this point she was more embarrassed than angry. It was over. Past. She was ready to move on.

Marilyn put down her cup of tea. "So you're over the whole Ellis affair then?"

Carolyn winced. "Don't call it an affair. Please."

"Okay. But the point is, you're not going to see him, and he's not going to pursue you, and it's over."

"Yes."

"So you don't need me to help you to process the whole mess anymore."

"No, I don't need you to help me process it anymore." Carolyn wanted to shake her head at her sister's assumption that that was what had been going on.

"Is it okay if we talk about something else?" Marilyn asked.

"I wish we would."

"Well, then, I have some news. We're going to move."

"You are? Where are you going?"

"Santa Cruz." Marilyn rustled in her place like a pleased hen. "Larry got a new position there with his same tax preparation firm. It's a big step up. Remember my telling you about this opening? This is the job I urged him to apply for before we married. He was too reluctant. When we came back from our honeymoon, I urged him, and when he finally applied, he got the job, as I knew he would."

"That's great."

"The girls aren't too excited yet, but this is as much for them as it is for Larry. They need to make a fresh start and find new friends. It's only an hour and a half from here, and I told them they'll like living near the beach. I'm going house hunting tomorrow. I'll let you know what I find. I'm hoping you'll be willing to help me decorate."

"Sure."

They talked comfortably and casually for another twenty minutes about the sort of house Marilyn was hoping to find, the job she planned to look for in Santa Cruz, and how Larry had gained eight pounds since the wedding, which was fine with her because he could stand to gain another ten.

Marilyn checked the clock on top of the television. She put down her mug and stood up. "I have to leave before the traffic gets too heavy. We're planning to go to the movies tonight. Larry is such a sweetheart. All I have to do is hint just once that I'd like to see something, and he goes online, buys the tickets, and tries to surprise me. But I always find out. I check the history on his computer so I know every website he goes to."

Marilyn paused by the open front door the same way she had a few days ago, letting the cold air in. "You know, I didn't say this earlier, but I should be angry with you for not answering any of my calls for a week."

"It wasn't a week, Marilyn. I turned off my phone for only a few days. I needed space."

"I know. And I gave you your space. That's because I know you, and I know what you need. I always have, and I always will." Marilyn gave Carolyn a lopsided smile and let herself out, closing the door with exaggerated softness.

Carolyn stayed on the sofa nibbling the last broken cracker and pondering all that it meant to be a twin. As similar as they were and as different as they were, they were intertwined. Marilyn was right. The two of them would be involved in each other's lives for as long as they lived.

For some reason, now that Marilyn had declared the "affair" over and Carolyn's pent-up anger at Ellis had disseminated, she felt sadness returning. All the small dreams she had entertained about possibly being loved again were gone. She was alone.

Carolyn heard footsteps at her door and guessed

Marilyn was returning for something she had forgotten.

The door opened. It wasn't Marilyn. It was Tikki. She stepped inside and gave her mother a crooked grin.

"Me again. Do you mind?"

"Of course not. Is everything okay?"

"Sort of. I guess. Pretty much." Tikki came over and cuddled up to Carolyn on the sofa, resting her head on her mother's shoulder. "I needed to come home again. I wanted to be with you. Sometimes, when life isn't making a lot of sense, you just need to be near your mama."

Carolyn felt a lump rising in her throat. She stroked Tikki's silky hair. "You're right. Sometimes you just need to be near your mama."

In that moment Carolyn crossed an invisible line in her heart. She knew the time had come; she was going to find a way to return to the Canary Islands. Yes, she was a single woman, a twin sister, and a mother. But she was also a daughter. And now she was the one who needed to be near her mama.

6

"A donde el corazón se inclina, el pie camina."
"To where the heart is inclined,
the feet will follow."

CAROLYN TUGGED HER wheeled suitcase behind her through the modern, bustling Madrid airport. She had two hours before her connecting flight left for Las Palmas on the island of Gran Canaria.

The combination of spending the past fourteen hours on planes, dashing through O'Hare from Terminal 1 to Terminal 3, and the whirlwind events of the past three weeks left her head feeling like a sieve. Every thought seemed to slide out. She would catch it and put it back in her mind only to feel it slide out again.

Carolyn noticed a small café that had dozens of oranges stacked behind a glass case. The man behind the counter was squeezing the fresh oranges by pressing down on a long lever on an elaborate juicer. The lure of the fresh-squeezed juice drew her over to the café. Carolyn stood in line behind a well-dressed businessman, and when it was her turn to order, she found it easy enough to use her limited Spanish and ask for *"uno"* and *"grande."*

She paid with euros she had exchanged at the

San Francisco Airport and found a small table in the corner. Parking her suitcase and her weary self, Carolyn took a long sip of the fresh-squeezed, heavy pulp orange juice. It was, she decided, the best orange juice she ever had tasted.

A slender woman took the seat next to Carolyn and gave her a quick glance. Carolyn smiled in response.

"Do you know what time it is?" the woman asked.

Carolyn checked her watch. "It's eleven forty."

The woman checked her cell phone, shook her head, and untwisted the top on the water bottle she had just bought. She glanced at Carolyn again. "By any chance are you on the one-oh-five flight to Chicago?"

"No, I just came from Chicago. I'm heading for the Canary Islands."

Carolyn wasn't sure why she had shared that bit of information. It piqued her fellow traveler's interest, though, and she replied, "That's one of the places I've also wanted to go. Have you been there before?"

"Just once."

"Did you enjoy it? I hear they have some beautiful beaches."

"They do. My mother lives there. In Las Palmas."

"That's nice. You have a place to stay anytime you need a vacation. Although the vacation part can be a downer, I suppose, if you don't get along well with your mother."

"Fortunately my mother and I get along very well. The only downer is that it's been far too long since we've seen each other."

"My mother lives in Topeka." The woman leaned back and looked down at her nails. "I should go to see her more than I do. It's been more than a year since I've made the trip. I travel a lot, but going home is like traveling back in time. I'm convinced I turn into a twelve-year-old as soon as I walk through her front door."

Carolyn smiled. She regretted all the years she hadn't been able to readily visit her mom. When her father passed away fifteen years ago and her mother made the decision to return to the Canary Islands, Carolyn was certain they would take turns crossing the ocean once every year to be together. Carolyn hadn't managed to make the journey once during the past fifteen years. Her mother had come back for Tikki's twelfth birthday and spent a wonderful month and a half with them. She returned again seven years ago for Jeff's memorial service. On that visit, Tikki and Carolyn both tried to persuade her to move in with them. But that was about the time of Marilyn's crisis in her first marriage, and she needed to be the one to move in with Carolyn.

In the wake of all the changes and sadness that had come to Carolyn in the past month, her heart had cried out to get away, to be with her mother.

"I hope you and your mom have a great visit."

"Thanks. I hope so too. I'm a little nervous about how everything is going to work out because she doesn't know I'm coming."

The woman pushed up her thin glasses and looked intrigued.

"Her birthday is tomorrow. It's her seventieth. I had lost track and didn't realize until my daughter brought it up three weeks ago that this was a significant year for my mom."

"Is your daughter coming as well?"

"No." Carolyn swished the remaining orange juice in her glass. "I wish she were with me. That was our original plan. At first we talked about coming in the fall with one of my aunts, but she is having knee surgery this week. Then, when we realized it was my mom's seventieth, we decided we should come now instead of in the fall. At the time my daughter was in the middle of a big life change, and it seemed like a good idea to get away."

Carolyn wasn't sure why she was telling all this to a stranger. She normally was much more private. But then, making the decision to take this trip and impulsively buying the expensive plane ticket was also out of the norm for her.

"It's too bad your daughter couldn't come with you."

"I know. She just received a promotion at the

bank where she works, and she couldn't take off the time." Carolyn wondered again why she was divulging all this personal information. She wouldn't be this talkative with someone beside her in a coffee shop at home. Somehow she felt anonymous in the airport on the other side of the world. Expressing her situation, she felt as if she were still talking herself into why this was a good idea.

"My mom's birthday is coming up," the woman said. "I suppose I should make arrangements to see her. I wouldn't try to surprise her, though. She doesn't do well with surprises. Does your mom like them?"

"I think so. We'll see how it goes. The plan is for me to just show up at her big birthday party luncheon tomorrow. I hope I don't give her a heart attack."

"If I did that to my mother, she would throw a fit." The woman smiled and took a long drink from her water bottle. She checked her cell phone again. "I better head toward my gate. It was nice visiting with you. I hope you have a fabulous time with your mother."

"Thank you. I hope you have a safe trip to Chicago."

"Thanks."

As the woman walked away, Carolyn noticed that she carried herself with confidence as she balanced on the narrow heels of her pale sage ankle boots. She wore nicely fitting jeans and a thin, loose-fitting dark blue sweater that fell to her hips. Her outfit was simple, but she carried it off with an air of sophistication. Carolyn looked down at her zip-up fleece and her black, slip-on shoes. Boring but comfortable. She might have stepped out of her comfort zone to talk openly with the woman, but she still didn't feel like a world traveler.

Carolyn finished her orange juice and watched people go by. She hadn't fully absorbed that she was in Spain. Announcements floated from the airport PA system in several languages, starting with Spanish. A couple near her were speaking in Castilian Spanish, in which all the "s" sounds were delivered with a flattened tongue that produced a "th" sound.

Carolyn wished Tikki were with her. It had been difficult to convince Aunt Frieda that once Carolyn had bought the ticket she was committed to attending her mother's birthday party rather than wait until the fall. It had been easier to break the news to Marilyn, who was so wrapped up in her house hunting and upcoming move that all she wanted to know was when Carolyn would be back to help with paint color selection.

Carolyn's fledgling confidence waned even more when she boarded the flight that would take her to Las Palmas. Everything about the flight felt different from her U.S. flight. Loud, contemporary music played throughout the plane as she entered and found her seat in row nineteen. The seats felt narrower, and the flight attendants' announcements were issued only in Spanish and German. The older couple that had the middle and aisle seats next to Carolyn spoke only German. They asked her something, but she couldn't understand them, so they gave up trying to communicate with her.

For the next four and a half hours, the man in front of her kept his seat reclined all the way. If she looked straight ahead, she could see every hair follicle on the top of his thinning scalp. Carolyn didn't dare recline her seat because the person behind her was using the tray table for his laptop computer and had managed to configure his legs in such a way that Carolyn could feel a foot or a knee pressing through her seat.

She tried to sleep. When that didn't work, she tried to watch the movie playing in the small screen suspended two aisles ahead of her. She hadn't bought a headset when the flight attendants came down the aisle, which made following the movie challenging. Carolyn also didn't take a boxed snack when it was held up because she didn't know if she had to pay for it, and if she did, her purse was stuffed into the overhead bin.

All her reserves felt drained by the time the passengers deplaned, and she followed the crowds through to the luggage claim area.

Carolyn's memories of this airport from more than twenty-five years ago were erased by the newer, more modern, and efficient airport she now strolled through. She was thankful when she saw her suitcase coming her way on the luggage carousel. At least she didn't have to try to file a lost luggage request in Spanish. Aside from being hungry, she had no major complaints.

Easily managing the two bags, Carolyn headed outside the terminal where the plan was for Rodrigo, one of Aunt Isobel's sons, to be waiting for her in a blue car outside of baggage claim. The plan sounded simple and easy last week. Now that Carolyn was outside of baggage claim, standing by the curb, looking right and left like a nervous squirrel, she thought the plan might have been too simple. No one was there to meet her.

Looking around, she noticed how the evening air felt warm against her skin. She drew in a deep breath of the faintly salt-laced air. Carolyn remembered now that the pace here was slower than at home. She wondered how much of her memory about the Canaries was still true.

A young couple speaking a language Carolyn didn't recognize shared a cigarette and helped each other to adjust their backpacks before walking off hand in hand. Two women wrapped in the dark robes and facial veils of West African Muslims stood next to Carolyn while three small boys wearing caps ran in and out of their stack of suitcases and boxes.

Dozens of blue cars drove by. Carolyn finally stopped trying to make eye contact with the driver in each car because many of them were apparently taxicabs. The drivers stopped, said something in Spanish, and Carolyn had to put up her hand in a "no thank you" gesture and shake her head.

The sky was darkening. Carolyn watched as the lights came on across the airport parking lot. The low, blue-tinged glow sparked inside each of the milky saucers seemed to hum with a quiet strength until the entire area was lit.

As much as she didn't want to admit it, Carolyn wished that Aunt Frieda had come with her. Frieda would have taken charge and, in her rapid Spanish, made all the arrangements.

A flock of small birds soared over the top of the terminal. The undersides of their bodies caught the fading light and turned from dark brown to a soft shade of yellow. As Carolyn watched them, a spontaneous plea sprang from her heart.

How much longer should I wait here? What if Rodrigo doesn't come? Help me. I don't know what to do.

Carolyn realized she was directing her thoughts toward God. She was asking for his help. It had been a long time since she had done that. What came out were not the recited prayers of her childhood. Nor were they the free-flowing prayers she and Jeff had shared since early on in their marriage when they were close to each other and to their Heavenly Father.

As soon as Jeff died, Carolyn found the only thing she could say to God was "Why?" When no answers came, she stopped asking the question and didn't ask for anything.

Until now. Here. All alone in this no-longer-familiar place, Carolyn found that it gave her comfort to simply ask God to be with her. Somehow she knew he was. That was the truth that had been instilled in her since childhood.

For another twenty minutes she waited, waving off the taxis that pulled up. She stretched her sore neck and ignored her grumbling stomach. A small white car came to a lurching stop at the curb in front of her. With the engine still running, an older woman pulled herself from the driver's position on the left side of the car and raised both her arms in champion style, the way Marilyn had done on the dance floor at her wedding.

Carolyn knew she had been found. One of the Women of the Canaries had come for her.

"¡Carolina, lo siento mi niña! ¡Pobrecita! Venga. Venga."

As the woman came around the front of the car, Carolyn could see that it was Aunt Isobel, the sweet, petite baby of the five sisters. She opened her arms, and Carolyn fell into them. In their warm

100

embrace, Carolyn was aware of how tall she was compared to her aunt. The distinct scent of onions mixed with rosemary and almond paste rose from Aunt Isobel as they hugged. The skin on her face felt like silk as she pressed her cheek against Carolyn's and kissed her twice on both sides.

"Lo siento," Isobel began again and followed with too many Spanish words for Carolyn to understand. She did recognize *lo siento* as an apology.

Drawing from old files in her memory, Carolyn pulled out the phrase *"No te preocupes"* and hoped that she was right and that the line meant "Don't worry about it."

"¿Más vale tarde que nunca, sí?"

"Sí," Carolyn replied, even though she wasn't quite sure what Isobel had said. She thought it was something like "Better late than never."

Isobel reached for one of Carolyn's suitcases, still chattering rapidly in Spanish. She opened the trunk of the small car, moved aside some gallon-sized water bottles, and hoisted the first suitcase into the narrow space. When it didn't fit, she kept talking and pointed to the car's backseat.

Carolyn opened the door to the backseat and stacked both of her suitcases upright like two toddlers strapped into car seats. Climbing in on the passenger's side, Carolyn waited until she could wedge a word in between her excited aunt's conversational barrage.

The opportunity came as they were pulling away from the airport and merging onto a main, well-paved road. The improvements to the road surprised Carolyn, but she knew from her mother's reports that a lot had happened to modernize the remote islands over the past twenty-five years.

"Aunt Isobel, I have to tell you that my Spanish isn't very good. I don't understand what you're saying."

"Ah." She clicked her tongue. "*Sí*. Ah. Rodrigo he have a baby. Today! This is early for baby. So I come for you but too much cars."

"A lot of traffic?"

"*Sí, sí*. Y . . . and . . ." She waved her hand, as if trying to brush away the challenge of explaining everything in her limited English.

"That's okay. You don't have to explain." Carolyn gave Isobel's arm a tender squeeze. She was amazed how firm the woman's arm was. No wonder this sixty-something auntie could hoist Carolyn's suitcases with ease. She was a strong woman.

Carolyn smiled. She was here. She was in the Canaries, riding beside her strong aunt. A long sleep awaited her, and then tomorrow she would see her mother.

"*¿Tienes hambre?*" Isobel glanced at her. "Hungry?"

"Yes. *Sí*."

"We have food and . . ." Isobel added another string of Spanish.

"I hope you didn't go to any trouble. I'm pretty tired. I'll probably fall asleep as soon as I eat something."

"No problema." Isobel glanced over and gave Carolyn another one of her warm smiles and squeezed Carolyn's knee. *"Mi niña."*

Carolyn recognized the phrase her aunt used. The words literally meant "my girl" and was an endearing term her aunts all used when they referred to any of the women in the family. Carolyn smiled back. She liked being one of the "my girls" of the Canaries.

The wide highway that led them into the city and the amount of traffic was nothing like Carolyn's memories of this place. She knew that her aunt and mother were living in the city now and not on the outskirts where their parents had lived when Carolyn last visited as a teen.

The high-rise buildings, traffic roundabouts, and huge, bell-shaped recycle containers at the end of the main streets all surprised Carolyn. So did the sight of the hills. The arid views of tall cactus anchored in the dusty brown curves of the dormant volcano were missing from this entry to the city. Instead, the landscape now was filled with apartment buildings stacked up like toy blocks in a variety of primary colors. Streetlights climbed up to the dark sky along black asphalt ribbons of new roads. Much had changed.

Carolyn stared out the open car window and caught sight of a few faded stars in the sky overhead. She thought of the multitude of vibrant stars she had once counted from a beach blanket at Las Canteras. She was certain those stars were watching her every move from the heavens. They were perhaps the only ones that saw her leave the group that last night on the beach. They saw when she slipped into the shadows and ran barefoot through the sand to where Bryan Spencer waited for her. And what happened after that, the stars saw too. They saw, but they never told.

And neither had she.

7

"Genio y figura hasta la sepultura."
"Character and presence from
the cradle to the tomb."

ISOBEL PULLED INTO a gated underground parking structure beneath a cement apartment building that ran the entire length of the block. She rolled down her window, pressed in a code on the keypad, and steered her compact car forward as soon as the gate lifted. They drove past rows and rows of parked cars before Isobel pulled into a narrow space and turned off the engine.

None of this arrival had been anything like Carolyn's previous visit. This gated, high-rise apartment was quite a departure from the flat-roofed home where Carolyn had stayed last time, with chickens in the yard and a back patio covered with a thick trellis of magenta-colored bougainvillea.

The wheels of Carolyn's suitcases squeaked as she rolled them into the elevator that took her aunt and Carolyn to the fifth floor. A security light came on, lighting the way while Isobel's heels clicked on the brightly polished floor. She wore classic pumps in a caramel brown shade and a full skirt in a soft orange and brown print. Her cream-colored blouse bore a variety of end-of-the-day crinkles. Even so, she looked fresh. Ready for a party.

And that's exactly what greeted them when Isobel opened the door to her apartment. From out of the living room and into the short entryway hall spilled every relative Carolyn had on the islands. Everyone but her mother.

Eighteen relatives greeted Carolyn with kisses and strings of lovely Spanish words that were more than she could absorb in the moment. For at least an hour she made the rounds, trying out her Spanish as they each tried out their English.

A bountiful assortment of tapas was set on the table. Carolyn filled a plate of the tasty appetizers and kept making her way around the room. Her second cousin Rosa pulled her aside and asked, "Are you tired? You must be."

"A little." The true answer was "a lot." But this was so grand and wonderful that she didn't want to show any sign of not appreciating the flourish of attention.

"Come with me." Rosa tugged on Carolyn's arm and pulled her into the small kitchen. Dishes and serving casserole pans were piled on the counter. One of the aunts was busy washing by hand while a not-so-thrilled-to-be-helping young cousin had drying duty. Carolyn offered to help with the dishes, but the aunt made it clear that Carolyn wasn't to get anywhere near the sink.

Rosa pointed to one of the four chairs at the compact kitchen table, indicating they should sit down. "You didn't know everyone would be here, did you?"

"No, but it's great. I had hoped to have a chance to see everyone."

"Just not all at once, right?" Rosa had a round face, short hair, and darling dimples that made her appear younger than her midthirties. "Everyone is happy you're here. They wanted to see you right away. Isobel should have told you."

"She probably did, but I didn't understand. My Spanish is pretty limited."

"Don't worry. It will come back to you while you're here."

"I don't know about that. Your English is really good. Where did you learn it?"

"Here and there. TV mostly. In school I had a friend who was from Florida; she taught me some."

"I'm impressed."

Rosa laughed. "Don't be. It's not a great accomplishment. I think if you just listen, you hear the language, and you remember it."

"It doesn't work that way for me. I think it's harder than you know. You must have a natural gift for it."

Rosa brushed off the compliment. "Do you want to go back out there? Or do you want to go to bed? You can do that, you know. You can tell them you have jet drag, and they will understand. We'll be together all day tomorrow."

Carolyn didn't try to correct Rosa on the "jet drag" comment. She simply said, "I'm ready to get some sleep."

Rosa took her by the hand and led the way down the short hall to where three closed doors appeared in a circle. That was the extent of the small apartment.

"This is the bathroom." Rosa opened the door in the middle, revealing a tall shower, freestanding sink, and elongated toilet.

"And this is your room."

Carolyn's suitcases had been placed against the wall like two miniature soldiers standing guard.

The room had a built-in closet, a twin-sized bed with what looked like a handmade patchwork comforter, a nightstand with a light, and a straight-back chair. That was all she needed. Simple. Clean. Inviting. This was the Canary Island style she remembered.

Rosa gave Carolyn another hug and wished her "happy dreams."

Carolyn slept in snatches, floating off for just so long and then waking when she heard the party still going on in the living room. During the deepest hours of the night, she woke when she heard footsteps of the neighbor in the apartment above them. When hints of light came through the window shade, she heard the screech of truck brakes and a baby crying in a nearby apartment. Each time she awakened, she rolled on her back and tried to fall asleep. It was a long stretch of much working at sleeping and not much actual sleep.

When she finally rose and saw that it was almost eight o'clock, she felt as bubbleheaded as she had when she first disembarked from the plane. As soon as Carolyn opened her guest room door, Aunt Isobel came trotting down the short hallway. She greeted Carolyn with a big smile, lots of cheerful words in Spanish, and a cup of dark coffee served in a small white cup balanced on a matching saucer.

"This is a nice surprise." Carolyn stood in the hall

in her pajamas and thin robe, sipping the coffee as Isobel watched. "This tastes very good. *Gracias*."

Isobel pointed toward the kitchen and said, "*¿Huevos?*"

"Sure, some eggs would be nice. Would it be okay if I took a shower first?" Carolyn pointed to the bathroom.

"*Sí, sí.*" Isobel showed her where the towel was hanging on a peg behind the door. She then showed Carolyn how to turn the shower on and off and how to adjust the temperature.

Carolyn finished the coffee and handed her efficient aunt the cup and saucer. She had to admit, it was pretty nice being greeted with fresh coffee and hopping in the shower while her breakfast was being prepared.

Carolyn didn't see a blow-dryer in the bathroom, and she hadn't brought one with her, so she towel dried her hair. The warm breeze that had come through her bedroom window gave her confidence that her hair would dry quickly in the perennially warm climate. The biggest blessing to having fairly thick and easy-to-manage hair was that she always could pull it up in a twist of some sort and fluff up the bangs across her forehead, and she looked as if that was how she meant to wear her hair that day. If her hair did dry without curving or sticking out in any peculiar way, she could wear it down, skimming her shoulders.

Dressed in her nicest skirt, her favorite blue

knit top, and matching sweater, she made her way to the kitchen, where Isobel had prepared a small feast for her.

"You didn't need to do this, you know. You're spoiling me."

Isobel beamed. Her cheeks stood out, smooth and round on her sweet face. She really was the most darling of all the sisters. "Isobel the Innocent" was what Marilyn had nicknamed her after looking at photos Carolyn had brought home after her summer visit so many years ago.

Carolyn took her first bite of scrambled eggs with fresh tomato slices and the diced-up potatoes with red peppers, onions, and lots of spices. Then she declared the meal *"¡Delicioso!"*

"¿Te gustan las papas?"

"Sí, I like the potatoes. You'll have to show me how to season them like this." Carolyn made a hand sign like she was shaking salt over the potatoes. "I like the spice."

"Ah! *Culantro. Mira. Aquí."* Isobel pointed to a wooden box precariously positioned in the frame of the window above the sink. Green shoots of various frilly shapes and sizes were growing in the box.

"You grow your own herbs. No wonder it tastes so fresh."

Isobel plucked a tiny sprig and rubbed it between her thumb and forefinger. She held her smudged fingers out for Carolyn to smell.

"Ah, cilantro. Of course. I love it. I don't think I've ever tried fresh cilantro with potatoes. I like it. *Me gusta.*"

Isobel looked pleased that Carolyn was attempting to express herself in Spanish. Taking three steps across the small kitchen's floor, the aunt pointed to a potted plant in the corner where it was soaking up the morning sunshine. *"Pimientos rojos."*

"You grow your own red peppers too. Nice."

A dull buzzer sounded, and Isobel looked surprised. She took off her apron and went to the front door. Apparently she wasn't expecting anyone that morning. Carolyn finished her last bite of eggs and was about to get up from the table when she heard a voice from the entryway that made her freeze in place.

Mom!

Hearing her mother's voice was like hearing a favorite song and feeling all the memories connected to that tune humming through her veins. She wanted to jump up and run into the other room. But she waited, heart pounding, not sure what to do.

Incredibly, the two women walked right past the open kitchen door without her mother noticing Carolyn sitting at the table. She considered calmly strolling out to the living room. That would make for a shocking surprise for her mother. And if the seventy-year-old matriarch fainted, at least she would do so in the privacy of Isobel's living room instead of in a very public restaurant where her birthday party was taking place later that afternoon.

Hearing the strength and verve in her mother's voice, Carolyn knew she wouldn't faint or have a heart attack when she saw Carolyn. Her mother was a bit like Aunt Frieda in that she most likely would enjoy the moment more if it happened in front of all the relatives. That realization motivated Carolyn to stay hidden and stick with the original plan, even though it was killing her to do so.

The two sisters talked briskly until at last it seemed that Aunt Isobel was giving in to what had been a friendly argument. A single set of quick footsteps headed toward the kitchen. Carolyn held her breath and watched the doorway.

Isobel entered with her eyes wide and her finger to her lips. She motioned for Carolyn to stay put. On the back of an envelope Isobel scribbled, *Sit. Rosa come.*

Carolyn nodded her understanding and leaned back as Isobel reached for her purse, and the two sisters left the apartment. As soon as Carolyn heard the front door close with a click, she let out a long slow breath and felt a wave of sadness. For the past seven years an ocean lay between her mother and her. Now only a thin wall had

112

separated them, and yet she hadn't been able to run and wrap her arms around her mother.

Soon enough.

Carolyn went to work, clearing the table and washing the dishes before returning to the bathroom to finish her nearly dry hair. As she brushed out her long brown strands and tucked the sides behind her ears, she thought, *The water here must be on my side. My hair isn't this smooth at home.*

Taking her time with her makeup and brushing her teeth, Carolyn then returned to the guest room to make her bed. She pulled up the window shade and had a look down on the large plaza between the apartment building she was in and an identical building across the way. Five floors down the garden spread out on either side of the huge, rectangular swimming pool. Only one person was in the pool, swimming laps on this beautiful morning.

Carolyn studied the carefully plotted garden boxes across the wide open area. Inside boxed beds of light-colored pebbles were planted varied palm trees, cactus, and tall bushes of colorful bougainvillea. Behind the end of the long, immense court Carolyn could see the tops of the hills and beyond the hills, the contented, blue sky. The sky's shade of blue was a soft pastel, a sleepy sort of blue. Not the vivid and stunning turquoise blue shown in calendars that featured tropical isles of the Pacific. Here the shades of Atlantic blue seemed subdued and understated, as if they had nothing to prove.

An hour passed, and Carolyn wondered if Aunt Isobel's plan for Rosa to pick her up was going to work out. To have come all this way and then to end up missing the big moment at her mother's party would be crazy. But then, Rodrigo's wife going into labor at the same time he was supposed to pick up Carolyn from the airport was a little crazy too. Was this how life was going to be while she was here?

The funny-sounding doorbell buzzed three quick times. Carolyn grabbed her purse and hurried to open the door for Rosa. Only it wasn't Rosa. It was an older woman with a sleeping baby in her arms. She spoke to Carolyn in a low voice, handing over the slumbering little one and trotting away before Carolyn could pull together two words of English or Spanish. The woman waved an arm as she went into the elevator and disappeared.

Carolyn stood in the doorway, frozen with surprise. Now she really didn't know what to do. She went inside and sat on the couch, holding the little one, who was lost in a dream. All she could do was wait for the woman to return or for Rosa to arrive.

This is crazy! ¡Loco!

The cherub in Carolyn's arms stirred. Carolyn

paced the floor, holding the baby up over her shoulder and patting its back. Just as the little one went back to breathing rhythmically, the sound of a key in the door caused Carolyn to stop her paces.

Rosa entered. "Hello! Are you ready to go?"

Her voice woke the baby, and the cries flooded the apartment.

"Who is that?"

"I don't know. A lady came to the door, handed this little baby to me, and took off before I could figure out how to tell her I didn't understand what she was saying."

Rosa came close and peered at the wailing baby's face over Carolyn's shoulder. "I know who you are. What are you doing here, Gabby? Where did your grandmother go?"

"At least you know who she is. The bigger question is, what should we do?"

Rosa took the little girl from Carolyn and shushed the babe, rocking side to side. She spoke softly in Spanish. "Gabby's *abuela* lives next door. She watches her daughter's children all the time. She probably thought you were Elena. Did you meet her last night? You look similar. Elena is over here a lot. She lived here last year when she was working on this side of town."

"So the grandmother just dropped off her baby for an unspecified amount of time?"

Rosa's techniques hadn't quieted the crying

baby. Gabby reared back her head. She was old enough and aware enough to know that neither of these women was familiar. The realization prompted more wails and more tears.

"We just have to wait for her to come back. She probably went to pick up the mail or for groceries."

"Groceries? We could be here for an hour."

Rosa shrugged. "Then we wait for an hour. Shh, Gabby. *No te preocupes, mi niña.*"

With a combination of soothing words and bouncing sways, Rosa calmed down the startled baby.

"So, I heard you had another surprise today. Isobel said your mother came here, and you hid in the kitchen."

"It was strange being so close and hearing her voice but not seeing her."

"I can imagine."

"Do you know why my mom came over? Where did they go?"

"They went to the beach. Your mother wanted to walk down the boardwalk and have coffee before the party. Isobel got away from your mother long enough to call me from the restroom and tell me what was going on."

"Everything is okay then?"

"Yes. You'll ride over with me."

"What time are we supposed to be at the restaurant?"

"Noon. But it's okay if we're late. They will be there most of the afternoon. Or if you want, you could go now. I'll stay with Gabby."

"But I don't know where to go."

"It's at La Marinera. Do you remember this restaurant? It's at the end of the boardwalk at Las Canteras. You can take a taxi. It will be no problem."

Carolyn wasn't sure what to do. It would be easier to wait for Rosa and go together, even if they were late. The baby started to cry again, and Carolyn decided she would try for the taxi. She certainly had managed to flag down enough of them at the airport last night when she wasn't trying to get one. She should be able to go out in front of the apartment complex and flag one down now. If she was unsuccessful, she could always return to the apartment and wait with Rosa.

Decision made, Carolyn exited the apartment and heard the heavy door close with a decisive click, separating her from one of the few English-speaking people she knew in the Canary Islands. She stopped and made a visual note of the number on the apartment door that belonged to Isobel. They all had looked alike to her when they had arrived last night. If she wasn't able to communicate well enough with the taxi driver, at least she would remember which door to knock on when she found her way back.

The elevator was slow in arriving at her floor. She rode alone to the first floor, chiding herself all the way for not popping out of the kitchen earlier and getting the surprise over with. She could have gone on the stroll with her mom and Isobel, and she would be at the restaurant with them now.

The uniformed guard by the apartment complex's gated entrance greeted her with *"Buenos días."* Carolyn nodded and mumbled the same back. Sounds of lunch-hour traffic filled the air as Carolyn stepped out on the wide sidewalk that ran the length of the main boulevard. The car motors' rumble was punctuated by the squeal of brakes and short blasts of a horn coming from a large delivery truck, which roared around the corner. The smell of diesel fumes mixed with the scent of sautéing onions that wafted from an open window of a first-floor apartment.

Rosa had instructed Carolyn that she needed to cross the street and flag a cab that was headed downhill, toward the beach. Rosa emphasized, "Pedestrians have the right of way. Don't wait for the cars to slow down. You put your foot out in the street, and all the cars will stop."

Carolyn stood on the sidewalk observing the rush of uphill traffic and knew she wasn't in California anymore. No button appeared on the street pole for her to press. The streets were not

118

equipped with painted white lines, and boxes with walking stick figures did not light up to help her navigate the intersection. No, this was a place for decisive action, and the longer she waited, the more intimidating the traffic became.

After several minutes of hesitation, Carolyn took the first step. She put her foot into the street, and almost immediately all three lanes of uphill traffic came to a halt. For a moment she was too stunned to move. Then, taking quick steps, she trotted past the attentive audience of drivers and took refuge on the median that separated the uphill and downhill traffic. The instant both her feet were on the median, the dash of the motorists began again at full speed.

Turning to face the downhill traffic, Carolyn repeated her best-foot-forward maneuver. Once again, all three lanes of vehicles immediately stopped. She had never seen anything like it. The power she could command with nothing more than her sandaled foot amazed her.

Unfortunately that power to command the will of oncoming cars didn't carry over in her attempts to hail a taxi. During her wait at the airport, Carolyn had discovered that the taxis could be any color. Many taxis had a small light attached to the roof of the car that was green when available and red when taken. Some cab drivers placed a card in the front windshield with the word *ocupado* when they were carrying a passenger.

In the glare of the overhead sun, Carolyn couldn't distinguish the red from the green on the marked taxis that came her way. She recognized the *ocupado* signs but didn't know what to look for in the window of an unmarked taxi.

For longer than she expected she would have to, Carolyn stood on the curb with her right arm extended, her palm open as her cousin had showed her, and waved up and down calmly at the fleet of oncoming cars. Certainly some of them had to be taxis. And at least one of those taxis had to be eager to pick up a passenger. However, every marked cab that passed was taken.

Just as her arm was beginning to feel the stretch, Carolyn managed to snag an open cab. She clambered into the backseat as the driver made eye contact with her in the rearview mirror and asked something in Spanish.

"Do you speak English?" Carolyn asked.

The driver replied in Spanish. Not English.

"I'd like to go to Las Canteras." Carolyn knew that if the driver dropped her off anywhere along the memory-laden beach, she could find her way to the restaurant at the end of the bay. La Marinera had been her mother's favorite restaurant years ago, and it made sense that it was her choice for her seventieth birthday celebration.

Without a reply, the driver flipped on the meter. With an unflinching jerk of the steering wheel, he merged into the flow of traffic. As the taxi sped downhill with all the windows open, she took a look at the surroundings that had been cloaked in dusk last night. Some areas were run-down and not at all appealing. Then a block later a modern building built of gray stucco with a red tile roof would appear.

Aunt Frieda often said that going "home" to the Canaries was like traveling back in time. Carolyn remembered that on her last visit most of the cars were older styles and none of the buildings had air-conditioning. The women still wore dresses whenever they were out in public and kept their shoulders covered the way good conservative women did in the United States during World War II. From what she was observing this time around, Las Palmas, Spain's ninth-largest city, was making hearty efforts toward expansion, development, and a more open dress code.

Leaning back and taking in the soft breeze on her face, Carolyn silently congratulated herself. She had made it all the way to the islands and even had managed to grab a taxi in spite of her limited Spanish. Tikki probably wouldn't agree that these minor accomplishments qualified as Carolyn's "getting a life," but as the taxi made its way to the old part of Las Palmas, Carolyn felt satisfied.

At home her life was insulated and familiar. Where she lived and worked hadn't changed for decades. Aside from a cruise to Mexico that she and Marilyn went on soon after Marilyn's divorce, Carolyn had done little traveling.

This was good. She felt strong.

The cabdriver slowly curved his way through the old part of the city, which seemed not to have changed much. The same shops were open for business, their narrow doorways displaying wares hung from the doorjamb and stacked on racks that held open the door. A Chinese restaurant had strung large, faded photos of the house specialties across the front window on a wire and held them in place with clothespins.

Carolyn remembered shopping with her mother for a new watch in one of the jewelry stores that displayed its name in cursive letters carved in wood over the door. She looked up and down the narrow streets as they drove past, certain she would recognize the shop if she saw it.

The driver pulled up to an open plaza area. Carolyn paid more than the amount showing on the meter since she wasn't sure if tipping was expected. By the quickly masked expression on his face, Carolyn guessed it wasn't. Next time she would know.

Heading for the beach, Carolyn stopped as soon as she came into view of the wide, sandy bay and drew in the scent of the sea. She was ready to retract her earlier assumptions that Las Palmas had changed. Here, at the Las Canteras beach, time had stood still. Everything was exactly as she remembered. Rows of neatly lined-up lounge chairs awaited customers within a roped-off section in front of a blue-and-white-striped cabana. A gathering of palm trees clustered beside the boardwalk and seemed to sigh with their own memories as the breeze rose to ruffle them.

Carolyn slipped off her sandals and buried her bare feet in the warm sand. She smiled at the way the sunlight sparkled on the clear, green water with an ageless verve. Along the shoreline, the Atlantic calmly curled and receded like a curtsy, leaving a fine white line of foamy petticoat lace on the tawny sand.

A vivid memory of her first visit to this beach rose to the surface of her thoughts. She was lying on her stomach beside her mother pretending to nap. In actuality she was peeking through the narrow gap between her raised arm and the beach towel. The object of her attention was the same as it was for all the other girls on the beach: bronzed, brazen, blond Bryan Spencer. He was playing soccer along the shore with a tribe of little pros. They were his lost boys, and he was their Peter Pan. Carolyn knew she wasn't the only girl who was willing to be his Wendy.

Quickly shaking off the memories along with the sand from her feet, Carolyn put her shoes back on and purposefully made her way along the busy boardwalk, eager to reach the restaurant. Businessmen strode past her in trim suits, talking shop and smoking dark cigarettes. Mothers with little ones in compact umbrella strollers kept up lively conversations with one another as they pushed on at an energetic clip. A dark woman covered in flowing cloth and headdress lowered her eyes as she passed Carolyn. She looked like she belonged in a Moroccan marketplace.

This was the Canary Islands she remembered. This mix of cultures and paces. This was her mother's home. And in a few moments she would step into La Marinera and give her mother the surprise everyone had helped to keep from their beloved matriarch, Abuela Teresa.

Carolyn felt her heart pounding with anticipation as she entered the restaurant's open-air front. A man wearing a white shirt and black bow tie greeted her and asked something in Spanish. She gave him her mother's name, and he responded with a smile of familiarity, nodding toward the back area where a party of at least forty of her mother's friends and relatives was gathered.

As Carolyn approached the group, she caught Aunt Isobel's eye, and as she did, her aunt rose from her chair, beaming and calling attention to her raised glass so that everyone would look at her. She offered a toast in honor of Abuela Teresa, as Carolyn stealthily sidled up next to her mother at the head of the table. Aunt Isobel turned to Carolyn and joyfully announced her by name.

All the guests cheered as Carolyn's mother turned and lifted her stunned gaze to see her daughter's face. She began to weep. Carolyn cried, too, and they embraced at last. They kissed each other's moist cheeks, laughing and crying at the same time. Carolyn leaned in close and whispered, "Happy Birthday, Mom. I love you."

Carolyn's beautiful, wonderful, strong-hearted mother took Carolyn's face in her two quivering hands. In a voice filled with wonder, she said, "Carolyn, you came all this way."

"Yes, I did. Just to see you."

Her mother's gaze flitted to the left over Carolyn's shoulder for just an instant. Carolyn recognized the instinctive glance. She knew that when a mother of twins saw one of her daughters, she always would check to see if the other one was right behind.

Carolyn shrugged slightly as if apologizing for Marilyn's absence. "It's just me."

"Just you," her mother repeated with a smile. "Just wonderful you."

She kissed the back of Carolyn's hand and pressed her cheek against it. "What a gift you have given me. And what a surprise!"

Aunt Isobel had moved into position beside Carolyn, and in an effort to keep the party moving along, she took Carolyn by the elbow and escorted her down the table to where an empty seat awaited her. There would be plenty of time for hugging and visiting during the week. The Birthday Queen had duties to perform. In a way, it all felt anticlimactic for Carolyn. She wished again that she had come out of hiding and joined her mother and Isobel on their stroll that morning. If she had, she wouldn't have been late or felt so conspicuous.

Carolyn reached for the cloth napkin folded on her plate and dried her tears. Up and down the table the guests had returned to their conversations, allowing Carolyn a moment to pull herself together. Drawing in a deep breath, she looked down the table to her mother, who sat with regal posture. Her mother wagged her finger at Carolyn playfully with an "I can't believe you did this" smile on her face.

Carolyn smiled in return and felt herself calming down. Leaning back, she placed her napkin in her lap. Then, lifting her chin, she looked up and for the first time noticed the guest seated across the table from her.

Time stood still. Her lips parted, and a single word escaped.

"Bryan."

8

"Dios los cría, y ellos se juntan."
"God makes them, and they find each other."

CAROLYN'S WHISPER OF Bryan's name had been only that, a whisper. Yet he seemed to hear her loud and clear despite the rousing conversations all around them. His expression made it evident that her immediate recognition of him and the soft echo of his name touched him deeply.

Lifting his glass to her, he smiled.

For several unflinching moments they held each other in a visual embrace, taking inventory of what the past quarter of a century had done to the two of them. Broad-shouldered Bryan still had a beachboy look about him, only much more mature and weathered, like someone who spent a lot of time outdoors. His once-blond hair was now much shorter and a less sun- bleached shade, a shorn version of the wind-tossed locks that once topped his head. He looked respectable and settled. Steady and tender. And while his face and hair had changed noticeably, his intense, blue-gray eyes hadn't.

"What are you doing here?" Carolyn hadn't premeditated her question. It slipped out like a sneeze.

127

"I came for a funeral. My stepmother passed away last week."

"Oh. I'm sorry to hear that." Carolyn was aware of how fast her heart was beating. She tried to come across as calm as Bryan seemed to be and repeated her sentiment. "I'm very sorry for your loss."

"Thank you. Your mother was at the funeral. She invited me to come today."

"Oh, I see." Carolyn nodded, letting this all sink in. She flipped her hair behind her ear and tried to sort out the details.

My mom didn't know I was coming. That means Bryan must not have known I was coming today either. This is all a coincidence, right? I can't believe he's here.

Bryan reached for a liter bottle of mineral water in the center of the table. "Would you like some?"

"Yes, thank you."

Bryan filled her glass and she took a sip, aware that her hands were trembling.

"So, how have you been?" Bryan's voice quavered, and for the first time he appeared as unnerved as Carolyn felt.

"Good. How about you?"

"Good."

Just then Carolyn's Aunt Sophie leaned over her husband on Carolyn's right side and held out her cell phone. On the screen was a picture of Rodrigo's newborn son. Carolyn stared at the picture without really seeing the image. Her contacts seemed to have gone blurry. Her uncle on her immediate right chatted in Spanish about the new baby.

"He's beautiful." Carolyn smiled at her aunt and uncle. She could feel Bryan watching her. Part of her wanted to turn her head and meet his gaze once again. Another part of her wanted to move to one of the empty seats at the far end of the table where she could watch him at a distance, as she had so many years ago. Being this close to Bryan still gave her butterflies.

Carolyn's uncle reached for a plate in the center of the table and presented her with some sort of fish that had been brought to the table with its head still attached. Only a portion of the white meat still clung to the spine, since nearly everyone had finished eating when she arrived.

"No, thank you." She fidgeted with the napkin in her lap and adjusted the silverware beside her plate. Narrow rivulets of perspiration zigzagged down her back, causing her blouse to cling to her skin.

Motioning for the waiter, Carolyn's uncle proceeded to order something he apparently thought Carolyn would want. From across the table Bryan pushed a plate toward her that had three small, round slices of crusty bread and a half-empty bowl of red dipping sauce.

"Pan y mojo," Bryan said. "You remember this."

She did. The crusty bread with the slightly spicy sauce made from red peppers was a familiar and comforting memory of the islands. Getting something in her mouth and her nervous stomach right away seemed like a good idea.

With a cautious glance to the head of the table, Carolyn saw her mother sitting back, hands folded in her lap, contentedly taking in the moment. A soft smile clung to her lips. She motioned to Carolyn by unfolding her hands, touching her heart, and then giving her daughter a tender, wistful look of motherly affection. Carolyn offered back a smile with two unreliable, wobbly lips.

"So, how long will you be here?" Bryan broke her interlude with her mom.

Carolyn swallowed and sipped the rest of her water without looking up to meet his gaze. "Just until the twenty-first."

Her fresh salad of mixed greens arrived then, along with a plate of grilled prawns ordered by her uncle.

"Will you be staying with your mother?"

"Yes."

"Have you been able to get over here to see her often?"

"No."

"When did you arrive?"

"Last night."

"Your mother certainly looks well."

"Yes, she does."

"It was nice that you could surprise her this way. I remember the women in your family were especially close."

"Yes, we still are."

"What about you? Do you have any daughters?"

Carolyn put down her fork. It seemed an odd question for him to ask, but he might well be stretching for topics to discuss. Carolyn hadn't exactly been helping him with the conversation.

"I have one daughter. Tikki. She's twenty-three."

"Tikki? That's a great name."

Carolyn repeated the same explanation she had given for years. "She's named Teresa Katharine for her two grandmothers, and 'Tikki' is her nickname. Her dad gave it to her when she was a baby, and it stuck."

Bryan nodded. Lifting his glass he nonchalantly said, "You married him, then."

Carolyn looked up. "Yes. I married Jeff."

He nodded again. His glance went to her left hand, where she still wore her simple gold wedding band.

Carolyn tried not to be obvious as she scanned his hands and saw that he didn't wear a ring. "And what about you?" She felt eager to move the topic along. The last thing she wanted to do was answer questions about Jeff.

Bryan leaned back and seemed a little less confident than he had come across earlier. "I'm not married. I have one son, Todd. He got married just last year to a really great girl. Woman, I guess I should say. They're doing well."

Just then a large cake was delivered to the table on a wheeled cart, and the conversation with Bryan came to a halt as all the attention went to the cake and Abuela Teresa. Right behind the cart Rosa appeared, waving at everyone and dispensing kisses and a dramatic explanation of why she was so late. Carolyn wondered what would have happened if she had stayed at the apartment with Rosa instead of taking the cab. Would Bryan still be at the party? What if he had left, and they hadn't seen each other?

She stole a quick glance at him as the candles were lit. His focus was on Carolyn's mother, who rose at the head of the table. With dignity, Abuela Teresa thanked everyone for coming, carrying on the conversation with first a sentence in Spanish and then the translation in English. She did it effortlessly as she told the guests she was a blessed woman. She didn't need to make a wish when she blew out her candles, she said, because God already had given her all her birthday wishes by allowing her to be there with them. God had even added a beautiful surprise, she said, by sending her an extra-special gift that came on an airplane over the ocean and was there, seated at her table. She extended her hand in a graceful gesture toward Carolyn.

Everyone applauded. Carolyn put her hand on her heart and smiled at her mother the way her mother had gestured to her earlier. Even with all the relatives and friends at the table and with Bryan sitting across from her, Carolyn still felt as if she was there for her mother, and her mother knew it. The specialness she had hoped to add to this day had unfolded. That realization had a calming effect on her wildly tossed emotions.

As photos were being snapped, the Birthday Queen faced her many-layered cake and blew out the seven tall candles, one for each decade. The cheers around the table were followed by toasts and laughter. Generous slices of cake were passed around. From underneath the table and from out of purses and bags an unexpected flock of gifts rose and made their way to the end of the table, where they all perched in front of the guest of honor. The gifts were presented to her with a humility and eagerness Carolyn didn't think she had ever connected with gift giving in the United States. The image that came to mind was of well-loved subjects presenting the first fruit of their harvest to their sovereign.

Carolyn had a few small gifts for her mom but had left them in her suitcase, thinking it would be nicer to give them to her in private. Now she wished she had brought them to add to the bounty.

Abuela Teresa opened each gift slowly, as had been her habit at every birthday and Christmas Carolyn remembered. Her mother made grand exclamations over each one, as if the present she just had unwrapped was the only one she had received and therefore was her favorite. Carolyn noticed the way her mother made eye contact with each gift giver and thanked them warmly. She had forgotten how much her mother relished the art of gift receiving. Carolyn never had met anyone who was as good at appreciating even the smallest gift.

The conversation went on around the table well after the cake had been served. Coffees were ordered. No one was in a hurry to go anywhere. One of the uncles was talking to Bryan in fragmented English, so Carolyn slid her chair back and decided this would be a good chance to make an exit for the restroom.

Her mother reached for her hand as she passed by. She pressed Carolyn's hand to her cheek. "You have made me so happy today."

"Good. That's what I hoped for."

"Isobel told me how she kept you hidden from me in her apartment."

"I know. It was terrible to hear your voice and be just on the other side of the kitchen wall this morning."

"Yes, but now we are together. I'm so happy. How long do I get to keep you?"

Carolyn didn't want to tell her mother how short this visit was going to be. She avoided giving a definitive answer. "Long enough for you and me to make every minute of every day count and enjoy it completely."

Her mother's brown eyes warmed, as she patted her clever daughter on the cheek. *"Mi niña. Te amo."*

"I love you, too, Mom."

Carolyn kissed her mother and forced herself not to glance at Bryan as she slipped away from the table and wound her way back through the restaurant to the restroom located near the entrance. Most of the lunch crowd had cleared out, making for quieter conversations between those lingering at the tables at the front of the dining area that faced the ocean.

She found the restroom and was once again reminded that she was no longer in San Francisco. The restroom was very small and gave every indication that it had been used excessively during the busy lunch hour. At least she was able to figure out how to turn on the water. She held a damp paper towel to the back of her neck and let the cooling effect help to calm her as she exited the bathroom. Carolyn felt as if she could go back to the table and finish out the luncheon with more polite conversation with Bryan, and that would be that. She shouldn't be this rattled. Bryan and all the memories connected with him belonged in the past.

Carolyn stepped out of the restroom and immediately saw Bryan standing a few feet away beside a potted plant. He seemed to be waiting for her. She coached herself to remain composed and to let him speak first.

Bryan rubbed the back of his neck. "Look, Carolyn, there's something I'd like to say to you."

She waited, feeling her heart speed up.

Coming closer to her and lowering his voice, he said, "I actually never thought I'd have the chance to say this to you face-to-face. But, Carolyn, I want to apologize."

She opened her lips to reply. When no sound came out, she pressed them together and remained frozen in place.

"I know this might come out all wrong, but I'm going to try to say it anyway." His voice quavered. "I didn't treat you the way you deserved to be treated, and I want to apologize for that. I could say that I was young—we were both young—but I don't want to use that as an excuse. What I did that last night on the beach, the way I treated you, wasn't good. I hope you can forgive me."

Carolyn felt so caught off-guard the only thing she could think to say was, "You don't have to apologize."

"I think I do."

"Well, we both were making impulsive choices, and I apologize, too, for not . . . for being . . ." She didn't know how to form the words.

"It's okay. You don't have to say anything else, Carolyn. I think I should take the greater responsibility in what happened. I know that I wasn't making very good choices at that time in my life. I think I'll leave it at that. I just wanted to tell you that I've long regretted how things ended between you and me."

"I do too." She felt embarrassed to be talking about this. His words and posture were so sincere. Inwardly, she was trying to untangle the Bryan that stood in front of her from the daring, rebellious Bryan she had known so long ago. What made the situation even more convoluted was that, ever since the fiasco with Ellis less than a month ago, she had convinced herself she couldn't trust any man, no matter how sincere he seemed to be.

"Well." Bryan let out a breath and leaned back. "I won't make this any more awkward than it is. I wish you the best, Carolyn, and I hope you have a nice visit with your mother."

"Thank you. I hope the rest of your visit is good too."

"Actually, I'm on my way home. My flight leaves in less than two hours. I need to get to the airport."

"Oh. Well, then, I hope you have a safe trip home."

"Thanks." Bryan rubbed the back of his neck again. "Well, good-bye, Carolyn."

Her throat tightened. At last the moment for closure had come. Now it was her turn to say her line. "Good-bye, Bryan." Those were the two lines that had never been exchanged that summer so long ago.

He wavered, appearing to want to lean close and offer a traditional kiss on the cheek in their parting. Instead he gave her a final nod. "I hope you'll tell that husband of yours that he's a blessed man."

"My husband?" Carolyn realized in the flow of their nervous conversation at the table she had said that she had married Jeff but then the focus had turned to Bryan. He didn't know what had happened.

Bryan looked at her more closely and seemed to be quickly glancing again at her ring finger. "I thought you said you married Jeff."

"I did. We were . . . but we're not . . . he's . . ." Carolyn really didn't want to answer any questions about Jeff at the moment.

Bryan's expression changed from surprised to a tender sadness. "I'm sorry. I didn't realize . . ." He glanced at his watch and looked back at Carolyn. "I hate to say this, but if I don't leave now, I'm going to miss my flight. I have to go. I wish I didn't have to leave like this."

"No, it's fine." Carolyn found a staid sort of

smile coming to her face as soon as she capped her emotions. The last thing she wanted was to be in that horrible place where she tried to explain the details of Jeff's death, and Bryan, the stunned listener, would flounder for the right thing to say. It was better to leave that topic unexplored.

He leaned in, this time giving her a gentlemanly cheek-brushing-cheek sort of farewell, which she interpreted as an expression of sympathy. There was no mistaking, though, that the closeness even for that brief moment was enough to cause Carolyn to blush. She glanced away, aware that she must be beet red.

She heard Bryan hoarsely speak the parting blessing Carolyn had heard many times from her mother and lots of other relatives on the islands. *"Dios le bendiga."*

"God bless you too." Carolyn looked up and watched him turn and disappear around the corner of the restaurant entrance. With numb steps she returned to the restroom and grabbed a long string of rough toilet paper to dry the tears that had come rolling down her cheeks.

What was that? I don't even know where to put that encounter and how it affected me.

The close-quartered restroom wasn't an enjoyable place to be for very long. Probing her deepest feelings was an even less enjoyable place for her to be, and a place she rarely let herself visit. This encounter felt too volatile to cram into the "To Be Figured Out Later" file, where she usually put all the life experiences she had been unable to explain or resolve.

Dabbing away the smudges of mascara from the small amount that still clung to her eyelashes, Carolyn returned to the table. She was determined to hold her feelings inside and make sure the rest of this day was about her mother. That's why she had come, after all.

Most of the guests were standing, as if they had started to make their departure but then remembered one more thing they wanted to tell someone. Rosa spotted Carolyn and motioned for her to come over.

"Your mom and Isobel want you to ride back to the apartment with them. I'll come in my car and help to move all the gifts to your mother's apartment. I can help you with your suitcases too."

"Okay. Thanks."

Rosa looked closer. "Are you all right? Your eyes are red."

"Oh, are they? I'm pretty tired."

"It must be the jet drag," Rosa said.

"Yes, I think you're right." Once again Carolyn didn't have the heart to correct Rosa.

"This will be good then. You can go to your mother's place and relax."

"I'm looking forward to it." Carolyn felt as if she had switched on to automatic pilot. All she wanted was to find a quiet spot to be alone and sleep.

It would be awhile before that happened, though, because every relative had a final hug, a kiss, and a word of affection and good-bye. Both Carolyn and her mother were showered with sweet words. Then it fell to Carolyn, Isobel, and Rosa to consolidate and carry the many gifts to Isobel's little white car, which was fortunately parked close to the restaurant. If Carolyn had told the cabdriver to take her to La Marinera instead of to Las Canteras, she would have ended up at this side of the bay much sooner. But she didn't regret her walk to the restaurant. She wished she could walk the same path again now, and let her thoughts sort themselves out.

Climbing into the backseat of the gift-loaded automobile, Carolyn rolled down the window and welcomed the cooling breeze on her face. In the front seat the two sisters conversed in Spanish. Carolyn didn't even try to pick up what her mother and Isobel were saying until she heard her name in Spanish followed by the name "Bryan." His wasn't a name that translated easily into Spanish and therefore stuck out in the conversation even more.

Abuela Teresa turned to face Carolyn with a winsome expression. "We are talking about you."

"Yes, I noticed."

"Isobel wanted to know how you know Bryan.

I told her about how you met when you were a teen."

Oh, dear. This is not good. Once any of my aunts has inside information, she delights in sharing it all around.

Isobel talked rapidly, glancing at Carolyn in the rearview mirror. Carolyn couldn't catch any of it, so she waited for her mom to translate. The two sisters went back and forth in the front seat for a few minutes before her mom turned again with a well-how-about-that sort of expression.

"Isobel's neighbor Maria cleans house for Bryan's stepsister."

Carolyn tried to make all the connections. "Wait. So, Maria is the one who has the baby, Gabby?"

"Sí," Isobel chimed in.

"And Maria cleans house for Bryan's stepsister. What's her name?"

"Angelina."

"Right. I remember. She's a lot younger than he is, right? She was a toddler when I was here last. So now she's married and Isobel's neighbor Maria cleans house for her. Got it."

"Sí, Angelina Esquierzo." Isobel said the name with flair as if Carolyn should recognize it.

"Is Bryan's stepsister famous or something?"

"She is married to a man who is, shall we say, high ranking in the local politics." Abuela Teresa raised her eyebrows and went on. "Maria said that, when she was cleaning the other day, she overheard an argument with Angelina and her husband. It was about her mother's will. Angelina assumed her mother would leave everything for her, but her mother left the house to Bryan. Isobel just made the connection now of who Bryan is. She didn't know he was Angelina's stepbrother."

Abuela Teresa turned to her sister and asked something in Spanish. Isobel had a long, animated response.

With eyebrows raised once again, Carolyn's mother said, "Well! This is getting interesting. Apparently the conclusion of the argument was that Angelina promised her husband she would offer Bryan a small amount of money if he would sell the house to her. Since he does not live here, it would be more difficult for him to clear all the paperwork on the land titles. While the house is old, the property is large enough to build four houses, and this is what Angelina's husband plans to do."

Carolyn felt sorry for Bryan. No thugs of any sort should be allowed to get away with such actions. A vivid sense of anger over failed justice rose up inside her. "What do you think he's going to do?"

"I don't know. He'll probably have to stay here for some time to work it out."

"But he left the island," Carolyn said.

"He did?"

"Yes. I saw him as he was on his way out of the restaurant, and he told me his flight was leaving in less than two hours."

Abuela Teresa and Isobel exchanged glances. Their expressions of shared surprise changed to a mix of concern and pity.

"That would be the answer then," her mother said with an air of finality, as if it was clear that he had signed the papers, taken Angelina's money, and left for the United States.

"Que lástima," Isobel said.

"Yes, it is," Abuela Teresa agreed. "Such a pity. If he left the island, we can be sure that was the last we'll see of Bryan Spencer."

The way her mother worded that last sentence, the finality of it all, hit the tender spot that had opened in Carolyn's well-protected heart when Bryan had apologized.

Before she could stop the flow, a spring of tears pooled in her eyes. She turned to the open window and let the sympathetic island breeze disperse them quickly.

What are you doing? Why are you crying? Get a grip.

For some reason she thought of the woman she had met at the airport in Madrid and how the woman said that, every time she went to her mother's house, she felt as if she turned into a twelve-year-old. Carolyn understood the feeling. From the moment she had looked across the table at lunch and saw Bryan's blue-gray eyes that had rocked her world so long ago, she felt as if she had turned into an eighteen-year-old version of herself.

She had to find a place to put all these emotions so that she could return to her forty-five-year-old self. And the sooner the better.

9

"El amor es ciego."
"Love is blind."

B Y THE TIME the women reached Isobel's apartment, the day had nearly passed, and Carolyn was feeling "jet drag" as well as emotionally drained. She purposefully put away all thought of Bryan and ignored the confusion she had encountered in her spirit when she had seen him.

Carolyn's mother lived in the same huge apartment complex as Aunt Isobel but in a separate building. This meant that they needed to go to Isobel's apartment to retrieve Carolyn's suitcases, return to the parking garage, drive around the block, and park in a different parking garage to take the elevator to her mom's apartment.

Once all those steps were accomplished, they were met by Rosa, who helped them to tote all the birthday gifts. As they exited the elevator on the seventh floor on her mother's side of the complex, they were met by the aroma of dinner cooking in a neighbor's apartment.

The other women commented on how good it smelled even though they were still full. Carolyn didn't have much of an appetite. Her mother searched for her key to open the door, and for the first time Carolyn observed that her mother had aged. At the party in her glowing glory, she didn't look as if the years had played their usual havoc with her. But they had. Her energy was depleted, and her steps were slower.

Isobel offered to help, but Carolyn's mother insisted on finding her own key and opening her own door. When she finally succeeded, they entered the apartment, and Carolyn felt a small smile rise up. She could be anywhere in the world, enter her mother's abode, and know immediately that her mother lived there.

Tikki had once told Carolyn that she had her own sort of "soul art" that she expressed best in the way she decorated her home. Clearly her mother expressed her "soul art" in the decoration of her apartment, and what made Carolyn smile was being reminded of how different her mother's art was from hers.

This is where Marilyn gets her love for bright colors, roses, calla lilies, and ornate lighting fixtures. I forgot that Mom liked so much red and lace. And look at all these knickknacks everywhere.

From an elaborate wire cage positioned between the double windows in the living room, a small yellow bird sang out a canary song, enthusiastically greeting them. That's when Carolyn truly knew she was in her mother's home. For as long as she could remember, her mother had kept a bird.

Carolyn put down her suitcase and went to the bird, peering into the well-maintained cage with a friendly smile. "Hello. *Hola.* And what is your name?"

"I call her Alma," her mother replied, coming up beside Carolyn. "She is my *Alma Gemela.* Do you remember what that means?"

"Isn't it heart something?"

"You're close. *Alma* means 'soul.' Soul mate. She's my little *Alma Gemela.*" Her mother gave a whistle, and the bird twittered back, hopping from the hanging swing to the branch affixed to the side of the cage and back to the swing.

Carolyn remembered the bird her mother had kept before moving to the islands. It was mostly green, and Tikki had named it "Tweetie." A brush of sadness came with the thought that her mother was naming her bird her "soul mate." Is that how she felt as a widow? Even with three of her sisters living so close? It made Carolyn wonder if her mother's leanings at age seventy should be taken as hints of what Carolyn would be like when she reached that stage. She was already a widow, after all. How much longer would Tikki be her soul mate?

She felt a grab in her stomach at the thought.

"Carolyn, where do you want your suitcases to go?" Rosa called from the hallway.

"I'll get them. You can leave them there for now."

"Would you like something to eat?" Her mother headed for the kitchen, and Carolyn followed her.

"No, thanks," Rosa replied. "I need to get going."

Isobel needed to be on her way as well. With a few more hugs all around, Rosa and Isobel left. Carolyn took her suitcases and headed for the room she assumed would be the spare room. The floor plan of her mother's apartment was the same as Isobel's except she knew that her mom had only two bedrooms instead of three. A short entryway hall opened to the combined dining room and living room on the right. To the left was the compact kitchen. The hall, like the stem of a three-leaf clover, led to a bathroom straight ahead and a bedroom on either side.

Opening the door that had been the guest room at Isobel's apartment, Carolyn found that instead of a guest bed waiting for her, the room had been turned into an overflow storage area. Boxes lined the wall where the bed had been at Isobel's. An ironing board was set up in the middle of the room, and several large, framed paintings were stacked facing the other wall.

Without saying anything, Carolyn left her luggage beside the ironing board and closed the door. She would be content on the couch with little Alma to keep her company. Returning to the open area that encompassed the small living room and dining room, Carolyn paused by the dining room table and viewed the mound of gifts.

I wonder if I could convince Mom to clear out some of the old collectibles around her apartment to make room for all the new gifts.

She had a pretty good idea her mother would protest and say that so-and-so had given her such and such knickknack, and what would she do if that person came to see her? She would be certain that the person would look for the gift and want to know that she still had it and that she displayed it prominently.

I'm sure I can find a way to convince her to part with some of the bric-a-brac. All I have to do is word it the right way.

Carolyn realized that having a task ahead of her made her feel more like her forty-five-year-old self. She had found she could always move ahead when she had something on her to-do list. It kept her thoughts on track, and if her thoughts were on track, her emotions usually complied and went along for the ride.

"Come sit with me," her mother called from the dark leather sofa in the living room. She leaned against the raised armrest of the traditional-style sofa and released a weary but contented sigh. "I cannot believe you are here. When I saw your face, my heart flew. Do you know that you look more and more like my mother? She was such a beautiful woman, just like you. She had the same high cheekbones and lovely smile. She would have enjoyed today so much. I do miss her."

Carolyn sat down, and they visited for a restful moment as her mother recounted her favorite parts of the day and the delights of her party. As she was talking about how much she enjoyed the cake, her mom began to cough. She leaned forward, and Carolyn patted her on the back, feeling the curve of her spine through her thin blouse.

"Are you okay?"

"Yes. I think I'm not used to talking so much."

"Would you like something to drink?"

"Yes, I would love some juice. Thank you."

Carolyn headed for the kitchen and heard her mom say, "And maybe a small bite to eat. I have cheese. Maybe I have some crackers. Better yet, I have some small pizzas. Yes, let's have those. They're frozen. And wouldn't you like a nice salad to go with our pizzas?"

Clearly the Birthday Queen was still holding court. Carolyn smiled to herself. She had a pretty good idea what her role would be while she was here. She didn't mind. Helping other people made her feel as if she was being about the work she was created to do. Besides, when was the last time the grand matriarch of the family had someone to care for her every whim? If Carolyn could spoil her mother for a few days, then she saw it as a much better birthday gift than another trinket to squeeze on a shelf.

"Would you like orange juice or this red juice in here?" Carolyn called from the kitchen.

"Orange juice, *por favor.*"

"Got it." Carolyn went looking for the individual pizzas in the compact freezer located in a small pull-out drawer at the bottom of her mother's old refrigerator. The freezer was stuffed so that every inch was used. She pulled out a small plastic bag that contained less than a tablespoon worth of chopped onions. Another plastic bag contained one chicken drumstick. She found a total of seven of the frozen individual pizzas and guessed either her mother had stocked up because they were on sale, or this was one of her favorites.

Carolyn reached up to open a cupboard in search of a glass. When she did, a plastic salad bowl tumbled to the counter. She scowled at the overpacked cupboard and was pretty certain she would find all the cupboards filled to bursting. Instinctively she wanted to empty the cupboards, rearrange them, and return only the items her mother truly loved and made use of. The recent renovations she had done to her home made her all the more motivated to assist her mother in experiencing the same joy that came from cleaning out and freshening up her home.

"Mom, would you like me to help you to organize some of your things while I'm here?"

"What things?"

"Your cupboards."

"What's wrong with my cupboards?"

"You have a lot of stuff that I'm guessing you don't use. It would lighten things up if you got rid of whatever you don't need."

"I need everything I have. It's all I have. Why? Is there something you see that you would like? You can take it, if you do."

"No, I'm not trying to go shopping in your kitchen. I'm trying to help with tasks that might be unpleasant or even difficult for you." Carolyn returned to the living room with the two glasses of orange juice and handed one of them to her mother.

"Do you think I'm so old now that I can't clean my own kitchen?"

"No, that's not what I'm suggesting. Not at all."

Even though her mother's voice didn't sound agitated, her expression was one Carolyn was familiar with. When her mother's eyes narrowed and her chin went forward the way they were now, Carolyn knew she should drop the subject. Not just drop it for the moment but drop it for good. For the duration of her visit, she would have to refrain from any cleaning and remove any suggestion of downsizing from her vocabulary. This was her mother's home. She needed to respect her mother and her mother's ways.

Returning to the kitchen, Carolyn shoved the plastic salad bowl back onto the second shelf. She unwrapped the hard discs that were the size of a salad plate and thought they looked sad and unappetizing. Poking around in the refrigerator, she found some leftover black olives and some hard cheese, which she added to the pizzas. She remembered the chopped-up onion in the plastic bag in the freezer and had more respect for her mother's method of saving every little bit because now she had something to use to spiff up their meal.

With the exception of an occasional trill from Alma in the living room, the only other sounds coming in through the open window were muted notes of life happening. Children's voices floated up from one of the apartments below. Sounds of footsteps and chair legs moving on the floor came from above. Consistent motor sounds from the busy city intersection seemed to roll out all the bass notes of this evening song. Outside, above her, all around her, life was humming along. This new pace, these new sounds, brought her unexpected comfort and contentment.

As soon as the timer was set on the oven, Carolyn tossed together a simple salad. She carried the two small plates out to the glass coffee table in the living room, thinking they could eat there instead of at the table, since it was covered with gifts. When she delivered the salads, Carolyn saw that her mother's eyes were closed.

"Mom?" she whispered.

She didn't reply so Carolyn tried again. "Dinner is served."

Still no response. Carolyn's heart froze. "Mom?"

She stepped closer and peered intently at the slouching matriarch. With slight, unhurried breaths, her mother's chest rose and fell. She was the picture of peace.

Don't scare me like that.

Carolyn sat on the couch across from her mother. She placed her open napkin across her lap, as she had been taught to do as a young lady. Then, as she had also been taught, she lowered her eyes and prepared to repeat the standard mealtime prayer. Her lips parted, but the ancient words didn't come to her.

Undaunted, Carolyn took the first bite of her salad and tried to remember the prayer she and Marilyn repeated every night at dinner. Being in the presence of her mother was bringing back familiar routines of the simple life they had shared. It was a good life. She had a good childhood. Her father worked in construction up until three months before he died of a pulmonary embolism. He was a mule of a man who demanded only one thing: respect. Carolyn's mother gave him not only respect but also sweet and tender affection. She loved her role as a wife and mother and gave the best of herself to her family.

Carolyn had hoped to emulate the same pattern for the life she and Jeff shared with Tikki. Respecting and loving Jeff was never a problem. Giving her all to her home and family became a challenge when she started to work full-time. If she could have stayed home, she would have. But she had no reservations about life in the San Francisco Bay Area requiring two incomes. The way Carolyn saw it, the fairy tale she and Jeff shared had simply ended too soon.

Carolyn chewed her salad slowly, thinking about how different her life would be right now if Jeff were still alive. It was a luxurious journey into the world of "what if," and one that she hadn't often allowed herself to take. Would Jeff have come with her on this visit for her mom's birthday? What would it have been like to sit next to Jeff at lunch with Bryan across the table?

Would I be sitting in the other room with Jeff right now, explaining to him at long last what happened between Bryan and me? Why didn't I ever tell Jeff? He never knew there was cause for Bryan to apologize to me.

Carolyn swallowed and put down her fork. *Bryan apologized to me.* Not once in the twenty-five years since she last had seen Bryan did she think she would encounter him again. And never in her wildest thoughts did she think that, if she did see him, he would apologize.

Soft light, the shade of melting butterscotch, spilled through the living room windows. The sheer, rose-pink curtains that hung to the floor billowed in response to the final puff of wind that seemed to come from the unhurried lips of the fading day. Alma fluffed her feathers from her perch and trilled a sunset song. Her mother's chest rose and fell with the ease of the ocean's tide.

Carolyn marked the moment in her memory. There was a sweetness in the room, in the company of her mother, that she felt nowhere else on earth. As much as she had longed for this serenity and had tried to duplicate a similar sense of calm in her own home and life, the extra blessing of peace that she felt here had eluded her best efforts.

What is it that I feel here? Is it love?

The faint scent of smoke wafted into the room. Carolyn popped up and hurried to the kitchen. The timer hadn't gone off. Yet, as soon as she opened the oven, she saw that the pizzas were past being done. She pulled them out, using a dish towel as an oven mitt, and swished the air, trying to clear the trace of smoke. The pizzas were a bit crisp around the edges but not bad. They looked edible.

Carolyn brought the well-done pizzas to the living room on two dinner plates and set them on the coffee table. The strong aroma roused her mother. She sat up straight and looked around, slightly confused. As soon as she saw Carolyn, she smiled and spoke in Spanish, her first language.

"Are you ready for some dinner? I started in on my salad, and I'm afraid the pizzas are crispier than I had planned."

Carolyn's mother answered her again in Spanish, saying something about the oven timer being broken. She slipped back into English. "I cannot remember the words when I am tired. I have not spoken so much English since I left America."

"We don't have to talk," Carolyn said. "It makes me happy just to be with you. It's been too long. Far too long. I should have come to see you sooner."

Carolyn's mother brushed away the regret-filled words. "No matter. You are here now. We will have our time together now and be grateful."

Carolyn thought about how her mother, the

oldest of the five sisters, had moved to the United States when she was fourteen. Their family came from deeply rooted Spanish ancestry and had been on the Canary Islands for two hundred years. Carolyn's mother and Aunt Frieda were the only two sisters who married men from the United States. The rest of the family moved back to the Canary Islands. Carolyn couldn't imagine growing up in one culture with a distinct language and then, as a teen, being immersed in a different culture and having to learn a new language.

"Tell me about Marilyn's wedding. I regret so much that I was not able to come."

"Everyone missed you." Carolyn gave her mom lots of details about the wedding, about Tikki's promotion at the bank in San Jose, about Larry's new job and the upcoming move to Santa Cruz. She had nothing but positive reports. It seemed in keeping with the tempo of their meal.

When they finished, Carolyn cleared the plates while her mother rose slowly and began her evening routine. Carolyn watched inconspicuously from the hallway while her mother approached a small, built-in shelf in the dining room's corner. A single candle rested on the shelf, and beside it was a small box of matches.

With a steady hand, Carolyn's mother struck the match and lit the candle. She placed both hands over her heart and bowed her head. Carolyn knew what her mother was doing. She was praying. She had done this as long as Carolyn could remember. Every morning the candle was lit, and her lips would move in respectful adoration, but no words could be heard. Then she blew out the candle and went about her day.

When evening came, she returned to the candle in the corner. Carolyn remembered her mother slipping her feet into red velvet slippers and padding across the linoleum floor in the kitchen as she approached the tiny, wedge-shaped shelf her father had built for her next to the refrigerator. It didn't matter if the TV was on in the next room or if Carolyn and Marilyn had friends over and were doing homework at the kitchen table. Their mother would close out the rest of the world, light the candle, whisper her prayers for the close of day, and then blow it out.

No images of saints or gold-trimmed icons ever appeared on the shelf. Only a candle and matches. And for a single moment twice each day her mother was blind to everything except God and her deep and abiding love for him.

As Carolyn watched her mother this evening, she longed for that same sort of elegant reverence for God to return to her life. It had been gone for so long. She missed the sense of God's closeness.

I wonder if that's what I felt tonight, as my mother slept on the couch. Every morning she welcomes God's presence into her life. Every evening she whispers her gratitude to his Holy Spirit. She has invited him here, and I think he has come. God is in her home and in her life.

Carolyn knew when that sense of God's presence had left her home and her life. She had been the one who closed off the relationship. Early in her marriage, she and Jeff had drawn close to God and to each other. They stayed involved in a strong and loving church. They raised Tikki to "love the Lord your God with all your heart, all your soul, all your strength," just as the Bible commanded. And Tikki had remained firm in her faith.

But Carolyn had shut off the avenues of communication with God. Not in an overt way that Tikki or anyone from church would recognize. The silence happened inside. In her *alma*. In her soul.

Carolyn watched as her mother blew out the candle and went over to the windows where she lowered the shades halfway, allowing the cool night air an easy entrance. Then she covered the birdcage, and Alma Gemela, her soul mate, ceased her song. All was still.

Just as it had long been still within Carolyn's soul, ever since the dark blanket of grief had come out of nowhere and covered her *alma* so completely.

10

*"Ni tanto que queme al santo,
ni tan poco que no lo alumbre."*
"Put the candle not so close that it would burn
the saint, nor so far that it will fail to light it."

CAROLYN FOUND AN extra comforter in the
hall closet and got ready for bed while her
mother was in her bedroom. She returned to the
living room and stretched out on the leather sofa
that was still warm on the two ends where they
had been sitting. Closing her eyes, Carolyn hoped
for sleep to find her before her mind decided to
evaluate any one of the many avenues of life
questions that had opened up for her that day.

A few minutes later, she heard her mother come
into the living room. Carolyn pretended to be
asleep. She knew it was a little girl thing to do,
but she did it anyway. Her mother drew close,
called her name softly, waited a moment, and
then left. Whatever she wanted would wait until
morning.

Carolyn woke when she caught the scent of an
extinguished match. Her mother was up,
whispering her morning prayers. Stretching her
neck and peering around the side of the sofa, she
saw the back of her mother's pink bathrobe with
her face to the corner. Carolyn recognized the

robe as the birthday present Marilyn had picked out and sent last year.

The pale buttermilk light of the new day poured through the lower halves of the open windows. Carolyn sat up and yawned. She had slept much better than she had at Isobel's, although she remembered waking sometime in the night, before it was light. It took awhile to find a more comfortable sleeping position, but she did, and somehow she managed to fall back asleep.

"Buenos días, mi niña," her mother greeted her as she lifted the covering from the birdcage and raised the window shades.

Carolyn blinked in the brightness. *"Buenos días."*

"Why did you not come share my bed last night?"

After growing up with four sisters, Carolyn's mother had often said she was used to sharing sleeping space and had made it clear in the past that she was more comfortable sleeping with another person than alone. That fact had slipped Carolyn's mind.

It shouldn't have because she felt the same way when Tikki had come home for Marilyn's wedding. Carolyn hoped Tikki would cuddle up with her instead of stretching out on the sofa. But Tikki had done the same thing Carolyn did last night. She had gone to the closet for her favorite down comforter and fell asleep with the remote control for the television in her hand. The two nights Tikki stayed with Carolyn during Marilyn's wedding were spent in the company of late-night talk show hosts and a bag of rice cakes instead of cuddled up with her mama.

"I'll sleep there tonight. I promise."

The two women went about the day without making a schedule, since they didn't have plans to be anywhere at a set time. This was catch-up day after the big party as well as conversation day, since they barely had touched on details of all the relatives and life happenings over their frozen pizzas last night.

After lingering over coffee, toast, and conversation, Carolyn said, "Is there anything you would like me to do for you while I'm here so that you can play the role of reigning Birthday Queen a little longer?"

"No, I have everything I need. I want you to rest and enjoy this as a vacation. This is your vacation, isn't it? I still don't know how long you'll be here."

"A week."

Carolyn knew her mother would frown in an exaggerated pout. That's why she had avoided telling her at the birthday party. To her mother, anything less than a month should not even be considered a vacation.

"If it helps soften the blow, I hope to come back and bring Tikki. Maybe in late summer or early fall. Hopefully we can stay longer then. Frieda wants to come too. And maybe we can get Marilyn to join us."

Their leisurely morning continued, accompanied by melodious birdsongs from Alma and calm breezes coming through the open windows along with an interesting mix of muted guitar music from an apartment nearby. Life here felt simple and unhurried. Carolyn could see now why her mother made the big decision to leave the Bay Area after Carolyn's father passed away to move back here. This tempo fit her mother's personality. This place composed a day-to-day music that Carolyn's mother knew by heart. She fit here. This was her home.

The guitar tunes from the neighboring apartment had picked up in their intensity. Carolyn recognized the style now as flamenco guitar. Brisk, passionate, and decisive. She went over to the window and looked down on the expansive plaza between the two long apartment buildings. It was as if she expected to see the guitarist seated on a stage in the plaza, playing the stirring notes to a gathered audience.

Instead she saw two women visiting with each other while three small children rode their tricycles in circles around them on the pavement. Four people were swimming laps in the pool. The water in the pool glistened in the noontime sunshine and beckoned to Carolyn. She resisted at first, but the guitar music seemed to send out a wordless message, inviting her to come.

Why not? I brought my swimsuit. I never get to go swimming at home. And I am on vacation, after all.

When her mother concluded the story about her cousin, Carolyn asked if she would like to go swimming.

"Swimming? No. Not today. I only like to go in the summer when it's hot."

Carolyn guessed the weather was in the low eighties. To her that was hot enough for a swim.

"Why don't you go? I have a few things to do here." Abuela Teresa gave a tug on her robe's collar. "Getting dressed would be one of the things I should do today."

"If you're sure you don't mind, I think I will."

"Of course I don't mind. As I told you, this is your vacation too."

It took Carolyn only ten minutes to get ready. She called out to her mother that she was leaving and then flip-flopped her way down the elevator and out into the warm sunshine. Seeing that she had the pick of dozens of lounge chairs, Carolyn spread out her borrowed beach towel. She knew that if she stretched out on the lounger to soak up the rays, she could easily talk herself out of dipping into the pool.

That's when she noticed the guitar music had ceased. She missed the stirring melody that had pressed her to make the decision to go swimming, but the notes had done their work. Here she was. With only two other people at the pool now, and neither of them appearing interested in watching her, Carolyn peeled down to her bathing suit and made her way to the built-in, notched steps in the pool's deep end. She lowered into the temperate water one backward step at a time until she was up to her waist and there were no more steps.

Then, letting go of the railing, she closed her eyes and leaned back so that she fell into the deep end, and the exhilarating rush of the water covered her. She felt eighteen all over again, remembering that she had spent time in the ocean nearly every day at Las Canteras. How long had it been since she had experienced this sensation of the cool water engulfing her?

She started to swim—face in the water, face to the side for a breath, right arm over her head, hands cupped, scooping her way through the liquid wall. For almost twenty minutes she stretched all the way to her toes, extending her arms and digging through the water. With each stroke came another memory of the golden summer that had tested her heart and tried her will.

The last time she swam under this expansive sky, she had just graduated from high school. While Marilyn had somehow kept a continuous string of boyfriends since her sophomore year, Carolyn had gone out only once to a winter banquet during her junior year. The only reason she had a date for that church event was because Marilyn's date had a brother, and the two of them were being generous to include their siblings.

Then the week before graduation Carolyn was babysitting for two boys who lived down the street. She agreed to take them to their Little League softball practice and drive them home afterward. Their coach, Jeff Duncan, was the most energetic, encouraging guy Carolyn thought she had ever seen. He reminded her of Richie Cunningham on *Happy Days* because of his All-American look with his short, reddish hair, upbeat personality, and perpetual grin. Jeff asked her after practice if she wanted to take the boys out for pizza. He said he was paying.

Carolyn assumed Jeff was inviting the entire team. No. It was just Carolyn and the two boys in her charge. By the time the pizza arrived, they found out they would both be going to Cal State Hayward in the fall. That's when Jeff asked for her phone number.

With each stroke as she swam from one end of the pool to the other, the memories kept coming. She knew she never would forget the night before she left for her summer on the Canary Islands because Jeff took her on a date. Their first date. He wore a tie and took her to a steak house that had rounded booths with tufted leather seats and candles in red, pear-shaped holders at the end of the table beside the bottle of A-1 Steak Sauce.

Carolyn blithely ordered a huge T-bone steak and a loaded baked potato but could barely eat. Jeff held her hand across the table, and in the glow of that patio-style candle, he told her that even though she was going to be gone all summer, he would wait for her because he had a feeling they were meant to be together.

When Jeff walked her to the front door of her parents' home that night, his smile diminished only long enough for his lips to form a kiss, Carolyn's first. That night Jeff unknowingly awakened an eagerness in her that she had long underestimated in spite of her twin's willingly shared descriptions of her exploits. With that ignited eagerness and curiosity, Carolyn arrived on the Canary Islands and first looked into Bryan Spencer's blue-gray eyes.

Out of breath and slightly trembling, Carolyn pulled herself from the pool. Worn and warmed, she surrendered to the sun-toasted towel waiting for her and listened to her pulse pound in her ears as all the glistening beads of water gave in to the force of gravity and skittered off her skin.

The pale blue sky spread its covering over her as a beautiful dream floated in on a cloud and lulled her to sleep. She couldn't tell when she woke up how long she had been gone. It could have been a ten-minute or a two-hour nap. But she knew she had dreamed of Jeff. They weren't sailing this time nor were they swimming. They were giving themselves to each other for the first time on their wedding night. Jeff's caresses had been slow, tender, and rhythmic. She was safe. She was happy.

Carolyn knew the second time Jeff kissed her under a tree on their college campus that he would love her with all of his heart for the rest of their lives. And so, with the desire to never do or say anything that might jeopardize that safety and harmony, she didn't tell Jeff what had happened beside the green fishing boat the night the Canary stars were watching.

Shaking off the lingering memories from long ago, Carolyn gave her still-wet hair a shake too. None of those thoughts mattered anymore. Jeff was gone. For that matter, Bryan was gone. None of it mattered. She needed to move on.

Tikki was right. I do need to get a life. I'm young enough to make a fresh start, aren't I? Grief takes so long to work through. When will I be past this sadness I feel like a weight at the bottom of my stomach?

For now, she decided that getting a life and moving on meant enjoying the time she had left with her mother and savoring her vacation instead of putting herself through some sort of adolescent-angst rehab.

Returning to the apartment, Carolyn saw from the kitchen clock that she had been at the pool for a little more than an hour. She felt as if she had gone to another world and back, returning with the resolution to remain in the present for the rest of her vacation.

On the table she noticed a handwritten list on the back of an envelope. Carolyn read the mix of English and Spanish words and called out to her mom, "Is this your grocery list? I can buy these things for you, if you like."

"You don't have to. Rosa does my shopping for me. She can do this when she comes later this week."

"I don't mind. I'd like to do this for you, Mom. The reason you need some of these things is because you have another mouth to feed this week that you weren't expecting."

Her mother shuffled into the kitchen. She was dressed, and her short, silver-laced hair was in place. She even had on lipstick. Yet she still looked weary from the party, not quite ready to take on the day.

"Let me do this, Mom. I don't have to buy everything on the list, but at least I can purchase something fresh for dinner and replenish some of your basics."

"Okay, if you like."

Carolyn changed while her mom finished the list. She handed it to Carolyn with stars next to the essential items. "Do not buy more than you can carry."

Carolyn's immediate thought was that she would buy everything on the list to save Rosa the trip later. Then she realized why her mother had said what she did. Abuela Teresa didn't have a car. Carolyn would have to walk to the market and back carrying the groceries, unless she wanted to take a taxi.

"Okay, I'll only buy what we need right away. And maybe a little sweet for the two of us for an afternoon treat."

Her mother smiled. She was such a lovely woman. Her dark eyebrows seemed to float unworried over her clear brown eyes. She had a long, thin nose and upturned lips. "Do you know where the *supermercado* is located?"

"No, is it far?"

"Only four blocks. Uphill. That makes the trip home easier."

Supplied with sturdy shopping bags, her purse, the grocery list, and her mother's set of keys, Carolyn set off in her practical, black, slip-on walking shoes, a pair of jeans, and a T-shirt, ready to casually explore the neighborhood on her way to the market. Her mother had settled in with her stack of thank-you notes and was planning to use the time to express gratitude to her generous family for their gifts. She encouraged Carolyn to take her time and to stop along the way at some of the small shops that lined the street just before she reached the market.

The sidewalks were surprisingly busy with people of all ages. Young mothers pushed strollers and carried weighted items in bags slung over their shoulders. An older man in a full suit and wearing a hat slowly made his way uphill with the aid of his cane. Two girls carrying schoolbooks chattered and laughed with the same lively animation found in thirteen-year-olds of any culture. A woman wearing a white lab coat and glasses hurried past Carolyn and entered a store that sold eyewear.

On the road that ran alongside the sidewalk, an endless stream of cars, trucks, and buses made their way downhill toward the beach. The afternoon heat had warmed the asphalt and added an intensified smell of diesel to the air. It seemed hard to believe that only half an hour ago, after a pristine swim, Carolyn had luxuriated in the sun by a pool that was located only a few hundred yards from all this noise and smelly heat. The immense, block-long, twelve-story apartment building seemed to serve as a rectangular barricade from the outside commotion, allowing space for a garden to grow and for guitar melodies to echo.

Carolyn stopped to look in the window of a small shop that sold jewelry. The assortment of beaded necklaces alongside beautifully boxed rings made of diamonds and other polished gems was surprising to her. The handcrafted items were displayed as proudly as the high-end jewelry.

She stopped again, a few shops later, in front of a salon. The front door was open, and Carolyn could see that the two employees had no customers that afternoon. She tried to translate the services listed on the card posted in the window. *Manicura y pedicura* were easily deduced. What she couldn't remember was the last time she had indulged in either service.

Why not?

Entering with a confident grin, Carolyn was greeted with an interested but unrushed glance from the two women standing by the counter that held a noncomputerized-style cash register. One of the women asked her something in Spanish.

Too timid to try her Spanish to ask for the service she wanted, Carolyn said, "Do either of you speak English?"

Both women shook their heads and looked shyly at her. Carolyn wondered if they both knew some English but, just like her, were timid to try it out.

Carolyn pointed to her feet and then wiggled her fingers. "I'd like a *manicura y pedicura, por favor.*"

The taller woman motioned for Carolyn to take a seat in the chair in front of the wash basin. If she leaned back, her neck would be cradled in the curve of the sink, and she could have her hair washed, just as she would at any salon back home. Apparently this was the manicure-pedicure station. It was nothing like the salon Marilyn frequented that had padded leather reclining chairs with built-in footbaths and massage rollers that could be adjusted with the push of a button.

Carolyn took off her shoes and made herself as comfortable as possible while the two women went to work with remarkable efficiency. A steady stream of conversation flowed between the two of them as a plastic basin was placed in front of Carolyn, and she plunged her feet into the warm water. She recognized one of their comments in Spanish: " . . . que grandes son los pies. " "What big feet."

It wasn't the first time she had been aware of her size since arriving in the Canaries. Most of the women, including her mother and aunts, came in at a little over five feet tall. Carolyn was five foot seven, which never seemed tall at home. Here she was noticeably taller than her women relatives. She and Marilyn, as well as their tall daughters, had her father's proud Dutch and Norwegian heritage to thank for the extra inches.

One of the attendants sat on a stool beside Carolyn and went to work on her hands, using a small folding tray as the operating pad. The shorter attendant took a servant position on her knees and went to work scrubbing Carolyn's feet.

She balanced one foot at a time on a towel across her lap and trimmed Carolyn's overgrown toenails with tender precision. Then she lathered her hands with lotion and expertly massaged Carolyn's feet.

The experience felt so different from the times she had gone with Marilyn to the stylized, machine-assisted nail salons at home. Here, even though the equipment was rudimentary, the touch felt personal and pampering. Not at all like she was receiving an automated service carried out in assembly-line fashion.

Carolyn's fingers were soothed with oil, one by one, with deliberate attention to each cuticle. The intense consideration was beyond anything she had experienced before with a manicure, and she felt like a princess. It took her a little while to settle into the pampering experience, but once she did, she loved every minute of it.

The nail polish she selected was soft pink. No bold statements in cherry red were in store for her big feet and neatly trimmed fingernails. The end results were exactly what she had hoped for: fresh and clean.

Feeling relaxed, Carolyn leaned back, resting her head on a folded-up towel one of the attendants had placed in the curve of the shampoo bowl. She closed her eyes and felt the breeze through the open door, as it did its part in the pampering process and dried her nails.

When she stood to leave a few minutes later, Carolyn saw that another woman had entered and was seated in one of two chairs in front of a mirror, ready to have her hair cut. Carolyn paid, and when her change was handed back, she tried to do a quick calculation. If she had her exchange rate figured out, she had just paid the equivalent of about seven U.S. dollars for the entire treatment.

She didn't know if it was customary to tip, so she tried to hand the attendant some money, but the woman looked confused as to what Carolyn was doing. Apparently a tip wasn't expected.

Carolyn smiled. *"Gracias."*

"De nada." The attendant then hurried from behind the counter and stood beside the open door. The other attendant left her haircut customer and joined her coworker. They seemed to be taking their positions, waiting for Carolyn to exit. It reminded Carolyn of the way flight attendants stood by the plane's door to say, "Buh-bye."

As Carolyn nodded to them and made her way toward the door, both women leaned over and kissed her on both cheeks and then said something in unison with a wide smile. Carolyn was so caught off-guard by their gesture that she couldn't leave.

"What does that mean?" She looked at each of them, startled. "I wish I spoke more Spanish so you could tell me what you just said."

One of the attendants said, *"Cuando una mujer . . ."*

Carolyn understood those words and repeated them aloud in English. "When a woman . . ." But after that she was lost. "I'm sorry. I don't understand."

The woman waiting for her haircut invited herself into the moment and explained to Carolyn what was going on. "It is the way the Women of the Canaries give praise to their sisters."

Carolyn looked to the other customer for more explanation.

"Have you never had this before?" the woman asked. "This kiss and congratulations?"

"No, what does it mean?"

"When a Woman of the Canaries shows herself a kindness, all her sisters must congratulate her. That is why they gave you a kiss. They are congratulating you for showing yourself a kindness."

Carolyn felt sweetly touched all over again. "That's beautiful."

"Now, when your sisters show themselves a kindness, you must congratulate them for taking such care. This is what we do for each other. It's a nice expression, isn't it?"

"Yes, it's a very nice expression." Carolyn departed with another round of *"gracias"* and *"adiós"* and stepped into the sunlight, headed the rest of the journey uphill to the grocery store.

What she had just experienced had so tipped her inward balance that she couldn't stop smiling from ear to ear. She entered the grocery store with her head held high.

I feel so lovely.

It was a wonderful way to start her shopping trip. The store was similar to grocery stores at home, with well-stocked aisles, push carts, and brightly colored cereal boxes stacked high on end displays. The main difference was that all the labels were, of course, in Spanish. With her mother's list in hand, she strolled up and down every aisle, trying to distinguish any familiar words on the labels that would confirm that what she had picked up was indeed a can of plain tomato sauce and not enchilada sauce.

The entire shopping trip took nearly an hour, and even though she tried to limit herself, Carolyn did end up filling all four of her cloth shopping bags. The two heavier ones she put over her shoulders, one on each side. The lighter two she carried in each fist. She let out the strap on her adjustable shoulder purse so she could wear it across the front of her the way bike couriers in San Francisco wore their document delivery pouches. She felt like a pack mule.

Downhill was nicer than uphill, as her mother had mentioned. Nonetheless her arms were sore as she rode the elevator up to her mother's apartment on the seventh floor. Setting down the bags in front of her mother's apartment, she felt the results of the strain she had put on her muscles. Even though she was perspiring, and her arms felt weak and wobbly, she had a feeling she was going to like the overall aerobic benefits of the jaunt.

Carolyn used her mother's key to let herself in. As she opened the door, she could hear her mother speaking to someone in Spanish and guessed she must be on the phone with one of the aunts.

Carolyn lifted the shopping bags again and walked quickly to get all four of them into the kitchen before her arms gave out. She had just deposited them on the counter when her mother called from the living room, "Carolyn, we have a guest."

Expecting to see one of her cousins, Carolyn brushed her hair from her perspiring face and forehead as she exited the kitchen. She pulled on the front of her shirt, billowing it outward in an effort to cool off, as she trotted into the living room where her mother was sedately seated with the guest.

A man in a Tommy Bahamas–style beach shirt rose from the sofa and turned to greet her. His presence seemed to fill her mother's living room. Among all the bric-a-brac and lace, he was definitely the most masculine object in the room. And the most handsome.

"Hello again, Carolyn." The blue-gray eyes softened at the sight of her.

This time she couldn't even whisper his name. All she could think was, *You came back.*

11

"Él que la sigue, la consigue."
"He who follows it, attains it."

Bryan went to Carolyn and awkwardly greeted her in the traditional style, lightly touching his cheek to hers. His closeness unnerved her, especially because she was aware of how rumpled and sweaty she was. She noticed he wasn't the freshest fish in the bucket either. Both of them obviously had been out and about that afternoon. Yet here he was, standing in her mother's living room. That was a surprise she never expected.

"My flight out of Madrid was canceled," he said.

Carolyn jumped in with the first thing that came to her mind. "They have good orange juice there. At the airport. It's fresh sneezed."

Her eyes widened, as she realized her mistake. "I mean, it's fresh squeezed. Freshly squeezed, I should say. Freshly squeezed orange juice. In Madrid."

Looking to her mother for some support,

Carolyn said, "Would anyone else like something to drink?" She was aware that her incoherent chatter gave the impression that she had drunk a little too much, as if she had been downing a bottle of Spanish *rioja* while she was gone.

"Nothing for me," Bryan said, with a slight grin lightening his expression. Her fumble seemed to have put him at ease.

"Nothing for me either. Why don't you join us?" Her mother smiled calmly, as if she were watching one of her soap operas on television instead of watching her own daughter presenting a comedy routine in the living room.

Bryan stepped aside and motioned for Carolyn to take his place on the sofa.

"I need a drink of water. I'll be right back." Carolyn tried to make a graceful exit to the kitchen, where she filled a glass with water and used a dish towel to dab away the perspiration on her face, neck, and chest. Billowing her shirt again a few more times, she took another sip of water and returned to the living room.

On her way back, she took a chair from the dining room table and positioned it beside the birdcage by the window so she could face her mom and Bryan. The look on his face reminded her of the expression he gave her the first time they met.

She was at her grandmother's house in a rural area outside of Las Palmas and had taken a basket of laundry outside to hang on the line. Bryan stood in the yard next door, not more than twenty-five feet from her, with all that wild beachboy hair, wearing a brown-and-yellow-striped T-shirt. He lowered his tanned arms and the slingshot he had been using to unsuccessfully snag a bird. When he turned to meet Carolyn's disapproving gaze over his aggression toward the birds, Bryan responded with the sort of amused grin that said, "So, I have your attention now, do I? Well, let me see what I can do with it."

His expression mimicked that look now, and Carolyn could feel herself sliding into her eighteen-year-old mind-set. She resisted the dip. After the resolutions she had made earlier at the pool, the way she felt affirmed at the salon, her victory at the grocery store, and the sense of empowerment from carrying all the groceries home, Carolyn wanted to be fully present as a forty-five-year-old woman. Or to be more precise, a forty-five-year-old widow.

"Your mother has been giving me some good counsel," Bryan said once she was settled. "Part of the reason I decided to return after my flight was canceled was because I have some business dealings I need to work through in Las Palmas. I realized I would be better off working on them here rather than back in the States. I also knew your mother would have some reliable resources for me to contact."

Carolyn waited for more details, but he ended his explanation there. She glanced at her mom, trying to get a feel for whether Bryan was aware that they knew about the fallout between him and Angelina over the terms of the will. Her mother's expression gave no hint one way or the other, so Carolyn decided it would be best if she kept quiet on the topic and just listened.

They chatted for a few minutes about Carolyn's impressions of the grocery store and the afternoon traffic. When she explained that she had walked to the store and back, Bryan looked impressed.

"Not having my car any longer is one of the luxuries I miss the most," Carolyn's mother commented. "I am spoiled, of course, in that I can call upon one of my sisters or nieces at any time and be taken anywhere I want to go. I do regret not having a car now while Carolyn is here. I'm afraid she's at the mercy of the relatives as well, if she wants to go someplace."

"I don't think that's a disadvantage at all, Mom. And I had no trouble when I took a taxi to your birthday party."

A sweet expression passed across her mother's face, as if she were lingering over a pleasant memory. "That was a wonderful party, wasn't it?"

"It was," Bryan agreed, casting a glance at Carolyn. "As a matter of fact, I was wondering if the two of you might be willing to join me for dinner some night this week. We could go back to the same restaurant, if you like."

"We would be honored," Carolyn's mom answered for both of them.

Carolyn looked at her mother and then at Bryan, offering him a nod. He knew how things were done in the Old World. By coming to ask advice from Abuela Teresa and inviting both of them to dinner, he was honoring traditions that had long since gone out of fashion. Carolyn knew her mom would like the way he was treating her. He was a smart man.

"But I have another restaurant for us to go to," Carolyn's mom said. "And I'll make the reservation for us, if you don't mind. I know the owner. Tomorrow night, then?"

Bryan looked at Carolyn. She nodded, not sure what other options were open to her. She was willing to get cleaned up right now and go out tonight, but if her mother's choice was for tomorrow night, then tomorrow night it would be.

"What time would you like me to pick you up?" Bryan asked.

In keeping with the traditional Spanish style of eating late, Carolyn's mom suggested eight o'clock and added, "If you don't mind us being among the first to arrive at the restaurant."

"I'll come by at around seven thirty. How does that sound, Abuela?"

Carolyn's mother dipped her chin, gracefully

receiving the way he addressed her as a respected elder as well as the "date" for tomorrow night.

After a few more minutes of casual chat, Bryan glanced as his watch. "I should be leaving." He stood, and Carolyn followed him to the door. She tried to keep her comments light and hoped she didn't pop out with some other "fresh-sneezed" phrases. The truth was that being around Bryan filled her stomach with flutters.

She had assumed the encounter at her mom's birthday party was a serendipitous, one-time event that had turned into a small gift for her when he apologized. Now she didn't know what to make of his return and the formal but nonetheless intriguing invitation to dinner. It made sense that he would decide to come back and settle the family problems with his stepsister, but he didn't have to come to her mother's apartment.

They paused at the door, and Carolyn said, "Thanks for coming by."

"I called your mom first, and she insisted that I come over. She assured me that I wasn't interrupting her time with you."

"No, not at all. And I'm sure she told you that you would be welcome anytime."

"Yes, she did tell me that."

"Good." Carolyn could feel a rivulet of perspiration trailing down the center of her back.

"I'm looking forward to tomorrow night. It will give us a chance to catch up."

"Yes, it was nice of you to invite both of us. I think my mom appreciated that."

Bryan looked to the side for just a moment. Turning his focus back on her, he appeared to want to say something purposeful, but he hesitated.

Carolyn wasn't sure what to say next.

Bryan's expression calmed. "It's really good to see you again, Carolyn. Really good."

She felt her face redden and wished she didn't blush so easily. "It's really good to see you too."

They lingered another moment before he said, "I'll see you tomorrow night, then. Seven thirty."

"Yes, seven thirty."

He opened the door and left without attempting another one of their previously awkward cheek-to-cheek farewells. As soon as the door closed and the sound of his footsteps was swallowed by the elevator at the end of the hall, Carolyn exhaled the long, slow breath she seemed to have been holding inside while they were saying good-bye. She still didn't know what to make of all this.

Returning to the living room, she found her mother sitting back with her hands folded in her lap. Her lips formed a thin line, but her enlivened eyes made it clear she had a secret.

"What did he tell you?" Carolyn asked.

"Let's have some tea."

"Tea? Now?"

"Yes, let's have some tea."

Carolyn knew it was useless to pester her mother for information until after the tea was prepared, so she set to work. As the kettle boiled, she put away the groceries and then prepared a small snack, or tapas, as her mother called them. When everything was ready, Carolyn carried the nibbles into the living room on a tray along with the steaming tea. It reminded her of how Marilyn had brought Carolyn the tea and apple slices a month ago when she was in such a slump over how things went with Ellis.

A warning sign went on inside her, reminding her not to project expectations on the dinner with Bryan tomorrow night simply because he had said he was glad to see her and looked forward to dinner. She never wanted to put herself in the same sort of vulnerable position she had been in with Ellis.

But this is different. Isn't it? For starters, he came right out and said he wasn't married when we were at the birthday party. At least I have that assurance to go on.

Carolyn put her thoughts aside and sat down gracefully, as she had been taught as a child. Her manners ended there, however. She leaned forward. "Okay, tell me. What's going on?

What's your big secret? You look like the cat that ate the canary."

Her mother frowned and cast a glance at Alma in her swinging cage. "Don't say that in front of my little friend."

"Then tell me what's going on. I can tell you're holding something inside."

Carolyn's mother took a slow sip of tea.

"You're incorrigible, you know." Carolyn shook her head.

"Incorrigible," her mother repeated. "That's a word I have not heard in a long time." She took a bite of a tapa, and Carolyn gave up. She remembered her mother playing these sorts of games with her and Marilyn when they were younger. Marilyn always found greater delight in the drawn-out taunting than Carolyn did.

Putting down her cup of tea and rising, Carolyn said, "I think I'll go swimming again. I need to cool off."

"His flight out of Madrid was canceled."

"Yes, I know. That's what he said." She stood beside her chair, not willing to sit down until her mother divulged new information. "Did he meet with his stepsister? Did he tell her he wouldn't sign over the property? Is that what he told you?"

"He asked me for references for lawyers in Las Palmas who spoke English." The teacup just happened to be at her mother's lips once again.

"So, he didn't sign the papers then. Is that it? He's going to fight to keep the property?"

Her mother raised her eyebrows and said nothing.

Carolyn gave up being frustrated and turned her thoughts to the humor of her mother's antics. "You are enjoying this way too much, I hope you know."

"Yes, I know." Her mother placed her teacup back on the tray, ready to tell all. "All right, I will tell you everything. Bryan has found himself in quite a dilemma. It's interesting. It will either help him or greatly harm him. Isobel and I had assumed that he signed over his part of the estate to Angelina, and that was why he left the islands. However, he hasn't yet signed the papers. It makes sense. Since the documents were in Spanish, he told his stepsister he wanted to take them back to the States and have them translated and looked at by an attorney."

Carolyn took a seat beside her mother on the sofa. "He told you all this?"

"Yes."

"Did he ask you to keep it confidential?"

"He said he trusted my discretion."

Carolyn felt like making a wisecrack about the way her mother and her aunts had been known to transmit information faster than the Internet. But then she knew that of all the sisters, her mom was the most trustworthy when it came to keeping confidences.

"I asked Bryan if he felt it would be appropriate for me to share with you what he was telling me, and he said he would leave that up to me. He said he felt he could trust both of us."

"Well, that's good," Carolyn said.

"Yes, it's good that you and I can be his advocates, but what happened to him is not very good."

"What happened?"

"When Bryan made the decision in Madrid to return, he didn't let Angelina know that he was coming. He rented a car and drove to his stepmother's home. It made sense for him to go there, since that is where he had stayed for the past four nights. He used the hidden key to get in, and when he unlocked the door, she was there."

"Who was there? Angelina?"

"Yes, she was at the house. And she was in bed. With someone. Someone who is not her husband."

Carolyn leaned back.

"Bryan left and checked into a hotel. A few hours later, he called Angelina to tell her that he wanted to settle the estate in a way that would be fair to everyone. She accused him of trying to trick her by returning in secret, and then she told him not to bother to tell any of the family about what he saw at the house. She already had alerted the family that he had returned without telling anyone because he was trying to go behind their backs to obtain the entire estate."

"Why is he the bad guy in all this? Do they all approve of her cheating on her husband?"

"None of the relatives knows. Bryan didn't tell anyone. He said it was something for his sister to tell her husband."

"Are you saying he protected her, and she put all the suspicion and accusations on him?"

"It appears that way."

Carolyn shook her head. "Why?"

"Problems like this are as old as the earth. I gave him some advice."

"What did you tell him?"

"Every family has an *abuela*. For him, it is a great aunt. I know her. She is a wise woman. I suggested he tell her what happened and let her determine the next step. His family should not be suspicious of why he returned. Especially when you and I know the real reason he returned."

"And what is that?"

"He returned for you."

The comment caught Carolyn off-guard, and she immediately protested.

Her mother left her bold statement out there in the open. She didn't try to argue with Carolyn, nor did she defend her declaration or state any evidence for her conclusion. She just sat and sipped the remainder of her tea.

12

"Quien a buen árbol se arrima
buena sombra le cobija."
"Whoever leans close to a good tree
is blanketed by good shade."

BEFORE CAROLYN COULD press her mother about her bold statement regarding Bryan's coming back for Carolyn, the phone rang. By the tone of her mother's voice and the way she was talking, Carolyn had a pretty good idea she was talking with Isobel. It was funny the way they interacted with each other on a daily basis, telling each other what to do and finding something new to squabble about.

Carolyn realized that, if her father were still alive, her parents would most likely have gone the way of many older couples, addressing each other more like siblings constantly spatting than as loving spouses who have spent half a century doing life together.

The call ended, and Carolyn's mother spouted, "Isobel, she is so persistent."

Carolyn smiled. "I have a sister like that too."

"Yes, I suppose you do."

"What did she want?"

"She wants us to have dinner at her apartment tonight. I told her we would come. We must bring a salad."

"Would you like me to make the salad?"

"We can make it together."

Carolyn knew right where the large salad bowl was. All she had to do was open the cupboard, and it tumbled to the counter once again. Her mother had meandered off to the bedroom, so Carolyn chopped and shredded. Her mother appeared just as Carolyn was covering the salad.

"How can you be finished so quickly?"

"I'm speedy."

"I was going to help you."

"That's okay. It's ready to go. I need to change."

"Try to be quick. I know they'll be waiting for us."

"I'm speedy, remember?"

Carolyn slipped into a fresh skirt and blouse. She wondered what she should wear for dinner tomorrow night.

If I'd known I would be going out to dinner so much while I was here, I would have packed nicer clothes.

As soon as the thought flitted through her mind, she chuckled to herself.

What nicer clothes? You don't own nicer clothes.

She remembered passing a women's clothing store on her way to the *supermercado*. Maybe she could slip away in the morning and do a little shopping. Carolyn reminded herself that she shouldn't build up expectations about dinner. She wasn't eighteen and shopping for a prom dress. She was a forty-five-year-old widow going to dinner with her mother and an old family friend.

However, I am a forty-five-year-old widow who just happens to have lovely pink toenails. And there's nothing wrong with treating myself to a cute little something that will go with these pinkies.

Bolstered by her thoughts, Carolyn mentioned her plan as she and her mother exited the apartment and strolled past the pool to the other side of the building where Isobel lived. The sky was its usual clear, pale blue, and the evening air felt balmy.

"I was thinking I'd do some shopping in the morning. I'm realizing I didn't bring enough clothes with me. I saw a shop today on the way to the grocery store."

"Curvas Peligrosas."

"Yes, that's the one. What does that mean?"

" 'Dangerous Curves.' Clever, isn't it?"

Carolyn loved the idea of buying something new at a store called "Dangerous Curves." "Would you like to go with me?"

"Only if we go in the afternoon. Tomorrow morning I have my dance lesson."

Carolyn laughed. She thought her mother was joking. "Dance lessons, huh?"

"Yes, dance lessons. I was hoping you would go

with me. The lesson begins at Lydia's home at ten."

"You're serious."

"Yes, of course I'm serious."

Carolyn still didn't believe her. "You really are taking dance lessons?"

"Yes. I have not told any of my sisters because I don't want to be assaulted with all their advice. I know they would have plenty. All of them dance flamenco. I'm the only one who never made the time to learn. So I decided to give myself a birthday present. I am going to learn to dance flamenco."

Carolyn stepped in front of her mother, causing her to stop walking. Putting down the salad bowl and her purse, Carolyn took her mother by the shoulders and gave her a kiss on both cheeks, duplicating the women's gesture at the salon. With an affirming grin, she said, "I don't know how to say it in Spanish, but congratulations for showing yourself this kindness."

Her mother's eyes sparkled with delight. *"Gracias, mi niña.* Where did you learn this?"

"Today at the salon." Carolyn wiggled her pink fingernails for her mother to see. "I was congratulated on my way out."

"Oh, Carolyn, this makes me happy. You have been here only two days, and you are becoming a Woman of the Canaries."

Carolyn picked up the salad bowl and her purse

from where she had placed them on the cooling pavement. Her mother linked her arm in Carolyn's, and they strolled the rest of the way to Isobel's apartment.

"So this means you will go with me in the morning to my first dance lesson?"

"Yes, of course. I wouldn't miss your first dance lesson for anything." Carolyn grinned at her mother, feeling as if the season of role reversal had begun. Wasn't it usually the mother who promised to stay with her daughter at her first dance lesson? Here she was, the one in the supporting role. To make her role perfectly clear, Carolyn added, "I'm only there to watch. I'll be your cheerleader, but I won't be your dance partner. So please don't try to sign me up for lessons too."

With a side glance at Carolyn and a coy look, her mother said, "We'll see about that."

It seemed best to drop the subject at the moment, since they had arrived at Isobel's apartment and the place was once again abuzz with relatives. It was a happy hive of activity and conversations. The only problem, Carolyn discovered, was that as soon as her stomach was full of all the great food, her jetlagged body insisted she lie down and sleep. The sound of so many relatives chatting in Spanish became white noise to her ears. She was too weary to try to pick up any familiar words.

Slipping away from the group, Carolyn motioned to her mother that she was going to lie down in the guest room. Her mother nodded, and down the hall Carolyn went. The peaceful, simple sleeping chamber was ready. The bed was just as she had left it, with the comforter pulled up to the pillow and folded over once. She took off her shoes, opened the window just right, slipped under the covers, and fell into the best sort of deep sleep.

She was awakened by her mother soothingly caressing her hair and patiently whispering, "Do you want to go back to my apartment, or stay the rest of the night here?"

"I'll go back with you." Carolyn forced her legs over the bed's side and fumbled for her shoes. She would have preferred to stay where she was and to keep sleeping, but she needed to take out her contacts. Plus she knew her mother would want Carolyn to stay at her place.

The grogginess had made Carolyn's vision blurry and her head fuzzy. She and her mother left the apartment with a kiss from her aunt and took the elevator down to the plaza. Once they were in the open air, Carolyn woke up. The night breeze felt cool and invigorating. They stopped by one of the tall cactus plants in the garden area. Carolyn's mother remarked that the plant had been up only to her hip when she first moved in. Every time she had walked to Isobel's apartment over the years, she said she took note of how it was growing.

"And now look—up to the sky it reaches."

Carolyn leaned her head back to take in the cactus's full height. When she did, she caught sight of a sprinkling of faint stars looking down on her from their heavenly canopy. Her thoughts immediately returned to Bryan and the first time they had walked along the beach at Las Canteras. That night the stars had seemed so close.

She remembered how he had hummed a song as they walked barefoot hand in hand. It was a song she had been listening to one afternoon when Bryan had helped himself to the headphones on her brand-new Walkman and listened to David Cassidy croon "Cherish." Carolyn loved that song, and when Bryan hummed it, she thought maybe she loved him. But that was midway through the summer, when her thoughts and feelings about Jeff had diminished and thoughts of Bryan monopolized most of her waking hours.

She tried to put those memories aside, as she and her mother made their way up the elevator to the apartment. *That was a long time ago. I was so naive. I didn't understand so much. If I'd come to the Canary Islands that summer with more experience with guys, if I'd been more like Marilyn, I might have seen where things were headed with Bryan. I would have understood why the relationship was never going to work out for us. I would have been loyal to Jeff and stayed focused on the dream that he had for us and our future. It was a good dream, and almost all of it came true.*

Carolyn hated the way her insides were curling up with these thoughts. She knew that she had idealized her life with Jeff. They had plenty of problems. But she still insisted on elevating their marriage to deal with the immense loss.

Now that Bryan had reappeared and had opened up so many locked-away memories of that summer of self-discovery and rushing emotions, she realized that not everything about her time with Bryan had been awful. Things had ended badly, but during the weeks they had spent together, many fun and wonderful things happened between them, like the water fight they had in her grandmother's backyard.

She smiled at the memory and kept thinking about it as she took out her contacts and then brushed her teeth. She looked at her slightly blurry reflection in the mirror. Thoughts of her summer with Bryan warmed her. Memories of Jeff comforted her. How could the two exist in the same moment without one being good and one being bad? That was how she had categorized them all these years. Her relationship with Jeff was good, and what she had experienced with Bryan was bad.

"Did I fall in love with Bryan before I fell in

love with Jeff?" Carolyn whispered to her reflection and noticed that the squint lines between her eyebrows lifted. Was this a truth she had never admitted to herself? Jeff knew he loved Carolyn long before she knew she loved him. Once she realized that what she felt for Jeff was real and lasting, her remaining mangled thoughts of Bryan and whatever she once felt for him were buried as if they were a land mine.

When Bryan apologized at the restaurant, it was as if that rusted land mine had been defused. Now she felt safe to walk through that territory in her thoughts.

What do I do with all this?

Her reflection had no reply. So, with a freshly washed face and minty-clean teeth, Carolyn shut off the lights and tiptoed to her mother's bed. A soft amber haze borne of a streetlight shone through the slightly ruffling curtains and spilled a path on the floor to the left side of the bed, the vacant place that had been her father's side.

Carolyn felt very young climbing in under the sheet and thin blanket. The year-round consistent mild temperature of the Canaries meant she didn't need much to cover her. The cool solitude and pristine simplicity of Aunt Isobel's guest room appealed more to Carolyn than her mother's roomful of dustables. Even in the dim light, she could make out the assortment of figurines lined up on the dresser. But this was where she needed to be tonight, and that knowledge made her glad she had come back to her mom's apartment.

Silence tempered the room. Only the muted sound of a neighbor's television could be heard, followed by the distant hissing sound of air brakes on a city bus.

Carolyn assumed her mother was asleep already. But then her mom rolled over and softly asked, "What is it, Carolyn?"

"Hmm?"

"There is something between you and Bryan. I can see it."

Carolyn didn't reply.

"*Dígame.* Tell me. What is it?"

"It's nothing. Really. It's in the past. It doesn't matter now."

"What did he do to you, *mi niña?*" Her mother reached for Carolyn's hand and held it.

Carolyn didn't move. She knew the time had come. She could tell her mother the long-hidden truth, and it would be okay.

Carolyn blinked in the darkness, and after a pause she said, "The last night here, on the beach, behind the fishing boats, he, well, we . . . but . . . he pressed me to . . ." Carolyn couldn't find the right way to explain what happened. Yet it didn't seem as if she needed to say anything else. Her mother knew.

"And did you?" A tenderness clung to her mother's question.

It took Carolyn a long, slow minute before she whispered, "Yes."

She could feel the grip of her mother's hand tighten. Inside her heart, Carolyn felt something begin to loosen.

"I didn't think things would go the way they did. I agreed to sneak off to meet him. But I didn't think about what might happen. I know I should have stopped him. But I didn't. And then it was over, and I . . . I don't know. I just was so naive. And afraid. I was so afraid."

Her mother reached over and stroked her hair.

"It ruined everything, you know," Carolyn said. "All the sweet times we had together during the summer—the innocent smiles, the jokes between us, the times we held hands, the stolen kisses at the camel ride—all of that was turned upside down. We didn't say anything to each other afterward. It was awful. I started to cry, and he . . . he just left. He walked away."

"Oh, *mi niña, mi niña*. It hurts my heart to know that you never felt you could talk about this."

"I was too embarrassed. I blocked it out and pretended nothing happened. He didn't come back, and then the next morning you and I left to go home." Soft, silent tears were falling onto Carolyn's pillow. She thought they were all her tears, but then in the glow, she saw the glimmers in her mother's eyes as well.

"That's why, when I saw him at your birthday

party, I was so shaken. It was the first time I had seen him since that night."

"Oh, Carolyn, I had no idea."

"I know."

"You hid your feelings so well."

"I know. I've gotten pretty good at that."

The two women breathed in steady tandem, both taking time before releasing any more words into the gauzy stillness.

Carolyn spoke first. She wanted to. This part of the story needed to be told as well. "Do you know what he did when I left the table toward the end of your party?"

"No."

"He came and found me. He apologized to me."

"He apologized to you?"

"Yes, he asked me to forgive him."

Carolyn's mother lifted her head. "And did you?"

"Yes. I told him I was sorry too."

"Then it is done." Carolyn's mother drew in a deep breath and released it slowly, as if she had in her lungs the power to blow away the past. "God has removed this from you. From both of you. You are free from the sadness, regret, and shame, Carolyn. Do you believe that?"

It took Carolyn a moment. She, too, drew in a deep breath and slowly released it before saying, "Yes, I believe that."

"Good. Then drink often of that truth. You have

been forgiven. Both of you. This truth will quench any lingering regret."

Tears filled Carolyn's eyes. She believed her mother's words.

"Hasta el justo se equivocal."

Carolyn knew that proverb. She smoothed away her tears and spoke the translation aloud. "Even the wisest make mistakes."

"Yes. You remember that one, don't you? It is true. Even the wisest. This is why we all need a Savior. We all need mercy. We all need grace. And you—you have always been so generous in giving grace to others. Jeff was good at this, too, was he not?"

"Yes, he was."

"So, now it's your turn. Give yourself some of that generous grace and be at peace, *mi niña*."

Carolyn drew closer and lightly rested her cheek on her mother's shoulder. This was a good place to be, sheltered by her mother's unconditional love, both of them blanketed by the long shadow of God's grace. Why had it taken her so long to open up to her mother? Why had it taken so long to return to this place? To this person? Now that she was here, she never wanted to leave.

Then, because she wanted to feel the freedom of being rid of all the regrets that harbored inside her, Carolyn added one more disclosure. She told her mother about her misjudgment of Ellis.

"And is he out of your life completely?"

"Yes. He was never really in my life. He doesn't know where I live. I made it clear as soon as I found out he was married that I wouldn't be seeing him again."

"Good. You do not want to entangle yourself with a married man."

"I know."

"Yes, well, your second cousin Tina did not know that piece of wisdom. She ruined her life for many years and hurt many people. Just now she is beginning to get her heart back."

Carolyn liked the phrase her mother used: get her heart back.

She thought about what had happened when Jeff died. Everything inside her was smashed to pieces: her faith, her hope, her peace. In the weeks following Jeff's passing, Carolyn's mother was the only one to whom she felt she could entrust the shards of her broken heart. She handed the sharp edges to her mother bit by bit for safekeeping.

For seven years her mother had held all the pieces with the same kind insistence with which she held on to every gift she was given. Carolyn was certain her mother had carried the fragments with her every morning to the corner of the dining room where she lit her candle and prayed. The dusty remnants remained there until it was evening. Then Carolyn imagined her mother gathered them up, blew out her candle, and took the treasured thing—her daughter's broken heart—into her bed, where she covered it and sheltered it beside her own heart during the dark night.

Now it was Carolyn who was covered and sheltered, safe and warm beside her dear, wise, praying mother. As they lay together in the thin hours of the night, Carolyn at last understood the unmistakable pull that had drawn her back to the Canary Islands to be with her mother.

Carolyn's heart had drawn her, and she was ready to get it back.

13

"Donde caben dos, caben tres."
"Where there is room for two,
there is room for three."

CAROLYN CAUGHT THE slight scent of smoke as her mother's morning prayer candle was extinguished in the adjacent room of the small apartment. She could hear her mother's footsteps as she made her way into the living room and uncovered the birdcage, poured the tiny seeds into the bird's dish, and opened the window all the way.

The peace that had come to Carolyn after their deep-hearted conversation in the night had remained. This was indeed a new day.

Someone needed to make the coffee. Willingly taking on the task, Carolyn made herself at home in the kitchen, and soon the fragrance of dark coffee filled the air, joined by the comforting scent of fresh bread turning warm and crisp in the toaster. With ease and contentment, Carolyn and her mother passed each other in and out of the bathroom, bedroom, and kitchen. It was dance lesson's morning, and her mother was determined not to be late.

They were just about ready to walk out the door to catch a taxi to Lydia's home when the phone rang.

"Let it ring," Carolyn's mother said. She had her purse in her hand and was ready to leave.

"Are you sure? It might be important."

"And it might be one of my sisters."

Carolyn hesitated, looking at the phone and then back at her mom. Reluctantly, her mother gave in and picked up the phone on the fifth ring. By her tone, Carolyn could tell it was not one of the aunts. The call was short, and when Abuela Teresa hung up, she looked as if her morning energy source had been unplugged.

"What is it, Mom? What happened?"

"Nothing bad has happened. It was Lydia. She had to cancel the dance lesson for today. I am so disappointed."

If Carolyn doubted her mother's enthusiasm for these lessons, all skepticism was put aside. It surprised her that the dancing meant that much to her mom.

"What should we do instead? Would you like to go somewhere? We could go shopping." Carolyn was thinking of finding something new at Curvas Peligrosas to wear tonight.

Apparently her mother had forgotten Carolyn's shopping request from last night because she said, "What would we shop for? You just bought groceries. I have everything I need, and more gifts than I can fit on my shelves."

"We can stay here, then. I'll help you around the apartment. Is there anything that needs to be done?"

"No. And I do not want to spend your visit cleaning out my closets or my cupboards."

"Okay, then what should we do?"

"Vamos a la playa."

Carolyn knew that Spanish phrase from her last visit. "You want to go to the beach?"

"Yes, let's go to Las Canteras. I have wanted to spend a day at the beach for a very long time. It is not something anyone else likes to do as much as I. That's why I made Isobel take me to my birthday party early. I wanted to sit and watch the people. But we sat for only ten minutes. She had no patience with me. She insisted we get to the restaurant, and there we sat instead of on a beach chair in the sand."

"Well, then, that will be my gift to you. We will

go to the beach, rent lounge chairs, and watch people all day. I will have all the patience in the world."

Before Carolyn's mother could reply, the phone rang again. She answered on the second ring this time, and a smile rose on her soft cheeks. "It's so good to hear your voice. How are you? Yes, my birthday was wonderful. I received your card. Thank you. Yes, she is. Your mother is right here."

"Tikki?" Carolyn took the phone, feeling her stomach do a pirouette. "Hi, honey. Is everything okay?"

"Yes and no. Do you have a minute?"

"Of course." Carolyn stepped over to the sofa and sat down, ready for an explanation of the "yes" and the "no."

"First, how are you doing, Mom? Is everything going well there?"

"It's great. But what about you?"

"Which do you want first? The good news or the bad news?"

"Start with the bad."

"I was laid off."

Carolyn felt her shoulders slump. "How could that be? You just received the promotion."

"That was part of the problem. I was there for two days when the bank did a company-wide cut in all loan departments and, of course, last hired, first fired."

"Tikki, that's awful."

"Well, not so awful. Here's the good news. I have a new job at Starlight Bank, which is the one I wanted to work at originally. They've offered me a position as assistant branch manager, which is also great because that's what I've been aiming for. It all happened so fast. I thought about it and prayed about it before giving Starlight a start date, and Mom, I decided I'm not going to start until May fifth."

"Okay." Carolyn couldn't figure out why Tikki sounded so thrilled with that start date. She would miss out on several weeks of income. "Why the delay?"

"I decided that you're not the only one who needs to get a life. I need to get a life too. So I'm coming to Las Palmas!"

"When?"

"Tomorrow! I took some money out of my wedding savings account and thought, Why not? If Matthew is going to take his sweet time to propose, I'll have all the money back in the account before I need it. I decided to do something life-changing with the money and knew I wanted to be with my mom and my grandmother. This is the perfect time. So I bought a ticket, and I'm coming. Can you or one of your aunts pick me up at the airport at four thirty? I'm on the same flight and airline you took."

Carolyn had no words.

"Mom, are you still there?"

"Yes, I'm here. I'm stunned."

Tikki's enthusiasm went down a few notches. "Do you mind my coming? Am I interrupting your time with your mom?"

"No, not at all. You're welcome here. You know that. I'll be at the airport to pick you up tomorrow."

"Great. And, Mom, how's the weather? It's pouring rain here."

"It's perfect here. Eighties during the day."

"I can't wait!"

"Be safe."

Tikki laughed. "Okay, Mom, I'll be safe. You be safe too. See you tomorrow."

Carolyn hung up and hardly knew what to think. At the forefront was a familiar feeling that came with her introverted nature. She felt as if her time and space were being invaded. It wasn't that she didn't love Tikki and want her to come, it was just that in the two days she had been there, Carolyn didn't have to be anyone's mother or anyone's sister. She got to just be a daughter, the only daughter of Abuela Teresa for the moment. The rare gift of that focused time had been so restorative and refreshing that Carolyn didn't want to share what she was experiencing with any of the other women in her family. Not even with her daughter.

The other thought that came quick on the heels

of her inclination to protect this time was the yet-to-be-defined Bryan piece. If part of the reason he had returned to Las Palmas, as her mother said, was to spend time with Carolyn, that was going to be more complicated with Tikki onboard. Tikki would want to go and see and do all she could while visiting, and that wouldn't leave much time for seeing Bryan. Not that his objective was to spend lots of time with Carolyn. She didn't pretend to know his objectives. She didn't even know how long he was planning to stay.

"Is everything all right with Tikki?"

Carolyn looked up at her mother, who was now standing in front of the open window.

"She has decided to come here, to Las Palmas. She arrives tomorrow afternoon."

Carolyn's mother sat on the sofa. "Well, now, that does change things a bit, doesn't it?"

"It doesn't have to. Whatever things you and I were planning to do in the next few days, I'm sure Tikki would enjoy doing them with us."

"Will she be okay sleeping here on the sofa, or do you think I should ask Isobel if she can stay with her?"

"The couch will be fine. She likes sleeping on the couch when she comes to visit me." Carolyn stood and walked across the room to return the phone to its recharger cradle. "I know my trip here was last minute and spontaneous, but this is really spontaneous. You know what? I wonder if she's trying to prove something to Matthew."

"Is that her boyfriend?"

Carolyn attempted to explain the intricate relationship Tikki and Matthew had shared for many years and the crossroads they were at since Tikki was ready to become engaged while Matt was lingering on the other side of the decision.

"This will be a good time for her," Carolyn's mother said. "For Tikki and for all of us. She is a social butterfly like her father. Meeting all the relatives will be fun for her."

Carolyn gave her mom a second look. "Are you saying you don't think I've enjoyed being around all the relatives?"

"It tires you. You're not a group or party sort of person. You never have been."

Carolyn didn't know what to say. Her mother was right.

"One never knows what a day will bring," her mother said. "I thought I was going to Lydia's for dance lessons, and instead, we're going to the beach and out to dinner tonight, and my granddaughter is coming tomorrow. I feel as if my birthday celebration has been extended for the entire week. By the way, how long is Tikki staying?"

"I don't know. She didn't say. I'm just glad you're enjoying all this, and it isn't frustrating you."

"Frustrating me? Oh, Carolyn, I spend hours and days all by myself, dreaming about what it would be like to have a social calendar filled with a week like this one. I'm in heaven. Come on, *vamos a la playa!*"

Twenty minutes later the two of them were repeating the steps Carolyn had taken when she caught a taxi to Las Canteras. They were dropped off at the same spot where Carolyn had been let off two days earlier. The view was as pristine as it had been that day and the beach just as inviting. Only this time she was prepared to sit and relax, basking in the warm sun. The two women walked slowly down the boardwalk, arm in arm. Carolyn's mother was the picture of contentment. This was her happy place.

She led the way to a grouping of lounge chairs lined up in a roped-off area of the pale yellow sand. All the lounge chairs were white with royal blue pads. Only a dozen of the forty or more loungers were filled. Carolyn steadied her mother as she slipped off her shoes, and together they made their way through the warm sand to claim two of the lounge chairs facing the sea. An attendant came over and settled the rental price, which included an umbrella.

The setup was ideal for them because it allowed Carolyn a little sun, if she wanted, while her mother remained in the shade, as she wanted. Carolyn stretched out beside her happy mother and smoothed coconut-scented sunscreen over her legs and arms.

"If I fall asleep, don't wake me unless you need something desperately," Carolyn said half-jokingly and half-seriously. She saw this as her only day of vacation in which she could enjoy partial solitude. Once Tikki arrived, everything would change.

Carolyn had been running various scenarios through her mind and was coming to a stronger place of acceptance and excitement about her daughter's last-minute decision. This could well be the mother-daughter visit that Aunt Frieda had so strenuously pitched at Marilyn's wedding. The golden opportunity might not present itself again for some time. Carolyn was resolved to enjoy every minute of it. For now, she was going to enjoy her personal quiet time and recharge her batteries.

From across the sand, Carolyn heard someone cry out. She looked around. Few people were on the beach and enjoying the beautiful day, so it was easy to spot the man coming through the sand in shorts and white T-shirt. Over his shoulder was slung a wide strap that was fastened to either end of a small ice chest. The weight caused him to lean in a way that looked painfully unbalanced.

"Aaaa-gua! Co-ca-co-la! Cer-ve-za! Aaaa-gua!"

"Is he selling water?"

"Yes." Her mother reached for her purse. "Water, Coke, and beer. Would you like something?"

"Sure, I'd like some water." Carolyn reached for her purse as well, but her mother stopped her.

"I'll get this." She lifted her arm as the beach vendor approached their area and waved him over to their chairs. With a friendly exchange of polite chatter and several euro coins, the man handed over two ice-cold bottles of drinking water.

Carolyn could understand parts of their dialog due to the simplicity of their conversation. He said something about its being a beautiful day for the beach, and her mother agreed. Then she said her daughter had come all the way from America to be with her to celebrate her birthday. Agua Man smiled broadly at Carolyn, displaying his crooked teeth without shame and appearing honored to meet someone from America. He asked her where she was from, and she said, "San Francisco."

He nodded enthusiastically and then showed great appreciation when Carolyn's mother tipped him for his services. Agua Man walked away still smiling and giving them a final wave. A few feet down the beach he called out again, *"Aaaa-gua! Co-ca-co-la! Cer-ve-za! Aaaa-gua!"*

Carolyn watched him plow through the sand in his short socks and tennis shoes. "It sounds like a song, doesn't it? The way he calls out. It's almost a melody." She softly repeated his call, starting out with a low voice and raising the end of *"agua"* to a long, held-out note.

"You see why I love to come here?" Her mother stretched out her arm in a sweeping gesture. "All that is the best about my island home sings to me here. Listen, can you hear the song of the ocean? I have missed not coming here for so long."

Carolyn took in the sweeping view of the wide, curving shoreline and the easy-rolling waves. A coral reef protected this bay from any onslaught of crashing waves driven from the Atlantic. Here the water was just right for children to play in or to sit beside as they created sand castles.

As her mother contentedly sipped her ice water and watched people, Carolyn thought about how little had changed on these islands for centuries. How many generations of children had come to this beach and played along the shore. To the far right was a picturesque view of a half-dozen small, wooden fishing boats turned underside up to dry in the warm sun. Each boat was painted a different bright color, chipped and faded with use but still evidence of the unique taste of the boat's owner.

Many of the houses that lined the shores were painted bright colors as well. A few shops, several hotels, and lots of sidewalk cafés stood shoulder to shoulder on the other side of the boardwalk. The few houses that remained tucked in between retained their painted shades of azure blue, canary yellow, and tangerine orange. The bright colors allowed the fishermen to spot their homes past the sand in the bay, as they returned from sea.

On the boardwalk, not far from where Carolyn and her mother rested, stood a statue of a fisherman's wife. The diminutive, round-figured woman in her dress and apron stood with both hands on her hips, fingers curled in a fist, as she squinted toward the ocean. Her well-crafted expression seemed to ask the ageless question many women knew so well: "Where is my man, and when is he coming back to me?"

Carolyn empathized with the statue. She knew that feeling. She had spent years with her hands figuratively punched in at her hips, asking God why Jeff had been taken from her. The answer was always the same. Silence.

"Are you all right?" her mother asked.

"Yes." Carolyn shifted her view off the statue and back to the ocean.

"What were you thinking?"

Carolyn knew there was no point in pulling back from the openhearted vulnerability the two of them had shared with such sweetness last night. "I was thinking about Jeff."

"I often think of your father when I come here."

"And you still miss him?"

"Every day. He has never left my heart. You know that. Jeff has never left your heart either. He never will. That's why he feels close in times like this. Every time I come to the beach, it's as if I open up my heart and let it air out. When I do, your father is right there on the surface of all my happiest thoughts."

Carolyn reached over and gave her mother's arm a comforting squeeze.

Her mother lowered her sunglasses, looked at Carolyn, and said, " '*Al vivo la hogaza y al muerto, la mortaja.*' "

"And what does that clever adage mean, or do I want to know?"

"You already know. You have been living this way since you arrived. This is for both of us. 'We must live by the living, not by the dead.' "

Carolyn tucked away her mother's sage advice. *Live by the living and not by the dead.* "Mom, what's the one that Frieda always says about not putting the candle too close to the saint?"

"That's one of her favorites. She used to quote it whenever anyone would talk about our mother as if she had no flaws. *'Ni tanto que queme al santo, ni tan poco que no lo alumbre.'* It literally means, 'Put the candle not so close that it would burn the saint, nor so far that it will fail to light it.' "

Not far from them several small children squealed with laughter. Her mother leaned back

219

in the lounge chair and put her glasses back in place, ready to rest. Carolyn watched as the children scrambled up the side of the overturned fishing boats, calling out who was king of the hill. She knew she had held the candle too close to Jeff in the past. She didn't want to ever hold it so far that it would fail to light up memories of him.

Two little girls, too young for school, sat together at the edge of the wet sand under the watchful eye of their *abuela*. They were blissfully making sand pies with nothing more than a plastic cup and a spoon. All they had on were big girl panties. Their torsos were a toasted brown, their sun-kissed, chocolate hair pulled back in braids.

Carolyn studied them, wondering if they might be twins. How different her life would have been here if their mother had managed to convince their father to move back here when she and Marilyn were young. Her mother had tried many times, but their father was convinced that America would provide better opportunities for his daughters, and so they stayed. She couldn't help but wonder what sort of life she would have had if she had grown up here.

The sun had so efficiently warmed her shoulders that Carolyn moved her chair closer to her mother's to tuck in under the umbrella's ample shade. For the next two hours, both

Carolyn and her mother dipped in and out of sleep. Carolyn could feel her muscles relax and her thoughts lighten.

When they woke, they gathered their tote bags and made their way through the hot sand to the nearest sidewalk café. Taking the last open table, they seated themselves under the shaggy palm frond umbrella that spread over the small, square table.

"They have my favorite dessert here. Panna cotta."

Carolyn thought dessert sounded like a very good idea. If Tikki were here, she would persuade them to fully engage in the vacation spirit and eat dessert first. That would start tomorrow. Today was set aside for only Carolyn and her mother, and that meant the first thing they would order would be a salad.

Lively conversations were taking place at the tables beside them. Carolyn watched two men who were at the table behind her mom as they spoke a language she didn't recognize. Her guess was that they were Italian. They were sipping espresso from tiny white cups balanced on white saucers. Both of them spoke loudly and were quick to use their hands to emphasize their points. Their conversation tactics fascinated her.

The waiter wore a crisply pressed white shirt, black slacks, and a bow tie. That intrigued Carolyn as well because, if she were sitting at an outdoor café in a place like Santa Cruz, the waiter might well be dressed in board shorts and a crumpled T-shirt. Here, even in the cafés, it was evident that the waiters took their position seriously as a career.

Carolyn's mother ordered for both of them: fettuccine with chicken and a bottle of mineral water along with a salad to share. The lettuce salad arrived at the table with cubes of mango, tomatoes and olives and slices of hard-boiled eggs.

"This is a meal in itself," Carolyn said. "It's so fresh."

"We won't have room for dinner tonight."

Carolyn looked at her watch. It was after two o'clock. She had a pretty good idea she would be ready to eat again at eight.

But then the generous servings of fettuccine were delivered to the table, and they realized they could have shared one order. The food was delicious, and Carolyn kept eating even though she was full. Her logic was that, after another nap on the lounge chair, she would walk along the shore or go swimming and burn off some of the goodness that had made itself at home in her belly.

Carolyn's mom reached across the table and gave her hand a squeeze. "Thank you for this gift. I think this is my favorite present this year. Having you here and coming to the beach with you is something I will remember for a long time."

Carolyn loved knowing that her mother felt honored.

"I believe I will have dessert," Carolyn's mother announced.

"How could you possibly have room?"

"I will make room. And when you have a taste of their panna cotta, you will make room in your stomach as well."

The prediction was only half right. Carolyn did taste the panna cotta, and it was as delicious as her mother had promised. The custardlike chilled mound of wobbly goodness was drizzled with an amazing dark chocolate sauce that woke up Carolyn's mouth and tried to entice her to eat more. But she couldn't. She found it impossible to make room for another bite. No matter; Carolyn's mother enjoyed every last dot of the special treat.

As they were waiting for the check, a man carrying two large plastic buckets by their handles approached the restaurant's entrance and was warmly greeted by two of the waiters. The man stood outside waiting until a man dressed in a chef's jacket came out to him. They shook hands, and the chef peered into each bucket. He exclaimed something in Spanish, plunged his hand in, and pulled up a large squid that seemed to still be moving.

Carolyn turned to her mother with wide eyes. "I guess the calamari will be fresh this evening."

"Of course. You didn't think they would use frozen fish here, did you? Carolyn, you know how highly we value our food here. Only the freshest will do."

A street vendor passed by holding up small wooden-carved palm trees. Her mother turned away. Carolyn gazed with curiosity for a moment until she saw the young man pause and head toward them. Following her mother's example, she looked away to discourage overly aggressive sales tactics.

They returned to their reserved loungers and picked up where they had left off as ladies of leisure. The sun had shifted, and while they were gone, their beach attendant had adjusted the umbrella for them.

Agua Man was making his return trek down the beach, and this time Carolyn waved him over. She was ready for another bottle of ice water and tipped him as her mother had for his belabored efforts to bring the luxuriously cold water to them. Carolyn took a sip and then placed the closed bottle behind her neck where the cool sensation felt wonderful down to her toes.

"I think this is the most relaxing day at the beach I've ever had," Carolyn languidly observed.

"You see? This is why I love it here."

After a nice half-hour lull to let her lunch digest, Carolyn made good on her decision to walk along the shore. She put on a cotton shirt and her flowing skirt the way she would cover up at home if she were strolling barefoot through the damp sand. All her modest instincts told her to cover up, to hide her flaws, not to provide a spectacle for observers.

The only thing was, she seemed to be receiving stares because she was so fully covered. Everyone else appeared to be enjoying the beach with innocent abandon, not concerned about their body rolls or bulges. Women of all ages and shapes comfortably walked around in bikinis even though their midriffs were thick and lapped over the bottom of their swimsuits like muffin tops. Men from a variety of European cultures confidently strode past her wearing nothing but Speedos and a pair of sunglasses.

The most unusual beach trend was that many women went topless. This cultural norm had shocked Carolyn when she first had visited this beach as an eighteen-year-old. She couldn't imagine ever taking her top off in public. She still couldn't.

During the several hours they had been people-watching, Carolyn had noticed maybe a half-dozen women—young and old—who took off their bikini tops as they sunbathed. The odd part to Carolyn was that no one seemed to stare. The absence of a top wasn't shocking or unusual to the locals. Nor did it seem as if the women were being exhibitionists. But Carolyn, covered up as she walked, was aware of the heads that turned to look at her.

It was strange. All of it. She still felt uncomfortable whenever her eyes fell on a woman who was sitting in the sand, gazing at the waves and not wearing her bikini top. It didn't seem right, moral, or normal. But for the women here, it didn't seem to be an issue.

Leaving her cover-up on the sand, Carolyn high-stepped her way into the waves, sporting her one-piece bathing suit and wondering if she was the only woman on the beach wearing a "normal" bathing suit. She couldn't imagine any of her friends wearing a bikini now that they were past forty. Even Marilyn, when she bought a new bathing suit for her honeymoon, would only settle on a one-piece that had a built-in tummy-tightening midriff panel. The way women here accepted their body shapes and sizes was very different from in the States.

The waves were placid this afternoon. The water felt brisk when she first entered, but as she paddled around, it felt good. The water wasn't warm enough for her to stay in more than ten minutes, but for those ten minutes she did a lot of kicking and paddling. She hoped she was burning off a little of that scrumptious fettuccine. She wanted to make room for dinner tonight with Bryan.

Just thinking about him and realizing she was going to see him in a few hours set her heart racing. Instead of fighting the adrenaline rush as she had all the other times, she now applied her mother's adage. *We must live by the living and not by the dead.*

Carolyn returned to where she had left her cover-up on the sand. Crystal droplets of the Atlantic Ocean fell from her skin and left a delicate trail from the water to her lounge chair. As she toasted her front side in the waning afternoon sunshine, she dreamed a new dream. Even in her subconscious state she knew, really knew, that it was okay for her to care again for another man. She was free to move on. Just as her mother had said, Jeff would always be in her heart, and she would miss him every day. But she was ready to get a life among the living and no longer among the dead.

14

"No hay mal que por bien no venga."
"There is no bad from which
good doesn't come."

WHAT CAROLYN NOTICED immediately
about Bryan when she opened the door to
him that evening was the soft fragrance of cloves
and fresh herbs that followed him inside. She
wasn't sure if it was Bryan's aftershave or the
breeze in the hall bringing in the neighbor's
cooking. Either way, he was bringing in with him
the strong and comforting essence of all that
hinted to her of "home" in the Canary Islands.

"Come on in."

Brian held both his hands behind him and
grinned. "First, pick a hand."

Carolyn pointed and Bryan held out his left
hand, presenting her with a bouquet of mixed-
colored roses.

"How pretty!"

"I thought your mom might enjoy them."

"Oh, yes." She quickly masked her surprise that
the flowers were for her mother and not for her.
"Of course. She'll love them. Thank you."

"And I thought you might enjoy these." He
pulled out his right hand and presented a second
bouquet of mixed-colored roses.

Carolyn's face warmed as she grinned at him. "Thank you."

"Looks like you got some sun today. You look nice."

"Thanks." Carolyn knew she was blushing, but when she had stepped out of the shower an hour ago she could also tell that, in spite of the sunscreen, she had obtained a bit of a "glowy" look and now had a tan line where her bathing suit straps had been.

"My mother is almost ready. Do you want to wait while I put these in water?"

Bryan headed for the living room while Carolyn slipped into the kitchen and put the flowers in two different vases. She knew which one he had handed her, and when she brought the bouquets into the living room, she placed her mother's on the dining room table and hers on the coffee table.

"These are really beautiful, Bryan. Thanks again. That was nice of you."

"When I left the hotel, I was practically assaulted by a vendor who's been by the door every time I've come and gone. I think he came after me this time because he saw that I was finally cleaned up and wearing nice clothes."

Carolyn commented on his freshly pressed, long-sleeved white shirt and dark slacks, but she didn't understand why he had said "finally cleaned up." "Have you been running around town looking particularly scruffy?"

"My luggage didn't make it back here with me. I called again today, and the airline said it should arrive in Madrid by tomorrow morning. Hopefully it will catch up with me before I leave."

Suddenly Carolyn understood why he had been not so fresh during his visit yesterday afternoon. But then, she hadn't returned from her trek to the *supermercado* in the freshest form either.

"If your luggage does come in tomorrow afternoon, let me know. My daughter is arriving on a flight around four."

"We should go to the airport together, then. That's about the time the airline predicted my luggage would arrive. Is she going through Madrid?"

"Yes, she is."

"Will she be having some of their fresh-sneezed orange juice while she's there?"

Carolyn grinned. "Probably not. Tikki never was a big fan of orange juice, sneezed or squeezed."

Bryan grinned back.

Just then Abuela Teresa made her grand entrance in a flowing dress with an embroidered floral shawl over her shoulders. She looked lovely, and Bryan told her so. He stood when she entered, and Carolyn said, "Did you see the roses, Mom? Bryan brought them for you."

"How lovely! Thank you, Bryan. That was a kind thing for you to do."

"I got some too." Carolyn motioned to her bouquet on the coffee table. When she turned, a strand of her hair fell in front of her face. She had carefully rolled her hair up in a French twist on the back of her head, but apparently she had been too lenient with the hairpins.

Carolyn might have imagined it, but Bryan seemed to give her a pleasant expression of approval when the strand came undone. He often had told her when she was eighteen that he liked her long hair. Maybe putting it up tonight in the same way she had worn it for Marilyn's wedding wasn't a good choice. Maybe she should have left it down.

Carolyn's mother paused at the dining room table. It still was scattered with birthday gifts. The vase of roses was wedged in between the boxes. She leaned closer and drew in a long breath of the colorful beauties. A slow smile rose on her face. She plucked one of the red flowers and carried it with her to the car.

To show continued respect for her mother, Carolyn took the backseat, folding her frame into the two-door rental car with as much grace as she could manage. Bryan had parked on the street and had no trouble pulling out into the flow of cars and heading downhill, toward the old part of town.

It surprised Carolyn that the restaurant her mother selected was near the harbor but didn't have a commanding view of the water the way La Marinera did. This restaurant was old and dark, with deep mahogany wood, high-backed chairs ornately carved, and thick cloth napkins.

The suave owner came to the table and greeted them with a flourish. Carolyn could tell her mother was eating it up. He moved through the room, scattered with early diners, like a celebrity, making recommendations on wine pairings for that evening's fresh fish and leaning over each group to tell a joke before moving on to the next table.

The restaurant's atmosphere revolved around the owner as well as his waitstaff and the presentation of the food. Instead of being at a dinner where the conversation between the people at the table was the main attraction, Carolyn felt as if they had been lured into becoming village extras on the stage of some Spanish opera. Waiters walked past them like sword swallowers, holding long, flaming shish kebabs. One uniformed attendant went from table to table pouring wine as well as water from handblown glass carafes by holding the vessel high above the table and hitting the intended mark of the empty glass every time.

"What do you think of my restaurant?" Carolyn's mother asked. "Do you like it?"

"I do," Carolyn said.

"Stellar choice," Bryan said, just as their first

course, a generous plate of smoked sardines, arrived. Carolyn's mother demonstrated how the small fish were to be lifted by the tail and held over the mouth. The proper way to eat the sardines was by scraping off the tender white meat with only one's teeth and swallowing the meat along with the shimmery silver skin. Done properly, all that would be left after a successful scrape would be the head and the spine. Those cartoonlike carcasses were stacked on a separate plate. In front of Carolyn, Bryan, and her mother were individual finger bowls filled with warm water and a slice of lemon. Here they dabbled their digits between sardines.

"This is quite a process. Have you ever had sardines before?" Bryan asked Carolyn after she had successfully consumed her second sardine.

"No, not like this."

"What do you think?"

"I like them. I like the flavor. And they're so tender."

"It's the fresh fish of the islands," Carolyn's mother said as she daintily moistened her fingers in her dipping bowl. "What do you think of the sardines, Bryan?"

"I think if we had some Cajun sauce, they would taste like crawfish. They don't taste like chicken, that's for sure."

Carolyn thought his comment was humorous, but her mother paid it no mind and asked him another question. "Have you had any of the *gambones con ajo* since you've been here, Bryan?"

"I don't think so. Is that shrimp?"

"Yes, prawns with garlic. Delicious."

Carolyn mentioned the squid they saw being pulled from the fisherman's bucket that afternoon at Al Macaroni Café on the boardwalk.

"They'll be serving fresh calamari tonight," Bryan said.

Carolyn laughed. "That's the same thing I said."

Bryan told her about a restaurant where he lived in Newport Beach called The Crab Cooker. "It's been there for as long as I can remember. I'm not saying it's the best seafood place in all of Newport Beach, but the fish always is fresh and that makes the difference, doesn't it?"

"That's what I always say," Carolyn's mother said.

The main course arrived on a cart. Fresh fish, of course. One large fish for all of them to share. The waiter stood behind the cart and lifted his curved knife and a long fork to the broiled fish that lay on a platter of parsley and what looked like basil leaves. The head and tail were still attached, causing Carolyn a slight sense of pity for the beautiful fish.

As the waiter expertly deboned the fish, extracted the steaming white portions, and arranged them on the three plates on the cart, Carolyn noticed her mother pull back. She gave an unpleasant expression for just a moment and folded her right arm over her middle.

I wonder if the sight of the waiter ransacking the fish in front of us makes her a bit nauseous too. At least I'm not the only one.

To each of the three plates the waiter added from a covered dish a generous helping of steamed baby carrots. He then stuck a fork into another dish that appeared to be nothing but a bed of crusted sea salt. Out came a small potato, cooked in the Old World fashion. Carolyn had forgotten about this.

"Are those *papas arrugadas?*"

The waiter looked up at her. *"Sí."*

Carolyn smiled as if the potatoes were a childhood comfort food. The waiter seemed to take note because he added an extra potato to one of the plates. That was the plate he served first, and he presented it to Carolyn.

"Someone has a fan," Bryan teased.

The waiter then took a different fork and knife and cut into the side of the fish's head. He extracted a small, not-quite-round, pearl-shaped object and placed it on the side of Carolyn's plate. She looked to him for an explanation, but all he did was nod as if they had done him a service by sitting at his table.

"He presented you with the cheek," her mother

said. Carolyn thought she detected a wistful tone in her voice. "It's given to the honored guest at the table. Tonight, that would be you."

"I'm supposed to eat this?"

"Oh, yes, it's a delicacy. He's waiting to see if you like it."

Carolyn glanced at the waiter and then at Bryan. He was watching to see what she would do.

Reaching for her fork, Carolyn gingerly speared the opaque, pea-sized fish cheek with a single tong and put it in her mouth. She knew she could swallow it like a pill and make all the appropriate "mmmm" sounds to please the waiter. But instead she placed it on her tongue, rolled it around to get the initial flavor, and then bit into it with her back teeth before swallowing.

"Well?" Bryan asked.

"Nice." She nodded to the waiter. *"Bueno. Gracias."*

He took another humble bow and wheeled away the cart.

"Did it have any taste at all?" Bryan asked.

"It tasted sort of like chicken."

Bryan laughed. "Cajun chicken?"

"No, chicken of the sea. Only with a squish." Carolyn and Bryan laughed like true Americans, openly enjoying the moment.

Carolyn could tell that her mother was holding back from correcting her unrefined daughter on her European table manners. Putting her attention to food waiting on her plate, Carolyn took a bite of the tender, flaky fish and made an appropriate, subdued sound. "Mmmm."

"When my son and I lived in Hawaii, he developed a taste for poi; you know, that gray pasty stuff they serve at luaus. That and the lomi lomi salmon. Two local delicacies that I never did come to like," Bryan said.

"When did you live in Hawaii?" Carolyn's mother asked.

"It was at least fifteen years ago. We were on Maui. In the Lahaina area."

"I hear Maui is a lovely island."

"It is. I was trying to start up a business with a friend of mine, but it never came together. Kai had some issues he was working through, and I lost someone my son and I were very close to. Todd was about ten or eleven at the time, and when Lani passed away, I knew we couldn't stay on Maui. We returned to California, and I haven't been back since. Todd has returned. He and his wife went there for their honeymoon."

"And what do you do now, Bryan?" Carolyn's mother asked.

"I work for a health care company as a systems analyst."

"And what is that, exactly?" Carolyn's mother hiccupped. She immediately covered her mouth and pardoned herself.

Carolyn wanted to laugh. So much for proper table manners.

"My job sounds more impressive than it is. I work out of my home and basically spend the day on the phone with medical assistants who run into any sort of problem with our software. Sometimes a whole office will have its system go down, and it'll take me a day or two to get them back up." He harpooned his last carrot. "I've been able to keep up with work some while I'm here. The time difference is the biggest challenge. But the best part of my job is that I can work pretty much anywhere."

Carolyn's mom shook her head. "The marvels of the computer world. I don't understand a thing about it. How did you manage to get such a job?"

"My roommate from Berkeley ended up at Microsoft. He opened some doors for me after my wife left. I needed to get established so I could obtain custody of our son."

"How long ago did your wife leave?"

"More than twenty years ago. She's remarried and lives in Florida now."

"So you raised your son by yourself?"

"It's more like we raised each other."

Carolyn had a funny feeling her mother was grilling Bryan rather than keeping up the conversation. She tried to redirect the topic by asking, "Aren't these potatoes good? I love the way baking them in the salt results in such crispy skin but leaves the inside so soft."

"They are good," Bryan agreed. "What about you, Carolyn? Do you work full-time?"

Carolyn told him about her long-held position at the school office and how she lived down the street from the school. She added that her sister, with her two daughters, recently had moved out after living with Carolyn for almost six years.

They chatted a bit about the housing market, and Bryan said he managed to find a house only a few blocks from the beach and how that made working from home even more desirable.

"I've been there almost twelve years, which is hard to believe. What about you? How long have you been in your house?"

"We moved in right after we married. So that'll be . . . ," Carolyn did the math. "Twenty-five years ago this July." She felt a tightening in her throat, and her spirit took a dive. *Twenty-five years. Jeff and I would have been married twenty-five years.*

"And how long ago did you and Jeff divorce—if you don't mind my asking."

Carolyn's fork paused midway to her mouth. She lowered the utensil. "We didn't divorce."

Bryan put down his fork as well and looked stunned. "I thought at your mom's birthday you said you weren't together anymore."

Her mother stepped in and answered for her, "Jeff has been gone for seven years."

"He . . . he was killed," Carolyn said plainly. She didn't know why she came out with it so bluntly. She never talked about Jeff's death that way. Her mother had handled the declaration with much more grace. Carolyn waited for the usual comment given at such a moment so she could thank Bryan for his condolences and they could move on with the rest of the dinner.

Bryan, however, didn't say anything. He reached across the table, took Carolyn's hand in his, and just held it. She looked away from his understanding gaze, but she didn't pull away her hand. Not at first. The waiter returned to offer dessert and coffee.

Her mother answered for them, and Carolyn pulled back her hand and finished the last few bites of her dinner. Bryan's gesture touched her deeply. Perhaps more deeply than all the wordy attempts of well-meaning family and friends over the years because, really, nothing could be said.

The table was cleared. All the crumbs were swept off the tablecloth with the use of a silver-handled brush and matching silver tray. More water was poured from a foot above their drinking glasses, and an entire new setup of silverware, coffee cups, saucers, and serving plates was set in front of them.

Next came an assortment of small slices of cake

along with ramekins of flan placed in the center of the table. Steaming coffee was poured from a long-spouted silver pot. A small pitcher of milk was delivered along with a small bowl of brown cubes of raw sugar.

Carolyn's mother leaned back, her hands folded across her stomach. She looked at Carolyn as if she was giving her an unspoken signal that one of them needed to say something more about Jeff's death. Carolyn preferred to be the one to give the explanation.

Tapping the flat of her spoon on the flan, she said, "I haven't talked about Jeff's death in a long time. But I want to tell you what happened."

Bryan's open expression made it clear that he wanted to hear.

Carolyn reached for her water and took a sip. She didn't know how to talk about Jeff without telling the whole story.

"Jeff volunteered for many years at a juvenile detention facility in Oakland. He spent a lot of time with the troubled teens there, doing all kinds of service for them—tutoring, yard work. He even washed dishes for a while. It made him happy to do something for them. They appreciated him—the staff, I mean. And some of the young men did too. Not all of them, of course, but he had some very meaningful conversations with some of those boys. They trusted him because he didn't have to be there. He wasn't an employee. They liked him, and he liked being with them."

Carolyn paused and wished she could stop there. She didn't want to tell this next part. Her gut tightened, and she swallowed back angry tears.

"One Saturday Jeff took several of the new boys to the back area for some softball practice. He had done that many times but not with these particular boys. They . . ." Carolyn didn't want to say it. She looked to her mother.

Her mother's expression showed her pain. She was clutching her stomach.

Carolyn looked down at her hands resting beside her plate and tried to say it as quickly as possible. "They turned on him for no clear reason. Two of the boys beat Jeff with a baseball bat. He never regained consciousness. He died three days after the attack."

And I never got to say good-bye.

Bryan reached across the table again and covered Carolyn's hand with his. Again, he didn't offer any words. Only his touch and his presence.

The senselessness of Jeff's death felt as real to her as it had that Saturday night when she received the call saying that her husband was in an ambulance on his way to the hospital. It wasn't fair. It wasn't right. Jeff was helping people. He was being a good Christian man. He had done nothing to deserve this.

The ache in her heart felt as large as the sea all over again. She wished she hadn't told Bryan. She wished she hadn't said the words aloud. Every time she spoke about it, the life-altering event felt real all over again. Real and horrifying.

Why did I think I was ready to move on? I'm not over this. I'm never going to be over this.

Carolyn slipped her hand out from under Bryan's so she could reach for the napkin and dot her tears. She didn't want to add the details about what happened to the assailants. It pained her even more to report that since the two convicted attackers were under age, they couldn't be tried for murder. She heard later that one of them had died from a drug overdose and the other one was in prison. That outcome should have brought a small sense of vindication to her, but all she could think when she heard the news was how sad Jeff would have been to hear that two of the young men he cared so much about hadn't made it out of the penal system with success.

Bryan continued to offer her his steady, unflinching gaze.

Her mother let out a small sighlike moan, which Carolyn took as a gesture of sympathy.

Something inside Carolyn made her want to apologize for bringing up such a terrible downer after the festive feel of the first part of their evening. Lifting her spoon to her lips, she tried to initiate some return to normality. She swallowed her flan without tasting it. "So, what should we talk about now?"

"We don't have to talk about anything. We can just be." Bryan leaned back and pushed away the rest of his dessert. The waiter came and poured fresh coffee. He delivered a small plate of square pieces of chocolate, compliments of the restaurant owner.

Carolyn looked around, trying to refocus. The restaurant was full of guests now. The other section that had been vacant when they arrived was atwirl with lively greetings by the owner. In the section of the dark restaurant where they were seated, all the diners around them were also at the dessert stage and were leaning over the candlelit tables, their conversations humming low and close.

Turning back to Bryan she said, "You know what this feels like, don't you?"

"I do," Bryan said. "It's like a hole in your gut."

Carolyn pressed her lips together and pushed aside her dessert as well.

"That's how it was with me when I lost Lani. She was a deeply spiritual woman. My son would call her a God Lover. She was an amazing woman, and she loved me and loved my son, but she wouldn't marry me because I wasn't a Christian then. She didn't hold my rowdy past against me. It wasn't a self-righteous thing. Lani just loved God and lived out what she read every

244

day in the Bible. She wanted that same abundant, eternal life for me. For us. Nothing less."

Bryan held up his hand to the waiter indicating he had had enough coffee and to leave his cup unfilled. "I went to church with her and listened, but it was so foreign to everything I'd known in my life that I remained skeptical. You know, I thought of you quite a few times during that season of questioning everything."

"Me?" Carolyn was caught off-guard.

Bryan looked at Carolyn's mother and then back at her. "I thought of both of you. Aside from Lani, Kai, and his parents, the two of you were among the few Christians I'd ever known. I remembered how you prayed before meals and talked about Jesus as if he were a real person."

Carolyn remembered how Bryan had told her that summer that he was a "hard-core agnostic." She had told him she didn't know what that meant, and he had laughed at her. Even though her Dutch dad had made sure they went to church every week and their Catholic-raised mom had nurtured a deep respect for God, it wasn't until she and Jeff became involved in a small group Bible study that Carolyn saw her childhood faith grow. She and Jeff prayed about everything. After his death, Carolyn found it difficult to pray and even more difficult to trust God the way she and Jeff used to.

Bryan said, "I had enough to go on to surrender

and put my faith in Christ, but the rebel in me held out. While I was demonstrating my independence, Lani was dying of ovarian cancer. By the time it was discovered, it was too late to do anything for her."

"But it was not too late for you, was it?" Carolyn's mother asked.

Bryan gave her a grin. "You already know the answer to that. It's never too late with God. It just took me awhile to finally bend my knee. I had to be willing to live inside the mystery."

"What do you mean by that?" Carolyn asked.

"Some things in life will never make sense. They won't be made right or explained. At least in our lifetime. They float around in a swirl of mystery. I wanted God to explain all that mystery to me before I agreed to trust him. But I discovered it doesn't work that way. He is God, and he doesn't have to explain anything. When I understood that, then I could surrender to Christ and step inside the mystery instead of stand back and resist."

Carolyn felt as if Bryan had just explained what she had been feeling the past seven years. She had tried to step out of the mystery and wait for God to give her answers. She remembered how Frieda had said at Marilyn's wedding that Carolyn needed to help God work out his divine plan for her. Carolyn had answered sarcastically that God didn't need any help from her because he seemed to do whatever he wanted. Apparently Bryan had come to the same conclusion, only his realization had brought him closer to God while Carolyn's had taken her further away.

Carolyn noticed that her mother was being noticeably quiet on a topic she usually had something to add to. Her chin was dipped, her arms folded across her midriff, as if she were intently focused or in deep concentration.

Carolyn tried to catch her mother's eye. "Mom?"

She responded with a catch in her breath.

"Mom, are you okay?"

Calmly but with force, she said, "I think I need you to take me to the hospital. Will you take my arm, Bryan? Please don't do anything that would draw attention to us. *¿Entiendes?*"

"Yes, I understand." Bryan was already around the table and pulling out her chair in a gentlemanly fashion. Carolyn's mother rose slowly and took Bryan's arm. Carolyn grabbed their purses and followed her stalwart mother, as she shuffled to the door, bent over and with her arm gripping her middle.

"Ándale," her mother said, giving them a breathy mandate to hurry.

15

"Barriga llena, corazón contento."
"Full belly, happy heart."

THE PROCEDURE TO admit Carolyn's mother to the hospital for examination went quickly. The large medical facility wasn't too busy that evening. Carolyn helped her mother dress in a hospital gown and settle in the bed appointed to her in the examination area. Once she was comfortable in the bed, Bryan came in. He took her hand in his. "Have you been in pain all evening, Abuela?"

"Off and on. It got worse as I was eating dessert. It's not so bad now."

"It's your stomach, right?" Carolyn asked.

She nodded. When the doctor entered a few moments later, Carolyn's mother repeated the symptoms in Spanish and answered the questions on the sign-in form. A series of tests was started, and Bryan and Carolyn were asked to leave. As they walked down the hall to the waiting area, Bryan reached over and took her hand in his, lacing their fingers as he had done that very first time at the beach. His presence meant the world to her at the moment.

"She kept pressing on her left side," Carolyn said, as they sat close beside each other on the couch. "I've been trying to figure out which organ is located there, just under the rib cage. Would that be her liver?"

"Possibly. I'm glad the doctor could see her right away."

"So am I. Hospitals make me queasy. Bad memories, you know."

"Yes, I know."

"Was Lani in the hospital a long time?"

"No. Only a few days. My worst memories in a hospital were just a few years ago. My son was in a serious car accident. All the doctors said it should have been fatal."

"But he's okay, I take it. You said he got married last year."

"Yes, he recovered. He has quite a few scars, but the way he came out of it was pretty miraculous. Seeing how his friends gathered around him really blew me away. A lot of people were praying for him. I wish I'd turned to the Lord when I was young, like Todd did. He's in such a better place than I was at his age."

"I often think my daughter has a much more developed relationship with God than I do. She doesn't question or doubt the way I have since Jeff's death."

Bryan nodded his understanding. Carolyn couldn't believe they were sitting there, in a Las Palmas hospital, holding hands and talking about God. Never in her wildest imagination did she foresee such a poignant moment as this with Bryan Spencer. Never.

"I hope my mom is going to be all right. If anything happens to her right now . . ."

Bryan let go of Carolyn's hand. He stretched his arm around her and welcomed her to lean on his shoulder. The scent of cloves and basil rose from the collar of his new shirt and helped to cancel the antiseptic fragrance of the hospital that had made her stomach clench.

Feeling comforted, Carolyn tried to remember how she felt when the young version of Bryan had put his arm around her on the beach. Those memories were fading, and she found herself very much at home with this new version of Bryan. She wondered how all this was translating for him. It was strange. Yet it felt familiar and not at all unusual that they would be there like that.

"Tell me more about your life." Carolyn lifted her head from his broad shoulder. "I don't want to sit here in silence and worry about my mother."

Bryan talked more about his son, his job, and the vintage Harley-Davidson motorcycle he was refurbishing. She noticed that he didn't say anything about his stepsister or the tense situation he was in with her and the issues over the inheritance. Carolyn didn't want to let him know how much she was aware of. It seemed better to wait and let Bryan tell her what he wanted her to know—when or if he wanted her to know it.

He asked her more about her life in Fremont, and she stuck with the lighter topics such as her recent decorating project and a few of the things she still needed to get fixed. After an hour of waiting, Carolyn said, "I'm going to check on her. I'll be right back."

She left the warmth of Bryan's closeness and conversation and went to where they had left her mom in an examination bed. Going to her mother's side, Carolyn took her cool hand in hers, and together they waited for the doctor to return. When he appeared, he offered Carolyn what looked like a sympathetic smile and explained the prognosis in Spanish. Carolyn didn't understand, but she nodded, knowing her mother would tell her everything.

As soon as the doctor exited, Carolyn asked, "What did he say? Did he find the problem?"

Her mother didn't answer. She had the look of a stubborn child.

"Mom, *dígame.* Tell me. What did the doctor say?"

"I have gas."

Carolyn squinted. "That's what the doctor said? He said you have gas?"

"Yes. Acute indigestion. He asked what I had been eating the past few days, starting with my birthday party, the fettuccine at lunch, and the dessert at dinner. He said I'm not used to so much rich food. I can go home and take the remedy he's given me to settle my stomach. Tomorrow it's nothing but tea, toast, and broth."

Carolyn was relieved, of course. But she knew her mother was embarrassed. This was much worse than if the diagnosis had required an overnight stay for further examination.

"What would you like me to tell Bryan?"

Her mother sighed. "The truth, I suppose. It's always best to tell the truth." She shook her head and muttered something in Spanish.

"Don't be flustered. You were obviously in a lot of pain. It was the right choice to make sure everything was okay. You have nothing to be embarrassed about."

She didn't look convinced.

"Would you like some help dressing?"

"No, I'm fine." She sat up, and a low rumble sounded from her midriff.

Carolyn ducked out and returned to the waiting area. "It's good news," she told Bryan. "Nothing serious. Just some indigestion."

"That's a relief."

"I'm sure she's embarrassed that she asked to come here over something minor, but I told her I was glad we brought her. She'll be ready to go in just a bit."

"I realized something while you were with her. We never paid for our dinner. We were in such a hurry to leave the restaurant that I didn't think to ask for the check. I called them just now, and the

252

person I spoke with asked that your mother call back and talk to the manager. Sorry about this. I was hoping they could take my credit card over the phone."

"You didn't tell anyone she was in the hospital, did you?"

"No. I got the impression your mother wouldn't appreciate that."

"Why don't I take your phone with me to the exam room, and my mom can call them now in case we need to stop by on our way home? How do I redial the last number called on your phone? This is way more sophisticated than the one I have."

Bryan showed her how to dial the restaurant, and she returned to the examination room where her mother was moving slowly. Her discomfort was obvious. She had her dress on but was slumped into the chair in the corner, appearing to have difficulty with her shoes.

"Let me put those on for you." Carolyn knelt down and lifted her mother's feet one at a time, maneuvering the shoes on and clasping the side buckles. Before she got back up, she felt her mother's hand on the crown of her head, as if in readiness to bestow a blessing on Carolyn.

"Dios le bendiga, mi niña."

Carolyn smiled and received the words. For so many years she had put herself in a position of service to help other people any way she could.

While she had received many thank-yous over the years, she didn't remember ever feeling this sort of hand blessing.

Rising to her feet, Carolyn smiled, and the two of them exchanged the sort of expression reserved in life for those you truly love, flaws and all, no matter what.

"Mom, if you don't mind, could you make a call before we leave here? Bryan realized we left the restaurant in such a hurry that we didn't pay for dinner. He called them, and they wanted you to speak with the manager." Carolyn pushed the button and handed the phone over to her mother.

She perked up and spoke with more liveliness than Carolyn knew she was feeling at the moment. The call didn't last long, but her mother was smiling when she handed back the phone. "It's all taken care of."

"Will they take Bryan's credit card over the phone?"

"No. The dinner was a gift, he said. For my birthday. No charge."

"I'm telling you, Mom, you are finding ways to keep celebrating all week long. That's great."

"I am a blessed woman."

"Yes, you are."

Her mother's stomach let out a low rumbling growl.

"You are blessed, and you are about to belch, aren't you?"

Her mother held her hand over her mouth, swallowing a series of small hiccups.

"Are you okay?"

"I will be. We need to get me home."

When they arrived at the apartment building, Carolyn's mother insisted that she didn't need help to walk up to her place. Bryan honored her decision. "How about if I call in the morning, Carolyn? We can decide what to do about going to the airport for your daughter and my luggage."

"That sounds good. Thanks again, Bryan. For everything."

He smiled back and then leaned over to her mother in the passenger's seat and brushed a kiss across her cheek.

Carolyn helped her mom to the apartment, taking slow steps. Tonight they didn't pause to examine the cactus or the night sky. Once inside, Carolyn filled a glass with water so her mother could take the medicine and went into the bedroom to turn down her mother's side of the bed and put out her nightgown.

Even though her mother was still in much discomfort and it was well after midnight, she had paused in the dining room, lit her evening candle, mouthed her benediction to the day, and blew out the light with a small puff and a hiccup. Carolyn covered the birdcage and closed the window halfway, as she had observed was her mother's custom each night.

By the time both of them were in bed and Carolyn was just about to drop off to sleep, her mother released a long, rolling belch.

"Mother!" Carolyn laughed.

A variety of gas-releasing sounds escaped from her mother's petite body with unexpected volume.

"Seriously!" Now Carolyn was sitting up and laughing. "What do you have to say for yourself, young lady?"

"I feel much better, thank you."

The two of them dissolved into a fit of giggles.

"I guess the medication is working." Carolyn waved her hand in front of her nose. "It's working so well, I think I'm going to sleep on the couch."

"I would if I were you." Another hearty belch sounded.

Carolyn cracked up. She reached for the pillow and took the folded-up blanket at the end of the bed. "Good night, Mom. If you need anything, call for me. But if you wake me up, it better be because you at least are having a gallbladder attack this time."

Her mother liked that one. She chuckled and hiccupped.

Carolyn felt her way along the wall to the light switch and set herself up on the couch. The confused bird called out a questioning chirp from under the cage blanket.

"Don't worry, Alma. I'll turn off the light, and

in two minutes all you'll hear is me peacefully sleeping."

Her prediction was right, and it was the warming rays of the morning sun that touched her face and woke her six hours later. She tiptoed into her mother's room to check on her.

"Are you feeling better?"

"Yes. *Barriga llena, corazón contento.*"

"I remember that one. You just said, 'Full belly, happy heart,' right?"

"Yes, I did. Your father used to repeat that saying whenever I made his mother's meatballs, do you remember?"

"I certainly do. I'm glad you're improved. How about if I bring you some tea? That's what the doctor recommended, right?"

"Yes. See if I have any mint tea, will you, please? I'll get up now, and we can have our breakfast together in the living room."

Carolyn was about to step out of the bedroom when her mother said, "Carolyn, what about you?"

"I'll make some tea and toast for me as well. I might have an egg or some yogurt."

"No, I am not asking about your belly. I am asking about your heart. Is your heart happy this morning?"

Carolyn paused only a moment before she thoughtfully answered, "Yes. Yes it is. My heart is happy this morning."

"Good."

That was all her mother had to say on the subject. She didn't elaborate on the intense conversation at dinner with Bryan or on the expectations of what might happen with him next. No hint was given that Carolyn should be looking forward to seeing Tikki that afternoon. Her mother's assessment for the moment was simply, "Good."

The first part of the day was just as good as her proclamation. Bryan called and asked if they wanted to join him for lunch. Carolyn's thoughts started to compare the invitation to the one Ellis had given Carolyn to meet him for "lunch" at the downtown hotel. She quickly told herself there was no comparison, and she believed it. Ellis and the world he belonged to were far away. The indecisive and insecure woman she had been with him was also far away. Carolyn felt as if she were stepping out of a thick fog into a place where she could at least see where to put her feet.

Bryan told her on the phone that he had found a beachfront café where he had gone earlier that morning for breakfast. He said he wanted to take Carolyn and her mother there before going to the airport, if they were interested.

Her mother waved off the invitation, saying she was under doctor's orders. No food for her. She wanted to take the day to rest up before Tikki's arrival. Carolyn agreed to take a taxi to meet him and asked the name of the café.

"Al Macaroni."

Carolyn laughed. "You discovered my mother's favorite sidewalk café. She took me there yesterday."

"Maybe that's where I heard about this place."

"Remember the fresh calamari delivered to the front door?"

"Oh, right. Yes, you were the one who told me about Al Macaroni. It's great, isn't it? But then you probably don't want to go there again today."

"No, I'd love to."

"Okay, good. Would an hour be too soon for us to meet there?"

"Make it an hour and a half, and it's a deal."

Carolyn bounced in and out of the shower, rummaged through her limited selection of clean clothes, and determined that she absolutely had to go shopping tomorrow to buy something new to wear. Tikki would be with her, and the thought of them shopping together made her feel even more buoyant.

Kissing her mother good-bye and grabbing everything she needed, Carolyn headed out the door and across the busy road like a pro. She flagged a taxi within the first three minutes and confidently gave him the information in Spanish. *"La playa de Las Canteras, por favor."*

She had the right amount of cab fare ready when she exited and thanked him in Spanish. With her old beach sandals on her feet and the ocean breeze in her hair, Carolyn walked with brisk steps down the crowded boardwalk to the café next to the statue of the fisherman's wife who stood frozen in time, peering out to sea with her hands on her hips.

Bryan was waiting at one of the tables under a shaggy grass umbrella. He stood when he saw her, and they greeted comfortably with a quick touch of their cheeks. Carolyn noticed right away that he had a phone earpiece in his left ear. Bryan motioned that he was on a call, and she mouthed the words, "I'll order for us."

Bryan nodded and said something to the person on the phone about equity and resale value. She guessed this wasn't one of his calls for work but rather it was counsel for the unsettled problem he had with his stepsister over the inheritance.

The waiter appeared, the same man in the crisp white shirt and bow tie who had served Carolyn and her mother the day before. He handed her two menus, but she didn't open them. With her newfound boldness after communicating with the taxi driver in Spanish, Carolyn ordered the same salad she and her mother had yesterday, *gambones con ajo* that her mother had mentioned last night at the restaurant, and a bottle of mineral water.

As Bryan concluded his conversation, she looked out at the sand and the water, once again feeling that sense of timelessness here where life's elements were at their most basic—sun, wind, sand, sea. She paused to wonder if

Columbus had ever come to this exact bay and beach when he was on the island. What other explorers or pirates had left their footprints in this sand in this place of soft, dusty tenacity?

"Sorry." Bryan removed the phone earpiece. "I needed to stay on that call."

"Don't worry. *No te preocupes.*" She grinned at her Spanish word-infusion. "I'm early."

Bryan checked his watch. "Yes, you are."

She noticed he was wearing the same Tommy Bahamas–style short-sleeved beach shirt he had worn to her mother's birthday party. It definitely looked beachy by this point.

"What did you order for us?"

"A salad."

"Healthy. Nice."

"And hopefully I ordered the prawns with garlic. Or if I didn't get my Spanish right, it could be something else."

"Like fish cheeks." Brian kept a straight face.

Carolyn grinned. "Yes, like squishy fish cheeks."

"Speaking of squishy fish cheeks, was your mom all right about your leaving her alone today?"

Carolyn's jaw dropped. She reached across the table and swatted at him.

"What?" He looked innocent. It was an expression she recognized because he had mastered it long ago.

"Why did you associate squishy fish cheeks with my mother?"

261

"No! I didn't mean she has squishy fish cheeks. When you said it, I thought of dinner last night and that made me think of your mom's episode. I wanted to make sure she was okay."

"Her 'episode.' I can't believe you just said that." Carolyn hid her grin. "Yes, she was fine with my leaving her today. And for the record, I didn't say squishy fish cheeks first. You did."

The bottle of mineral water arrived, and Bryan did the honors of filling their two short glasses. He lifted his glass and said, "Truce?"

"Truce." Carolyn took a sip and kept an eye on him over the top of her glass.

"What? Why are you looking at me like that?"

"You're still you," she said.

"And you're still you. Only a whole lot more beautiful than I even remembered."

Carolyn hadn't expected his compliment on the heels of their bantering. She hid her smile with another sip of mineral water, but she couldn't hide her happiness. It could be just one of his roguish lines of flattery or even a small joke. She didn't care. It made her glad to be a woman and glad to be alive. It made her glad to be there, with Bryan.

Just then the impressive salad arrived, a repeat of yesterday's bountiful feast, and Bryan said, "Good choice. This looks great." He reached across the table and covered Carolyn's hand as she was about to pick up her fork. "Do you mind if we give thanks?"

Carolyn couldn't remember the last time she had paused to pray before a meal. She somberly bowed, feeling self-conscious as to what the mix of humanity gathered at the other tables might think of what they were doing.

Bryan's words of gratitude to "Our Heavenly Father" were as clean, true, and elemental as the sun, sand, and surf. It felt as if he was gently taking Carolyn by the hand and leading her back inside the mystery, into a place of vast, unexplainable life ruled by an untamable God.

Upon his "amen," Bryan released his warm hand, and Carolyn looked up. Her eye caught on the statue of the fisherman's wife. That's when Carolyn knew that Someone had been standing on the shore for a long time, staring into the ocean of her sorrow, scanning the horizon, and waiting for her to return.

She had been out at sea far too long.

16

"De tal palo, tal astilla."
"From such a stick, such a splinter."

THE REST OF Carolyn's time at lunch with Bryan was as natural and enjoyable as if they were established friends who met at the same table every week for conversation sprinkled with charm. Carolyn was tempted to bring up the unexpectedness of their reconnection or comment on how easy it was for them to talk. She felt she should let him know how much she was enjoying their time together.

But she didn't want to spoil any of the easiness and spontaneity. She thought of all the times Tikki had told her about her "DTRs" over the years with the guys she had dated, including Matthew. Every time those conversations had taken a toll on the natural momentum of the relationship. Carolyn preferred to enjoy the moment and not try to figure out what it all meant or what was next.

As they drove to the airport, Bryan opened up to her a little about the problem with his stepsister. "Do you remember Angelina?"

"Yes. She was only five, I think, when I was here last time."

"That sounds about right. She and I are working out the details of her mother's will. It looks like I might be staying here for a while. Did your mother tell you?"

"Yes, she did."

"Did she tell you all the complications?"

"Yes, she told me. It sounds like it's going to be difficult to work everything out."

"I hope not. The attorney your mom sent me to has already started to work on the case. We'll see how it goes. I don't know how long Tikki is planning to be here or how much time you'll have, but I wanted to let you know that I'd like to see you some more—you, your mom, and your daughter—if it fits in with your schedule."

"I'd like that too. I'm sure we can make plans after I talk with Tikki. Her phone call letting me know she was coming was short and sweet. Right to the point."

"Tell me more about her. Does she look like you?"

"Yes, I think she does. Although, when I look at her profile—her forehead, nose, and chin—I see Jeff's side of the family. She has the brown eyes and nice legs from my side of the family. And our hair is similar."

Bryan glanced over at her and then back at the road. "You've always had great hair. And nice legs. You're right about that. The women in your family have very nice legs."

"Thank you." She knew that men noticed such things, but it had been a long time since she had heard a man mention her physical attributes in the conversational flow. Bryan did it in such an even-paced way that Carolyn didn't feel uncomfortable.

"I'm looking forward to meeting Tikki. I still think that's a great name. Good for Jeff for coming up with that one."

As much as it felt strange and natural at the same time for Carolyn to meet up with Bryan and to carry on casual conversations, she found it also felt strange and natural for him to praise Jeff and to say that he liked her daughter's name. The past and present seemed to be merging more and more. It felt very much like her impressions of Las Palmas that first day when she saw how the old overlapped the new. Each still held its place, and yet it was becoming more challenging to see where one ended and the other began.

Bryan parked his small rental car in the outdoor parking area, and they walked together to baggage claim.

"When I arrived the other night, my aunt was delayed in picking me up," Carolyn said. "This airport at dusk seemed like a different place than it does now."

"Really? How so?"

Carolyn looked up. No starlings swooped in unison overhead. The flickering, blue-hued streetlamps weren't in use yet. The mix of cultures and languages didn't startle her as much as it had when she first arrived. The traffic stopped when they put their feet into the crossing.

"It just felt different," Carolyn said. "It was unnerving."

"And how does it feel now?"

"Familiar."

They entered the terminal, and Bryan took off his sunglasses as he shot her a sideways glance. "Are you sure you're talking about the airport?"

"Yes. Why?"

"I thought for a moment you might be talking about me. Unnerving a few days ago . . ."

"And now you're feeling more familiar?"

"Sure, something like that."

"Yes," Carolyn agreed. "Something like that."

They found the listing of where the luggage from Tikki's flight would be delivered and joined the group gathering around the conveyor belt. "It looks as if her flight might have come in a little early," Carolyn observed.

"I'm going to check with the attendant over there to see if this is where my bag will come in," Bryan said.

"Okay. I'll wait here with Tikki as soon as I find her."

Carolyn made her way around the oval conveyor belt, checking left and right for her daughter. She headed back the other direction as the crowd grew thicker.

"Mom!" From across the open area in the baggage claim, Carolyn saw her beautiful, energetic daughter waving and rushing toward her. Tikki dropped the large shoulder bag from off her arm and threw her arms around Carolyn.

The elated greeting surprised Carolyn at first, but then she realized Tikki had just come a very long way by herself and might have been wandering around alone, as Carolyn had when she arrived. Of course her mother was the happiest and best thing she had seen since leaving home.

"You're here." Carolyn greeted her with kisses and a strong hug.

Tikki's hair was a scramble of tussled strands scooped up on top of her head. She had what looked like a coffee stain down the front of her T-shirt and her mascara was smeared under both eyes. Regardless, she beamed when she looked at Carolyn.

"Yes, I'm here. And look at you! Mom, you're radiant."

"I'm a little sunburned, I think."

"No, it's not that. You look happy."

"I am happy."

"Wow, that's so cool, Mom. You've only been here a few days, and you're already looking better." Tikki picked up her shoulder bag and corrected her last statement. "I mean, it's not that you looked bad before, it's just that you look really good now. Vibrant. Healthy."

"Thank you. Now what about your luggage? It's coming in on carousel four, right?"

"Yes, it's the carousel behind you. It looks like they're already sending stuff through."

"How was your flight?" Carolyn asked as they positioned themselves to watch the luggage come around.

"Why didn't you tell me how long it takes to get here? I slept as much as I could but . . . Hey, there's my bag. Let me grab it." Tikki slid between two shorter people and pulled her suitcase off the carousel.

"Is that it?" Carolyn asked.

"Yup, that's it. Just one suitcase. I'm here for only eight days. I figured whatever I didn't bring, I'd have an excuse to buy it here."

"Good, because I've discovered I'm low on clothing options, and I was hoping you would be interested in doing some shopping tomorrow."

"Sounds great. I'm open to anything. I'm just so glad to finally be here. Get me a bed and about six or seven uninterrupted hours of sleep, and I'll shop with you wherever you want to go."

"Are you hungry?"

"No, not really." Tikki looked at her mom, who was searching for Bryan. "Are we ready to go, Mom?"

"I'm looking for our ride." She spotted Bryan. He was waving at her and pointing to the luggage belt, indicating that he had spotted his suitcase.

"Did I tell you that Matthew called me?" Tikki asked.

"No. When?"

"About four hours before I left for the airport."

"What did he say?"

"Not much. I think he was kind of shocked that I was going through with this and actually coming here. But I've been thinking through all of this for hours, Mom. The entire way here I thought, you know, you and me, we're Women of the Canaries, right? We can have a great time just being here together. We don't need no stinkin' men."

Just then Bryan walked up next to Carolyn, pulling his suitcase behind him.

"Bryan, this is my daughter, Tikki."

"Hola. ¿Cómo está usted?" Tikki politely extended her right hand and added in English, "You look familiar. Now, which uncle are you?"

Bryan grinned. "I'm not a relative. Just a friend of the family. And to answer your question, I'm fine, thanks. How are you?"

"I'm good. Tired, you know, but good." Tikki tilted her head. "What was your name again?"

"Bryan. Bryan Spencer. Here, let me take that suitcase for you."

"Sure." She turned over the handle to her suitcase and gave Carolyn a who-is-this look as the three of them started for the parking lot with Bryan leading the way. Carolyn picked up her daughter's questioning expression out of the corner of her eye but kept looking straight ahead.

"Bryan?" Tikki called as he was about to step off the curb. He stopped before crossing the road to the parking area and turned toward her.

"What did you say your last name was?"

"Spencer."

Tikki's eyes widened. She turned to her mom and then back to Bryan. "You're not *the* Bryan Spencer, are you?"

He chuckled. "That depends. What does it mean if I admit to being *the* Bryan Spencer?"

"You're the one who took my mom on a camel ride."

His eyes lit up, and he smiled at Carolyn. "You heard about that, huh?"

"Only what my aunt Frieda will tell me. But I'd certainly like to hear all about it. Maybe you can fill in the interesting parts that my mom won't talk about."

Bryan's expression dimmed for only a moment, as if a mist of regret passed over him. Then it looked as if he remembered that he and Carolyn had confronted and cleared all the regrets from their summer so long ago. His smile widened. "It sounds like the three of us are going to have to visit those camels in Maspalomas so you can see what it's like for yourself."

"Good," Tikki said. "That was at the top of my list."

"Oh, you have a list, do you?" Carolyn asked.

"Of course I have a list. You know me. So, Bryan." Tikki hurried to catch up with him, as they crossed over to the parking area. "My aunt Frieda said you were quite the beachboy back in your day. I heard all about your wild hair."

Carolyn cringed.

Bryan laughed off Tikki's comments. "Yeah, I guess it was pretty wild." He opened the small car's trunk, rubbing the back of his neck and puzzling how to fit the two suitcases inside.

"Tikki, come here, will you?" Carolyn gestured

for her daughter to join her out of Bryan's earshot. "Please don't say anything else to Bryan about his hair or what Aunt Frieda remembers about him. He's been really kind to your grandmother and me and—"

"I'm sorry. I didn't know. I was just making stuff up to have something to say. Can I blame it on the jet lag?"

"Yes, you may blame it on the jet drag, as your cousin Rosa calls it. I know all about that. And it is a real drag. Just be nice to him, okay?"

"Okay."

Carolyn turned to go, but Tikki reached for her mother's arm and pulled her back, looking her in the eye.

"Wait a minute." Tikki's expression blossomed. "He's the reason you're so happy, isn't he? You still care about him, don't you? I mean, really deeply care."

Carolyn glanced over at Bryan, who was stuffing one of the bags into the backseat. She looked back at Tikki and felt herself blush.

"You do! You like him. And you can't tell me that rosy glow is sunburn. That is not sunburn." Tikki gave her mom a hug. "Wow, Mom, this is so cool."

"It's just what it is right now, Tikki, so please, you know . . . be nice to him and chill."

"Okay, Mom. I'll 'chill.' " Tikki laughed. She linked her arm in Carolyn's, and they walked back to the car without saying anything.

Bryan had shoved his suitcase into the trunk and was leaning on the trunk's lid, trying to close it all the way. As Tikki ducked into the backseat, she leaned close to Carolyn and whispered, "He's cute, by the way."

Carolyn grinned and whispered back, "I know."

The rest of the evening turned into a miniature reenactment of Carolyn's first night on the islands, with a gathering of relatives and lots of food. Only this time the gathering was at Carolyn's mother's apartment and drew in less than half the family members. Apparently the short notice had diminished attendance. Tikki and Bryan shared the novelty of being the guests of honor. Both of them handled the language and the social interactions much better than Carolyn felt she had. The other difference was that the clan left much earlier this time.

Bryan followed Carolyn into her mother's kitchen, as she cleared the dishes and stacked them in the sink. "You have a great family. I'm sure you know that."

"I didn't know much about them until I met them the night I arrived. They were the same way with me as they were with you and Tikki tonight. So open and loving."

She ran the water in the sink and turned to thank Bryan for the nice day, the great lunch, and the ride to the airport. As she turned to face him, her heart pounded. He was so close. She could have easily kissed him. She wanted to kiss him. The rush of such powerful, immediate feelings overwhelmed her. It had been so long since she had felt this intense rise of passion.

Bryan reached over and slowly pulled a wayward strand of her cocoa-colored hair off her forehead. "You come from a good tree, Carolyn."

She didn't know what to say. It was as if a blast of adrenaline was coursing through her veins.

"You better turn that off," Bryan said.

"You're right. It's too soon, isn't it? I shouldn't be feeling this way."

He gave her an odd look. "I meant the sink."

"Oh!" Carolyn turned off the faucet and realized that she had just said aloud to him the thoughts that had been on the surface when he touched her hair. She couldn't bring herself to turn and look at him again. Out of the corner of her eye, she could tell that he had moved to the other side of the kitchen and was leaning against the counter.

"Listen, what do you think about asking Tikki if she wants to go into Old Town tomorrow? I have a meeting on that side of town at ten. The two of you might like to see the Columbus Museum while I'm in my meeting, and then we can find something to eat, if you like."

"Sure, that sounds like a good idea. I'll see what she thinks." Carolyn plunged her hands into the water and washed the plates, stacking them in a strainer on the counter.

Bryan pulled a dish towel from the hook on the wall and dried the dishes. The intimacy that caused her to feel toward him was almost too much to hold inside. This was one of the things she had missed the most about Jeff. The way they shared the everyday things in life and kept a continual conversation going through it all. The circles of past and present had overlapped again, and the results were beginning to mess with her mind as well as her emotions.

Bryan's cell phone rang. He put down the towel, put in his earpiece, and stepped to the far side of the small kitchen, where he pulled out a chair and sat at the table.

"Did you already do a scan of the history?" he asked. "How long ago did you run the interface?"

At first Carolyn thought it was odd that someone was calling him so late at night. Then she realized that this was a business call. With the time difference, his clients would still be at work.

Tikki entered the kitchen and went to her mother, wrapping her arms around her and dropping her head on her mom's shoulder. "I love you. And I love being here."

"I love you, and I love your being here too. I love that we're both here." She kissed Tikki on the side of her head. "Are you ready for some sleep?"

"Definitely." Tikki straightened up and noticed Bryan at the kitchen table. She looked to her mom for an explanation as to why he was sitting with his head down and hand over his ear, appearing to be deep in thought.

"He's on the phone," Carolyn said in a lowered voice. "He's working. It's still office hours in the United States."

"I thought he lived here, in the Canary Islands."

"No." Carolyn quietly explained the circumstances of his stepmother's funeral and how he came to the birthday party.

Tikki looked amazed. "Mom, this is fairly epic, isn't it? Both of you returning to the Canary Islands at the same time?"

"I don't know if I'd call it that. Hey, listen, would you like to go to the Columbus Museum tomorrow?"

She shrugged. "I suppose. Would that be before or after the shopping?"

"Before, probably."

"Sure, I'm open for anything. Is Bryan going?" Carolyn nodded.

Tikki's expression brightened. "Then I'm definitely going because I'm starting to get the feeling that you two need a chaperone." She picked up the dish towel and gave it a twist and then attempted to give Carolyn a playful snap on the backside.

Carolyn stuck her hands in the soapy water and

flicked the dishwater at Tikki in retaliation. The two of them kept at it and started laughing like they hadn't done together in the kitchen for a long time. At the same moment they both realized how loud their laughter was and covered their mouths, shooting apologetic glances at Bryan.

He looked over and smiled at Carolyn, making it clear that he loved seeing her with her daughter like this and that the commotion didn't bother him.

"Okay, that verifies my prediction," Tikki whispered to her mother. "You two definitely need a chaperone. I can see where this is going." With a wink she added, "By the way, Mom, you rock."

17

"No hables a menos que puedas
mejorar en el silencio."
"Don't speak unless you can
improve on the silence."

THE INVITATION STILL stands," Bryan said to Carolyn's mom the next morning, when he arrived back at the apartment. "You are welcome to come with us."

"Yes, I know. And thank you. But I have been to the museum, and I would rather stay here this morning. Now, did Carolyn tell you that you're welcome to come for dinner? Since she has arrived I haven't cooked for her once. I promised to make *ropa vieja* for her tonight."

"Doesn't that mean 'old clothes'?" Bryan asked.

"Yes. Very good translation with your Spanish. Have you ever had *ropa vieja?* My mother was the one who made it the best. I try, but I still don't think mine is as good as hers."

"It's shredded flank steak in a tomato sauce base," Carolyn explained. "One of my childhood favorites. And don't let her fool you. Hers is better than her mother's by a mile."

"Are you sure you don't mind?" Bryan asked.

"Of course not. You took us to dinner last night."

"But I didn't even have to pay."

"No matter. Let me cook for you today. This is the least I can do to thank you."

On their way to the car, Carolyn convinced Bryan that her mother loved to cook her Old World recipes and would give herself wholeheartedly to the task all day. "It's therapy for her. Trust me."

"My mom's right," Tikki added. "You couldn't have given Abuela a nicer gift than to say you would like to come and eat the food she's prepared."

"You know, my stepmother used to be the same way. She enjoyed cooking a big meal and gathering everyone together to eat. It's one of the things I remember about her."

"I heard that she recently passed away," Tikki said. "I'm really sorry, Bryan. Losing a parent is absolutely the worst, isn't it?"

Carolyn felt a grab in her stomach as Bryan drove them toward Old Town. The grab wasn't because of the downhill traffic. It was because she rarely had heard Tikki speak so openly about losing her dad. Carolyn wondered if Bryan had that effect on Tikki. She had noticed that her cousin Rosa was surprisingly open with him at the family gathering last night. It seemed that people found they could let down their guard around Bryan and say what they really felt.

Tikki talked about how much she missed her dad and how hard it had been growing up without him during high school. Bryan listened appreciatively. "Your dad sounds like he is an amazing man."

"Was an amazing man," Tikki corrected him.

"I like to say 'is' because the core of who Jeff is, his soul, is still very much alive. It's just no longer on this planet."

Tikki seemed to like Bryan's thought. She caught Carolyn's eye and gave her a comforting smile. They were all quiet for a moment, and then Tikki asked Bryan about his stepmother.

"I didn't know my stepmother very well. The only time I ever saw her was the summer I was here before college. I spent as little time as possible at her house. Which is ironic because now she has left the house to me. It's sort of a last twist of a dart, though, because she left the house to me and the land to my stepsister."

Carolyn turned to him. "I had the impression she left you the house and the land."

"No. Did I tell you that?"

Carolyn tried to remember. The information probably came from Aunt Isobel's report of the cleaning woman's version. She knew little of the facts and didn't want to probe.

"I misunderstood. Sorry."

"No need to apologize. It's been complicated, so I thought maybe I'd miscommunicated. The house was left to me, but the land was left to Angelina. She offered me a firm price right away for the house to buy me out. I considered going ahead with the arrangement, but I decided to take my time and have it appraised first. That's why I'm on my way to the meeting this morning. It's the first step to settle the terms of the agreement."

As they entered the old part of town, Tikki made the same sort of observations Carolyn had on her first day. Tikki pointed out the butcher shop with chickens hanging inside in front of the large windows. She commented on the narrow streets and all the sandstone-colored buildings.

Bryan pulled out his phone and handed it to Carolyn so she could help him navigate his way down the narrow streets past a variety of dusty shops and into a parking structure.

"The Columbus Museum is about three blocks from here," he said, as they climbed out of the car. "I thought I'd walk down there with you and then come back here for my meeting. When the meeting is over, I'll join you at the museum."

"Can I make a suggestion?" Tikki asked. "How would it be if Mom and I went with you to your meeting and waited in the lobby? That way we could all go together to the museum because, no offense, Mom, but Bryan's Spanish is a whole lot better than yours. If you and I get stuck someplace and nobody speaks English, we couldn't pull together a complete sentence."

Bryan looked at Carolyn. "It's fine with me. As long as you don't find waiting in the lobby too boring. I thought you might rather see the museum."

"My mom is the one who is going to enjoy the museum. She's the history buff. I'm more interested in seeing inside an office building and how they conduct real estate business over here."

"That's right. Your mom told me you work in a bank's loan department."

"Actually, I just took a new position at a different bank. I'm the assistant branch manager."

"Then, by all means, you should come with me. I'm sure it will be an experience for all of us. And to be honest, I appreciate the company."

The building they entered was a fairly modern structure, six stories, in the middle of a row of office buildings that looked like something constructed post–World War II. Exiting the elevator on the fifth floor, they walked down the polished, white-tiled floors and entered through the propped open door.

A young woman sitting up perfectly straight at the front desk greeted them formally. She had her hair pulled back in a neatly styled bun and wore a simple blue blouse. Bryan gave her his name, and she motioned for them to be seated on the straight-back, chrome-legged chairs lined up on either side of an end table where a few magazines were stacked next to an ashtray.

The woman rose with a manila file folder in her hand and walked to one of the two closed office doors. She wore her pressed cotton blouse tucked into the waist of a navy blue pencil skirt with a hemline just above her knees. Carolyn noticed the woman's matching navy blue pumps. Her prim appearance reminded Carolyn of how in this culture women dressed conservatively but then went topless on the beach. She was sure incongruities existed in the United States, but here they seemed more obvious to her.

The woman tapped on the closed door located several feet behind her desk. She let herself in, barely opening the door wide enough for them to see who might be on the other side. Carolyn wondered if this was how the elementary students at her school felt when they were called into the principal's office.

"Listen," Tikki whispered. "Do you guys hear that?" She nodded her head toward the open door they had entered as if there were something down the hallway Carolyn and Bryan were supposed to hear.

Carolyn caught the faint sound of something tapping unevenly. "What is that?"

"Typewriters. When was the last time you heard that? I'd guess at least three of them are going. It's like we've stepped back in time. I mean, talk about going old school. It feels like everything around us should fade to black and white."

The office door opened, and the secretary held it as hospitably as a flight attendant, waiting for Bryan to enter. The door closed, and Carolyn and Tikki were alone with the tapping typewriters and the secretary in the pencil skirt.

"How long do you think he'll be in there?" Tikki whispered.

Before Carolyn could answer, they heard raised voices coming from behind the closed door.

Tikki and Carolyn exchanged looks of alarm. "That's not how we do business where I work," Tikki said. "What do you think is going on in there?"

Carolyn sat perfectly still, listening, trying to catch any Spanish words she could.

The door opened, and Bryan stepped out with a look of determination and his square jaw set. Carolyn and Tikki rose, ready to follow him out. A middle-aged man wearing a linen business suit and noticeably shiny black shoes stepped out after Bryan with a scowl on his smooth face. As soon as the man noticed Carolyn and Tikki, his expression lightened. He looked them over and said something to Bryan, who paused in his exit only long enough to reply in Spanish and reach for both Tikki's arm and Carolyn's to escort them out.

Tikki pulled back from Bryan's reach. "Are you sure you need to leave like this? It's a business transaction, right?" She turned to the man, who now looked as if he might start laughing any minute. "I'm confident the two of you can come to more of an agreement than this."

"Calladita se ve más bonita," the man said.

Carolyn caught the word *"bonita"* and knew that meant "pretty." Tikki seemed to go with that single word as well and offered the businessman a broad smile in return and replied, *"Gracias."*

The man broke into a demeaning smirk, and Carolyn knew they needed to leave. This time she was the one who reached for Tikki's arm and ushered her out of the door with Bryan right behind them. Carolyn walked quickly, sensing the imbalance in the situation. She had intervened more than once with volatile situations between parents and the principal in her job at Mill Creek Elementary. She knew when it was time to help someone exit the building.

Bryan didn't speak until they were down the elevator and out on the street, still walking at a fast clip.

"I probably shouldn't have said anything," Tikki said. "Sorry. My training for the bank just took over. I saw it as an opportunity to preserve negotiations by introducing a third party."

When neither Carolyn nor Bryan responded right away, Tikki said, "I guess they don't do business here quite the same way. At least he lightened up a little and said something about Mom and me being pretty."

"I don't think that's what he was saying," Carolyn said.

"Are you sure? Bryan, do you know what he said?"

"Yes, but I don't want to tell you."

"Come on! You have to tell me. What did he say?"

Bryan slowed his pace. His jaw looked more relaxed. He glanced at Tikki. "I'll tell you, but you won't like it."

"I can handle it. What did he say?"

"He said, literally, 'You look prettier when you're quiet.'"

Tikki looked stunned. "You can't say things like that to potential clients."

"We're not potential clients of his. Definitely not."

"I just can't believe someone who runs a business, any sort of business, would treat a complete stranger like that."

"I wasn't exactly a complete stranger."

"Are you saying you met him before, and he still treated you that way?"

"Let's just say that we weren't formally introduced at our first meeting. He knows my stepsister."

Carolyn connected the dots and quietly said to Bryan, "Was he at your stepmother's house the day you returned to the island?"

Bryan nodded and kept walking. In a low voice he said, "Of all the gin joints . . ."

Carolyn caught the *Casablanca* reference and knew what Bryan meant. Of all the appraisers on the island that Bryan could meet with, he had ended up walking into the office of the man who was having an affair with Angelina.

"I wonder if my mom or one of my aunts could recommend another appraiser for you."

"That would be great." Bryan let out a huff of air and seemed to relax. "Nothing is ever as easy as you think it's going to be, is it?"

"That's for sure," Tikki agreed.

The three of them had stepped into a cobblestone plaza where the buildings along the narrow walkways were painted a soothing shade of sunset yellow. Tikki seemed enraptured.

"What is this place?" Tikki pulled out her cell phone and stopped to take a photo of one of the buildings.

"This is the Vegueta section of the Old Town. Come here; you're going to love this." He led them down an alley and around a corner where they all stopped in unison, and Carolyn exclaimed, "Oh, look at that! How beautiful."

The morning light streamed through the narrow space between the old buildings and hit just right on a simple plaza fountain. From the center of the fountain rose an old but sturdy pillar that supported a bowl from which the water spilled into the pool below.

Behind the fountain was a large building with a stunning, ornate doorway that reached up to the second story. The facade was carved out of a green stone with lots of curves and raised relief work in the shape of what looked like leaves. On two pedestals on either side of the huge entry sat two small statues that, from a distance, looked like some sort of fierce animal holding up a shield.

"That's the Casa de Colón," Bryan said. "That building was the home of the governor of this island, Gran Canaria. Part of the building has been turned into the Museo Colón. The assumption is that Christopher Columbus, or Cristóbal Colón, stayed in this house while repairs were made to his ships before his great voyage."

"Are you kidding me?" Tikki stood still, taking in the whole plaza. Carolyn recognized the look in her daughter's eyes. It was that breakthrough moment when she realized she was on the other side of the world and standing in a place where history had unfolded hundreds of years ago. "This is amazing. When you asked if I wanted to go to a museum, I didn't picture anything like this. Look at that fountain. Is that elegant or what?"

Tikki took more photos just as a refreshing breeze came their way and tossed the silver beads of water from the fountain into the air, as if daring her to catch their escape with her trigger-happy finger.

Bryan drew closer to the fountain, and Carolyn joined him. They were only a few feet away when the loveliest thing happened. A single bird flew over them and lighted on the edge of the fountain bowl. A moment later a second bird joined the first, and together they sipped from the flowing water.

"Stay right there," Tikki said. "Now slowly turn and face me. Smile!"

Carolyn heard the rustling of the birds' wings as they flew off together into the sunlight. She stepped away from Bryan and Tikki, curious to see what was down the next alley. The birds were nowhere to be seen, but a simple structure caught her attention. It was painted a deep mustard yellow for the first five feet up the front. After that first rise of color, the building was painted white and had gray rectangular stones inset from above the tall wooden doors all the way to the roof. A small, mission-style bell hung inside a rounded alcove, and above the alcove was a simple cross.

Carolyn returned to the fountain where Bryan and Tikki were both taking photos with their cell phones, comparing the angles and the exceptional morning light.

"It looks like a chapel is around the corner. Do either of you want to see it with me?"

Bryan and Tikki joined her, and together they walked over to read the elaborate sign posted to the side of the wooden doors. Tikki read the words,

EN ESTE SANTO LUGAR
ORO
COLÓN
1492

"What does that mean?" Tikki asked. "*Oro* means 'gold,' right?"

"Not in this case." Bryan had the best sort of smile. All the tension from the encounter at the office was gone from his expression. "Here it means 'prayed.' The sign says, 'In this holy place prayed Colón,' as in Columbus."

"Are you telling me that Christopher Columbus came to this chapel when he was on the Canary Islands?" Tikki asked.

"Apparently so. I don't suppose anyone can prove it. But what a profound image this place conveys. Before embarking on his journey into uncharted waters, Columbus came to this chapel to pray." Bryan tried the door and found it locked. "I wish we could go inside."

"Can we?" Tikki asked. "I'd love to see inside."

"No, the door is locked. I wonder if it's still used for worship. Wouldn't that be something? To pray in the same chapel where Columbus prayed."

Carolyn was finding it hard to come up with the right words to say in response to Bryan and Tikki's shared delight. She had always enjoyed history. Being here, stumbling on this "holy place," felt like she had come upon a treasure chest. She wanted to open it and go inside as much as they did. It thrilled her to think, as Bryan had said, that while unknown worlds awaited Columbus on the other side of the Atlantic, before he set sail, he came here, to this humble chapel, and he prayed.

Tikki snapped more pictures. Bryan pulled out his phone and paused to read the screen. "I need to return this call," he said. "I'll just be a minute." He stepped a short way across the cobblestone square and stood under an old gnarled bougainvillea bush that covered him like a canopy.

"Stand by the door, Mom. I'll take your picture."

Carolyn posed, and as she held her smile, the doors behind her made a creaking noise. She turned and saw the face of a short, elderly woman peering out into the brightness of the plaza.

Tikki seized the opportunity to fumble with an unmatched assortment of Spanish words in an attempt to see if they could enter.

"Sí, sí." The woman opened to them, and the sacred place swallowed them whole. In the darkened, gold-embellished chapel, Carolyn could smell the beeswax of the flickering candles lined in straight rows at the front altar. She and Tikki stood in shared reverence, not moving from the back where they stood next to the elderly woman.

She said something to them and then walked a few feet down the center aisle, picked up a dusting cloth, and went back to her labor of love, rubbing oil into the pews. The faint scent of lemon rose from her efforts.

"Oh, I miss Daddy right now so much." Tikki's whispered confession surprised Carolyn. It seemed out of context from what they were experiencing. For Carolyn, this was like stepping into world history. Apparently for Tikki the moment awoke something different. Something hidden away in her personal history.

"Why do you say that, honey?"

Tikki linked her arm in Carolyn's, bit her lower lip, and blinked. Then, releasing her mom, she took small steps forward down the ancient aisle. "I miss Dad because of this." She took another measured step forward and then another, heading toward the altar with her hands clasped over her stomach.

Carolyn understood. Jeff wouldn't be there to walk his baby girl down the aisle and give her away one day, some day, on her wedding day.

"I know, sweetheart," she whispered. "I know. I'm so sorry."

The two women let out a shared sigh of lingering sorrow.

"Not that it seems to matter at the moment, since I've eliminated my only prospect." Tikki wiped her tears. "It's just that I really loved Matthew. I know that I loved him, Mom."

Carolyn wrapped her arms around Tikki and stroked her hair as her daughter cried out the sorrow of her loss. In the same way that Carolyn's mother had offered Carolyn her presence and her unflinching, grace-infused shelter that night in her bed as Carolyn wept, Carolyn followed the path of wisdom and offered a shoulder for her daughter to cry on.

And that was enough.

18

"Al buen entendedor, pocas palabras bastan."
"To the good 'understander,'
few words are needed."

FOR THE REST of that day and all of the next, Carolyn felt like everything in her life was put on hold. Her first few days on the island, when she was with her mother, Carolyn seemed to move ahead in great leaps, reconciling hurts from her past and feeling hopeful for the future. The time she had spent with Bryan had opened up a wellspring of healing and given her bursts of energy and glimmers of loveliness.

After Tikki's tears in the chapel, the focus of Carolyn's time and energy was redirected to her daughter. She didn't mind being present for Tikki; it just took a lot of time to listen as Tikki tore apart her life and asked her mother to help her construct a new blueprint for the future. Carolyn was amazed at the way her strong, independent daughter now doubted herself on every level. She wondered if she had done the right thing taking the position at Starlight Bank. She wished she would have talked to Matthew in greater depth before she left so that she wouldn't feel odd about being far away from him. She regretted draining her savings account to make the trip.

The only way Carolyn could describe it to Bryan, when he left her mother's apartment after the splendid dinner of "old clothes," was that Tikki toppled.

"I understand," he said. "Let me give you my number. I'm going to be around. Why don't you call me when you have time to talk?"

Carolyn hated being the one to initiate the slowing down in their times together, but she loved that Bryan understood and that he calmly gave her the space she needed. The affection that had warmed inside her for him after all these years only warmed more.

The frustration was that her vacation days were limited. If there really was going to be something more with Bryan than just a few chaperoned dates, Carolyn had less than a week to see it sprout. She didn't want to think about the possibility of boarding a plane, leaving the Canary Islands for the second time in her life, and not knowing, also for the second time in her life, if she would ever see Bryan Spencer again.

Carolyn's mother had curled into a more withdrawn version of herself than Carolyn had experienced her first few days there. It made her realize what a gift it was for her to have her mother all to herself for the time that she did. Their day at the beach would always be just as her mother had said: the best gift for her birthday that year.

Carolyn appreciated that her mother was being as understanding as Bryan about the shuffling of Carolyn's time and attention. But she didn't like it. She treasured her first days there when she had experienced her mother's full attention, which had always been a rare thing while growing up with an extroverted twin.

So, on the morning after the museum tour, the dinner of *ropa vieja,* and a long talk into the deep night, Carolyn tried to convince Tikki to go swimming with her. That flopped. She brought Tikki tea and toast, but it remained untouched as Tikki stayed under the comforter on the sofa and watched Carolyn's mother go about her morning steps with the candle, the bird, and the window.

Close to noon Carolyn invited Tikki to go with her to Curvas Peligrosas. She showed Tikki the limited options in apparel that she had packed, and Tikki agreed that Carolyn needed something new to wear. Something that would make her look younger and more "hip."

"Then come with me, Tikki. I need your opinion. Besides, your Spanish is better than mine."

"My Spanish is terrible. But I'll come."

The exercise seemed to do them both good. They were a block from the clothing shop when, in the middle of a nearly one-sided conversation of self-evaluation, Tikki stopped. "Thank you, Mom."

"Sure. What for?"

"You've been listening to me for almost twenty-four hours straight."

"That's okay, honey. You have a lot to process."

"I want to be done with all the processing. I just want to be here."

"Okay, we can do that."

"Do you remember at the Columbus Museum yesterday the phrase in the display that had the hourglass?"

Carolyn remembered. She repeated the line for Tikki. " 'The time spent has been good. The time to come will be better.' " It was the saying Columbus repeated to his crew every night at sunset, when the ship's hourglass was turned. Carolyn took it to heart because she wanted to start saying it to herself and believe that it was true of her life.

"I like that." Tikki stopped in front of the beauty salon and looked at one of the pictures in the window. Turning her head right and then left, she seemed to be studying her own reflection.

"Do you want to go in?" Carolyn told Tikki about her manicure and pedicure, and how she was congratulated when she left.

"Yes, I do want to go in. Do you?"

"I think I'll go on to the clothing shop and check it out. It's just a few doors up this same street." Carolyn didn't see a reason to have her nails redone so soon. Besides, she liked the idea of Tikki having her own experience of feeling like a Woman of the Canaries who was showing herself a kindness.

The two of them went their separate ways. Carolyn spent nearly an hour in the shop named "Dangerous Curves" and tried on at least thirty different tops before deciding on two that she liked. She tried on one dress, and it fit perfectly. Carolyn couldn't figure out how to ask if the saleswoman could keep her items on hold, so she bought the dress along with the tops and returned to the salon, eager to report her findings.

When Carolyn stepped into the salon, she didn't see Tikki. An older woman was in the barber's chair, and a slim young woman with short dark hair sat by the window reading a magazine. Carolyn wondered if Tikki had gone into the restroom in the back. She was trying to figure out how to ask that question when she heard Tikki's voice.

"Mom!"

Carolyn stopped dead still. The young woman by the window put down the magazine and stood.

"Tikki?"

"What do you think?" The extremely short-haired version of Carolyn's daughter gave a spin. "It was my own *Roman Holiday* moment. You know, when Audrey Hepburn ducks into the salon and has all her long hair cut off shorter and shorter? That's what happened. What do you think? I love it. I can't remember the last time I had my hair this short."

The style was darling on Tikki, and she looked like a different person, which was apparently her objective in light of all the soul-searching she had been doing. Carolyn said all the right affirming words, and Tikki beamed.

But inwardly Carolyn felt as if something primal and familiar had been severed forever. They didn't look as much alike anymore. Tikki was becoming her own person.

Bolstered by her haircut, Tikki took a dip into the clothing store, where she found a skirt, a blouse, and a belt. An entire outfit, ready to be worn, as she tried out the new Tikki.

Carolyn's mother raved about Tikki's hair. It was beautiful watching the way Tikki blossomed under her *abuela*'s praise. Fully rested after her stint with the indigestion, Carolyn's mother was picking up steam, as she said they should go down to the beach and walk the boardwalk in their new outfits and watch the salty air play with Tikki's new hair.

"Will you come with us, Grandma?"

"I don't see why not. We can eat at Al Macaroni or La Marinera. Either one. You haven't been to either, and they are both my favorites."

"I know. I haven't even seen the beach yet." Tikki fingered the ends of her hair in the back.

"We should go," Carolyn's mother said. "This is the best time of day to be on the beach."

"I'll get my stuff ready." Tikki scooted off to the bathroom.

"Carolyn, are you going to change?"

"I think I'll stay here, if you don't mind. It will give you and Tikki a chance to have some time, just the two of you."

"Did you and Bryan have plans?"

"No. I said I'd call him sometime. But I just need a little pocket of quiet. I might go swimming or take a nap."

"You always did the best job of refueling your spirit by being alone." Her mother leaned over to where Carolyn sat on the sofa. She gave Carolyn a kiss on the top of her head. "Rest, my daughter. Be at peace."

"Thanks, Mom. Thanks for being so understanding."

"You are the understanding one, Carolyn. You're a wonderful mother."

"I learned from the best."

Tikki had been hanging back in the dining room, as Carolyn and her mom exchanged their kind words. "Are you two done with your mama-moment yet?"

"Yes," Carolyn said, grinning at her mom.

"I'm ready to go when you two are."

"I decided to stay here," Carolyn said.

"Are you sure you're not going to sneak out and meet a certain young man while we're out?" Tikki teased.

Before Carolyn could find a quick answer, her mother said, "I almost forgot to tell you both. Lydia called. She rescheduled my flamenco dance lesson for tomorrow morning at ten. I would like it very much if both of you would go with me."

"Flamenco?" Tikki looked intrigued. "I'll go with you for sure. Is it too late to sign Mom and me up for lessons too?"

"You're both welcome to join in my lesson."

"How fun! Mom, you're taking the lesson with us, and don't try to get out of it."

Carolyn had stretched out on the sofa. Her eyes were closed, as she pretended to be asleep.

"You don't fool us," Tikki said. "Did she pull this stunt as a child?"

"Every so often, yes," Carolyn's mother said. "Usually when she wanted to get out of something."

"You want to take these lessons, Mom. You do. And you want to take them with us. This is a Women of the Canaries activity like Aunt Frieda always talks about. You can't pass this up."

"Okay, okay. Go to the beach and let me take a nap, and I promise I'll go to dance lessons with you two."

Alma, the little yellow bird, broke into a trilling cantata, and Tikki laughed. "See? Even Grandma's bird is happy that you're going to finally dance with your daughter after all these years of promising me you would."

"It's a conspiracy," Carolyn muttered, still

keeping her eyes shut. "All of you are in on it. Even the bird. You're determined for me to reveal how uncoordinated and clumsy I am."

"Hush," Carolyn's mother said. "You're supposed to be taking a nap."

Carolyn wasn't sure if her mother was directing her comment toward her or the bird. It didn't matter. She was already onboard the sleep train.

She hadn't traveled very far down the track when the phone rang. She fumbled to reach it before it stopped ringing. As she had hoped, it was Bryan. He told her he had just met with the new assessor her uncle had referred him to, and the meeting had gone well.

"After yesterday's debacle, anything would be an improvement. How's your day been?"

Carolyn told him about the long conversation she had had with Tikki late last night and how the intended shopping trip turned into Tikki's own personal *Roman Holiday,* and now she and her grandmother were out celebrating at the waterfront.

"Are you interested in meeting up for an early dinner?" he asked.

Even though she knew she would be teased endlessly by both her mother and daughter if she went out, Carolyn said, "Yes, I am. As long as we don't go to anyplace at the beach where we would be under the watchful eye of not one but two chaperones."

"I know just the place. It's in Old Town. I heard about it today. And since this sounds like it's going to turn into our first official date, I'll even change my shirt since it's streaked with dirt. I was out at the house with the assessor going through some of the stuff that needs to be repaired. This is a bigger project than I thought it would be. Anyway, how about if I meet you at your mom's apartment in an hour and a half?"

"I'll be ready."

Carolyn loved that Bryan was marking this evening as their first real date, and she even had a new dress to wear. The soft pink, V-neck jersey dress from Curvas Peligrosas had a wide waistband and a flowing skirt. It fit just right, and the rosy hue even matched her nail polish. She borrowed one of her mother's lace shawls and left a note for her mom and Tikki affixed to the refrigerator, just like she and Marilyn did growing up and as Tikki had done when she was younger.

When Bryan arrived, he pulled his hand from behind his back and produced another bouquet of mixed-colored roses.

Carolyn laughed. "The guy in front of the hotel is on to you."

"Yes, he is. He asked if these were for *mi novia*."

Carolyn knew that word. *Girlfriend.*

"And what did you tell him?"

Bryan grinned. "I told him to give me the correct change this time."

Carolyn found a glass pitcher, placed the roses in water, and left them on the kitchen table. As they walked out the door, Bryan said, "You look really nice, by the way."

"Thank you. So do you."

"So this is it, huh? Our first real date."

"We did meet unchaperoned at Al Macaroni the other afternoon before going to the airport."

"That didn't count. You met me there. I think this counts as our first date." Bryan reached for her hand the way a childhood playmate would grab hold of a friend's hand to run down a hill. Bryan didn't run, but he led her to the elevator and with a teasing look said, "It took you, what, only twenty-five years to agree to go out with me? A less determined man might have given up before now."

"You should get your facts straight, Mr. Determined Man. As I see it, it took you twenty-five years to work up the courage to ask me to go on a proper date."

"Oh, so that's how you see it, huh?"

"Yup, that's how I see it."

"What about our day at Maspalomas? I asked you out then. I came over to your grandmother's, and I stood in her kitchen, and I asked if you wanted to ride camels with me. That would have counted as our first date except you had to invite your uncle to come with us."

"Did you forget, Bryan? My uncle was

necessary. He was the only one we could find with a car."

"That's a pretty flimsy excuse, if you ask me. That was a fun day." Bryan gave her hand a squeeze. "Do you remember that day?"

"Yes, I do. It was a very fun day."

"Let's go again and take Tikki, like I suggested at the airport. You tell me what day works for the two of you, and this time I'll be the one with the car. Unless you want your uncle to come with us again."

Carolyn laughed. She couldn't picture her seventy-four-year-old uncle clambering into the saddle on the camel the way he did on their last trip. He loved to clown around and enjoyed acting as if he were going to fall out of the saddle.

They chatted easily, as Bryan drove back into the Old Town section and parked the car in a covered parking structure. He came around and opened Carolyn's door for her and then took her hand once again as they strolled across the cobblestone plaza. They passed the fountain again. This time, in the glow of dusk, the fountain had a completely different look—old, gray, and weary. She liked the view in the morning light much better.

Bryan led the way past the chapel where Columbus prayed, and a short distance away he stopped in front of an old wooden door that appeared to have been refurbished recently.

"This is the place. What do you think?"

"What is it?"

"The restaurant."

Carolyn looked around for a sign indicating it was a restaurant. All she saw was the house number and a glass-covered box built into the wall. She realized that the paper posted inside the glass box was the menu and restaurant hours.

"You really have to know what you're looking for around here, don't you?"

"That's why I asked for recommendations." Bryan released her hand and pressed down on the latch, opening the left side of the thick wooden door. They stepped together into a darkened alcove.

As their eyes adjusted, Carolyn whispered, "Are you sure this is a restaurant?" Directly ahead of them was a wrought iron gate that opened to an inner courtyard.

Bryan pushed on the ornate gate, and it opened. He stood back and invited Carolyn to enter first. She felt as if she were stepping into another world. A half-dozen tables filled the quiet inner courtyard. The tables were shaded by taut, white garden umbrellas set at the same angle, like sails against a west wind. Shade plants in deep green hues thrived in huge pots positioned across the courtyard. Carolyn's line of sight rose to the second-story inner balcony that ran the length and width of the rectangular enclave. Vibrant purple bougainvillea anchored in planters on the second story spilled their thick strands of paper-thin blossoms over the edge of the balcony. Some of the plants reached their delicate fingers all the way down to the patio.

Straight ahead of them, Carolyn spotted a larger-than-life-sized statue of a man in garb from centuries ago, standing with his right hand raised to shield his eyes, as if he were gazing out to sea. There was no mistaking the artist's intent to capture the expression of a restless explorer on the face of this Christopher Columbus statue.

"I think we seat ourselves." Bryan pointed to the closest open table.

Carolyn noticed another couple at one of the tables on the right side of the restaurant. That helped her feel a little better about being in such an exclusive, clandestine place. Bryan pulled out the chair for her, and she sat as daintily as she knew how, tucking her hands beneath the edge of the white linen tablecloth.

"This is quite a place. How did you find out about it?"

"I asked the appraiser today while we were out at the house. We were talking about renovations, and he told me about the renovations done on this building. He knows the guy who bought it more than a decade ago. It had been vacant for years. When he started the renovation, the builders found hidden tunnels."

"Tunnels?"

"They led to the chapel." Bryan looked as if he were revealing to her secrets about pirate coves and smugglers' dens. "Whoever lived here and dug the tunnels had a way of getting desperadoes to a place of sanctuary, refuge. Can you imagine?"

"Do you mean the chapel where Columbus prayed?"

"Yes. Mind-bending, isn't it? The history of this place, I mean. Can you imagine who might have been crawling through those tunnels five hundred years ago? And here we are, sitting on top of them, now that they're filled in, and about to order dinner."

A man in a long-sleeved white shirt and black necktie greeted them but didn't offer any menus. Bryan said something in Spanish, and the man gave an honored bob of his head and left.

"Did you just tell him to make the dinner selection for us?" Carolyn asked.

Bryan nodded. "He's the owner. He did all the renovations. He's also the chef. The appraiser I met with today tipped me off and said that to get the best of the best here, I should honor our host and leave all the selections up to him."

Carolyn leaned back and let the peace of this inner garden pour over her. It felt as if they were guests at a private dinner party. "This is pretty amazing. I've never been to a place like this, and I've never left the choice up to the chef."

"You don't have any food allergies, do you? I suppose I should have asked that."

"No, I'm on good speaking terms with just about every sort of food I've ever tried. What about you?"

"No food allergies. I don't like beets or watermelon, but that's just a preference thing. I am allergic to bee stings, though. So is my son. If I get stung during dinner from a rogue bee hiding out in one of these creeping vines, rush me to the hospital right away."

"Okay. But you know, it could become rather suspicious if we keep dining out all over town and leaving in a dash to go to the emergency room without paying the bill."

Bryan grinned. "Good point."

Their suave host appeared at the table with a wheeled cart and prepared a tossed salad complete with anchovies, chopped tomatoes, and thinly sliced carrots. He served Carolyn first, then Bryan. A plate of baguette-sized bread slices was placed in the center of the table along with a smooth red *mojo* sauce served in a white dish shaped like a fish.

Bryan reached across the table for Carolyn's hand and prayed just as he had at Al Macaroni. Once again his easily spoken, sincere words comforted Carolyn and made her feel as if she were inching her way back into a place of familiarity with God.

The calm that came with his prayer remained with them throughout the delicious dinner of chicken in a white wine sauce and zucchini baked with a crusty sort of top.

They were nearly finished with their delightful dinner and equally delightful conversation when Bryan said, "You know what, Carolyn?" He put down his fork. "I need to confess something to you."

Carolyn felt a grab in her gut. Everything had been going so smoothly. What did he feel he needed to say? Hadn't they waded through those murky waters days ago and come out on the other side? She hoped he wasn't about to apologize to her again for something that was part of their ancient history. As she saw it, all the old tunnels in their past had been filled in, and the relationship was renovated, just like this house. All she wanted to do was enjoy the cool comfort and beauty of the new space.

"I debated whether I should tell you this."

She put down her fork; she suspected she wouldn't be hungry anytime soon.

"You know how I said at your mother's party that for a long time I wanted to apologize to you?"

Carolyn pressed her lips together and gave a slight nod.

"Well, I actually did try to apologize to you a long time ago." He rubbed the side of his neck.

"You told me that summer when we were here that you were going to Cal State Hayward in the fall. You told me that's where Jeff went to college, and you were excited about being out of high school and on the same campus with him."

Those details were all true. It surprised her that Bryan remembered them.

"After I left the Canaries that summer and went back to my dad's house in Los Angeles, I, uh, shall we say 'borrowed' some money and rode my motorcycle up to Hayward."

Carolyn's eyes widened. She knew that had to have been at least an eight-hour motorcycle ride.

"It took me two days of hanging around the campus until I found you."

Her heart raced. "You were on campus?"

He nodded. "I saw you. You were walking across an open quad area all by yourself. You had on this flowing white blouse with long tails and a row of tiny buttons down the front."

Carolyn knew the blouse. It was her favorite. She called it her "poet's shirt" and felt artistic every time she wore it, which was often that first year of college.

Should I be freaked out that he was there? That he remembers what I was wearing?

That Bryan went to Hayward and waited around for two days before he spotted her was shocking enough. Knowing that he remembered what she was wearing doubled her shock. She didn't know if she should be overwhelmed by his sentimental gesture or a little alarmed that he went looking for her.

Bryan lowered his gaze as well as his voice. "You see, I had convinced myself that you and I belonged together. In my eighteen-year-old wisdom, I thought all I had to do was show up on campus, apologize for the way things went between us that last night here in the islands, and then ask you to . . ."

She waited for him to finish his sentence.

Bryan looked up. "I don't know what I thought. Maybe I was hoping you would be so happy to see me that you would forgive me and . . . I don't know . . . hop on the back of my bike, and we would ride off into the sunset. Something like that."

Carolyn let a small grin meet his eyes. She was dying to know why he didn't say anything to her that day. When he didn't add any more to his story, she ventured further, saying, "I never knew you were there."

"I know."

"I didn't see you."

"I know."

"So, what did you do? I mean, when you saw me, I guess you changed your mind . . ."

"I didn't change my mind when I saw you. I changed my mind when I saw Jeff."

"You saw Jeff?"

"Yes. As soon as I saw you, I started heading

toward you." He offered a shy grin. "I have to tell you, I was pretty nervous. I kept going over the lines I'd been rehearsing all the way up. You were walking across the grass toward a bench. There was a guy sitting there. The minute he saw you, I could see the look on his face. I wasn't the only one smitten with you. I pulled back and watched him come to you and wrap his arms around you. He kissed you. And you kissed him."

Carolyn felt herself blushing.

"When I saw the two of you like that, only ten days after you and I had been together, I knew I'd lost my chance. I needed to go. It wasn't right for me to cause you any more pain than I already had. So I left."

Carolyn didn't know what to say.

Bryan leaned back in his chair. "You can see why I debated whether to tell you. But it's bothered me that, when I walked away from Cal State that day, I didn't find a way to still offer an apology to you. It's also bothered me that for the past twenty-five years you probably thought I didn't care about the way things ended with us. I did care, Carolyn. I still do care."

Carolyn reached across the table and gently placed her hand on his. "I'm glad you told me that."

Bryan opened his clenched hand and turned his palm up. Carolyn laced her fingers with his. For a long moment they sat in a comfortable silence.

"I would give anything to go back in time and

do things differently," Bryan said. "But we can't go back. Only forward. And that's what I'd like to do, Carolyn. I'd like to move forward. But I need to know what you think about that. What do think about us moving forward?"

They were still holding hands across the table, their last few bites of chicken left to cool in the evening air. Carolyn wasn't quite sure what he was asking. She hesitated before finally saying, "How do you see us moving forward? I mean, realistically?"

"I have some ideas. But first I need to know that you're interested in even talking about it."

"I am. Talking, at least, for starters." In an effort to lighten the moment she added, "I mean, this is our first date, after all."

"It might be our first official date without a chaperone, but you and I both know that a lot of life has rushed past us in a very short time. I want to be deliberate about the way I live. I also want to pay attention to what comes my way. You came my way. Or I came your way."

"Or we both just came here, and there we both were."

"Exactly," Bryan said. "We're both here, now. The old feelings I had for you—they're still there. And I have a pretty strong notion that you still feel something for me." His eyebrows rose slightly as he waited for her affirmation.

Carolyn felt comfortable telling him. The words

came out in a hushed voice. "Yes, I do still feel something for you. Something new and surprisingly sweet has been growing in me every time I see you."

"So what does all this mean? What is God doing?"

Carolyn didn't reply. She had given up long ago trying to explain anything that God did. "I don't pretend to even try to guess what God is doing. I do know that being around you these past few days has been wonderful. I wish there was a way to keep going forward like you said. I don't know how that would be possible."

As soon as the words were released into the air between them, Carolyn felt a sadness creeping in. She would go home in a few days, and then all this would be over.

Bryan didn't seem to feel the same sense of finality. He leaned forward and covered Carolyn's hand with his other hand, holding it between both his hands, as if it were something fragile and precious.

"I've been thinking quite a bit about this. Please just hear me out. Take as long as you need to think through what I'm going to say before you give me your answer. That's all I ask, that you think about this. And pray about it."

"Okay."

Bryan smiled. "Okay. So, here's what I'm thinking . . ."

19

"Quien bien te quiere, te hará llorar."
"The one who loves you a lot
can make you cry."

IN THE HUSHED quiet of the night, Carolyn lay on her side watching the shadows fade into the silken haze of her mother's bedroom wall. Steady sounds of ruffled breaths came from her mother as she slept, unaware of all that had happened to Carolyn that night while she was at dinner with Bryan. Her only report to her mom and Tikki, when they mercilessly needled her for date details, was that she and Bryan went to a restaurant in a renovated house that had tunnels. And the coffee was very good.

All the other details she kept to herself. She wasn't ready to outwardly process any of Bryan's well-thought-out plan for how their relationship could move forward. True to her agreement at the restaurant, she had heard him out, and now she was going to give herself a day to think about everything.

He could wait, he said. He had smiled and said that, if he had waited this many years, he could wait another day or two to know if he would have a second chance with her.

In so many ways, though, it didn't feel like a

second chance to Carolyn. It felt like part two of an affection that had blossomed in two young hearts before either of them knew what to do with that attraction.

Part of the challenge for Carolyn was that, if she would be willing to open her heart again all the way with Bryan, she knew it would mean she would need to come into a place of reconciliation with all that she didn't understand about God and his uncomfortable ways. To overlap her life into Bryan's world would mean praying together and living inside the mystery, as he called it. She couldn't remain in her cloister of spiritual neutrality if the two of them were going to move forward.

She also knew that meant she would have to accept God on his terms. And they weren't easy terms. He was God. He could do whatever he wanted. He wouldn't be tamed by her demands or swayed by her cries. She would have to surrender to him.

And something deep inside her rebelled against that.

Carolyn sighed. *I need to sleep. I need to wait until I'm fully rested before I decide if I can agree to Bryan's plan. I need sleep. Sleep.*

A gentle pat on her hip woke Carolyn. She opened her eyes slowly in the brightness of the sun-flooded room.

"Mom, are you pretending to be asleep again, or are you really asleep?" Tikki asked.

"I was really asleep. What time is it?"

"It's almost nine. Grandma is anxious to get going. She doesn't want to be late."

"Late for what?" Carolyn noticed that Tikki was dressed, her new cute, short hair was styled, and she had makeup on.

"Don't give me that! Late for what! Mom, you are going to take this dance lesson with us, and you can't get out of it. I can't believe you forgot."

Carolyn pushed up on her elbow and pulled the clip from the back of her tussled hair. She yawned. "I can be ready in ten minutes."

"Good. Hop to it. *¡Ándale! ¡Muy pronto! ¡Arriba!*"

"Okay, okay. I got it. I'm going to hurry. Go tell Grandma I'm getting ready."

When the three of them were in the taxi forty minutes later, Carolyn could tell her mother was nervous. She didn't know if the nerves were over the possibility of their being late to Lydia's for the first flamenco dance lesson, or if it had to do with the lesson itself.

The only reason Carolyn was doing this was for Tikki. She had a feeling the reason her mother was doing this was to finally feel as if she was on par with her sisters.

Once they were out of the cab and walking down a cobblestone alley that led to Lydia's home, part of the reason for her mother's nerves became clear as she reminded Carolyn and Tikki of their manners.

"I want you to know that Lydia is a highly respected woman, and I must show her honor."

"*Sí, Abuela. No te preocupes,*" Tikki trilled, letting her grandmother know she didn't have to worry.

"And I will try my best not to embarrass you," Carolyn promised.

"No one is going to be embarrassed. All of us will try this, and we will learn something new today. *¿Sí?*"

"*Sí,*" Carolyn agreed.

"*Sí,*" Tikki echoed.

They arrived in front of tall narrow doors that showed the wear of many years, and for the first time Carolyn felt a tinge of gladness that she was taking this flamenco dance lesson with her mom and Tikki. This immersion in her mother's world was one of the reasons Carolyn had made this long journey. She didn't come for Bryan—obviously, because she had no idea he was going to be here. She came to be with her mother in her mother's world, and this was her chance to experience more of that world before she went home. This is what she had hoped Tikki would experience as well. And here they were.

The weathered doors opened in response to her mother's tapping of the round metal ring against the wood. In the movies, plundering pirates would break down doors such as these and find chests filled with gold and jewels.

The treasure behind these doors was Lydia, a lovely woman with smooth brown skin who opened to them and welcomed Carolyn, Abuela Teresa, and Tikki into her home. Lydia pressed her cool cheek to Carolyn's as she greeted her, sending feathery kisses into the air. First the right cheek to right cheek and then the left cheek to the left cheek. She spoke in rolling Spanish, taking efforts, it seemed, to make sure every "r" received sufficient tremors on her tongue before escaping her perfectly shaped lips. Lydia's graying hair was pulled up in a smoothed-back bun. She led them into her home with an air of refinement, as if they were entering her castle.

The interior was far from castle status. The condition of the home surprised Carolyn. It was old and showed every sign of its age more obviously than Lydia did. The tile floor raised in irregular bumps. The paint was peeling on the walls, and the room they were directed into was dark and crowded with old furniture. This was how Carolyn remembered the feel of her grandparents' house. Old and dark. It made her realize why her mother and Aunt Isobel preferred the open, light, and airy feel of the new apartment complex where they lived.

Lydia set to work moving back a sofa and an end table. Tikki and Carolyn stepped in to help her make room on the floor for their dance lessons. Lydia rolled up the faded rug and motioned for the three women to come stand in front of her in the newly cleared space.

With perfect posture, the five-foot-and-a-few-inches woman struck a pose in front of them. Her left arm was bent with ease in front of her tightened stomach, and her right arm rose in the air like a graceful calla lily. Her hands were fixed in a ballerina's pose, with the thumb straight, first finger slightly bent and the remaining fingers curled in easy succession.

All her directions were in Spanish, and all her motions were fairly easy to follow. Not that Carolyn could imitate the grace and ease with which Lydia moved through the positions. Carolyn did notice that her mother came by the movements naturally and seemed to already have an idea of what she was supposed to do.

"Are you sure this is your first lesson?" Carolyn asked her mother as she switched her right-hand position to over her stomach and tried to get the elbow of her left arm bent just right.

"Yes, why do you ask?"

"You look like you already know what to do."

"It's in our blood. Did you understand what Lydia just said? This is a dance of life."

Carolyn pulled back her shoulders and willed that the half of her blood that ran as red as Spanish *rioja* wine would flow through her veins and tell her hands and arms what to do.

No sooner had Lydia showed them the basic

arm motions than she switched tactics. Now they were to stand with their hands on their waists just above their hips. The position reminded Carolyn of the statue beside Al Macaroni of the fisherman's wife standing with her hands on her hips, gazing out to sea at twilight.

Lydia explained something else, and Carolyn said, "Mom, can you translate? I'm not catching much of what she's saying."

"I'm lost," Tikki added.

"She is explaining that this is the dance that draws out of you what is held deepest inside. Most women cannot dance flamenco with true . . . what is the English word? Fortitude? Honesty?"

"Guts?" Tikki ventured.

"Yes, that's close. Most women cannot dance with this sort of passion in their gut because they have not loved enough or lived enough or lost enough to know this depth."

Before Carolyn could process that thought, her mother went on to say, "We're going to concentrate on the feet now. We will move only the feet. Our hands, she said, must stay here, at the waist."

"Cinco paseos," Lydia said, and Carolyn's mother echoed, "Five steps."

Carolyn followed the steps with her left foot lunging forward, then she stepped to the side with her right, then forward and to the other side and then back. As she pounded the floor in her practical, black, slip-on shoes, she realized her steps were too big. Her feet weren't straight. She was clomping about instead of sliding from position to position. Tikki and Carolyn's mom seemed to pick up the steps more readily, which was no surprise.

"No, no, no." Lydia stopped and pointed to Carolyn's feet and tapped her right leg so that Carolyn would begin with the right, not the left. Lydia demonstrated once more, and Carolyn tried again and fumbled again. She let out her frustration in a growl.

"Tranquila, Carolyn," Lydia said with complete calm and a motion for Carolyn to breathe. *"Tranquila."* She continued her instructions in softly spoken Spanish, making small gestures with her lovely hands.

"She is saying these five steps embody the journey of life. We begin always with the right. One step to the right, followed by the left foot coming along behind. Then the left foot moves back to where it began, and the sympathetic right foot follows the left foot halfway with a small step. And then with confidence the right foot follows the rest of the way to the left foot with the fifth step. This is made lightly and with confidence."

Lydia stood tall and straight in the final position, as Carolyn's mother said, "And we end up back where we began, but we are wiser and more experienced because of the steps we have traveled."

"I love this!" Tikki said. "This is my life right now. I need to return home wiser and more experienced, that's for sure."

The three women went through the *cinco paseos* again. Carolyn knew her shoulders had slumped, and her head had jutted forward and was bobbing along after each step. She knew that nothing about her position, posture, or pace looked anything like her instructor's. But she was trying. She was going through the motions. That had to count for something.

Lydia stopped. She stepped closer to Carolyn. A deep passion blazed in Lydia's fiery eyes. With a swirl of faithfully rolled "r's," Lydia expressed herself as if she were imparting to Carolyn the ancient secret of life and womanhood.

"She is telling you that in life, it is not enough just to do the steps. You cannot merely go through the motions. You must dance from the stomach up. The way you are moving, she says you are a loose woman. This is no way to dance or live."

"A loose woman?" Tikki teased Carolyn, giving her a pat on the side. "You hide it so well."

Lydia placed one open palm on Carolyn's stomach and the other on the small of Carolyn's back. She pressed firmly on the soft flesh that Carolyn kept hidden behind the tummy control panel of her jeans.

Carolyn's mother explained Lydia's stream of words. "She is telling you that this is where life happens within you as a woman. In your stomach. In your gut. It is here, in this deep place, where a woman invites her husband and where her babies are cradled before they are born. This is where she nurtures and brings forth new life. Here is where a woman holds all her secrets and hides her hurts and her dreams. Your dance must come from this same place. From the stomach up. When you dance like that, then you will begin to live like a Woman of the Canaries."

"Oh, that was beautiful." Tikki rounded back her shoulders and drew in her stomach. "I love that. From the stomach up. Come on, Mom, you loose woman, you, we can do this."

Carolyn placed her hands on her sides and pulled in her stomach muscles. Lydia stepped away and gave a nod for her to begin. With her chin up and leading with the right foot, Carolyn and Tikki began in sync, taking each step from the stomach up. Right, left, left, right, right. Back where she started, wiser for the journey.

Carolyn's mother sedately applauded the two of them.

Tikki broke out in the best smile. She had tiny glimmers of delight in her eyes. "You did it, Mom! Look at you! You're dancing! You and I are dancing. Oh, this makes me happy."

Carolyn smiled and received a nod of approval

from Lydia before she moved on to the next step.

"Las cruces." Lydia demonstrated how the left foot begins and crosses behind the right in a series of invisible crosses that seemed to be marked on the dark wood floor.

"This is where in life the sacred intersects with the common," Carolyn's mother explained, as she repeated the motions. She made the steps look easy and graceful. Her shoulders were back, and she was dancing as Carolyn knew her mother had always lived, from the stomach up, with the sacred and the common intersecting naturally.

Lydia moved on, introducing the *chulero*. This side step included a lunge of the minutest proportions but a lunge nonetheless.

"This is my favorite one so far," Tikki said as she struck a lunge pose and held up her hand as if she were holding a sword. *"En garde!* I dare anyone to try to mess with us."

Lydia put a quick halt to Tikki's joking around and had her three pupils line up again and repeat the steps all the way through three more times. *Cinco paseos, las cruces, chulero.* Tikki had it all memorized, and Carolyn's mother was right there with Tikki, anticipating the next move and making the smooth transitions. Carolyn felt she was admirably holding her own. She was a little slower, but each step was taken with her head held high.

"This next movement is with the right arm."

Carolyn's mother gracefully repeated Lydia's demonstration and raised her right arm while keeping her elbow bent slightly.

"Keep your wrist tilted over your head, fingers in harmony with each other, thumb relaxed."

Lydia looked up to her hand, slowly turned her wrist so that the palm faced her as if she were holding an invisible ball. She drew her hand to her face as if giving it a sniff, and then with a confident staccato motion, she looked as if she were throwing away whatever invisible item she had been holding in her hand.

Lydia did the motions again, rapidly explaining each movement as Carolyn's mother slipped into her easy undercurrent of translating for Carolyn and Tikki. "This is the garden. Life, your life, is the Garden of Eden, and you are Eve. Now reach up your hand. You pick the apple, you smell it . . ."

With bravado, Lydia thrust her arm across her front at an angle, as if quickly throwing away the apple. All the while her face was still turned to where her right arm had been in the air.

"She says you are Eve, and it is your turn. What will you decide? You sniff the apple, and you throw it away! Then you do this."

With a snap, Lydia's left arm went up with fingers gracefully posed. Her left index finger victoriously pointed to the heavens.

"That's cool," Tikki said. "Do it again."

Lydia demonstrated, and Carolyn's mother

translated Lydia's running commentary. "Every woman has this moment in her life when she must make her choice. You hold in your hand the apple. You smell it, and what will you do? It is your turn to make the decision. Will you take the bite? No! You are a strong woman. You throw it away and take a stand of victory because you did not fall for the trap."

They all watched as Tikki repeated the motions. Then Carolyn's mother did them with grace. All eyes turned to Carolyn. Lydia stepped closer and once again pressed her hand to Carolyn's stomach and then to the small of her back. Carolyn stood tall as she reached up, picked the invisible apple, drew her arm past her nose, and threw the apple away. Her left arm rose to the ceiling, index finger pointed toward the heavens.

Lydia gave her nod of approval and said, *"Ahora con la música."* She walked over to the end table in the corner and pressed a button on an old-fashioned boom box. Passionate flamenco guitar music filled the room. All three of the students lined up and improved their posture. They began with the *cinco paseos.*

As they moved into *las cruces,* Carolyn felt her stomach tighten. It was there, in that simple room with the paint-chipped walls and the passionate music surrounding these three generations of women, that Carolyn witnessed something ancient yet invisible. The sacred was intersecting with the common. They were being invited to step inside the mystery.

They performed the lunge in unison and continued the steps as they each reached for their imaginary apple. Carolyn suddenly knew what her "apple" was: the lie she had bitten into many times over the past seven years. She hesitated only a moment, and then with a snap, she "threw it away" and thrust her victorious left arm into the air.

Unexpectedly, a wave of tears came over her. She clutched her stomach with both arms, as if a deep place inside of her had been punctured and something was being released from her spirit.

Lydia was the first to notice Carolyn's reaction to the music, the motions, and the meanings. She came to Carolyn's side, slipped her arm around her, and made a soft cooing sound like a dove.

"Mom, what's wrong?" Tikki and Carolyn's mother gathered close. "Are you frustrated? Because you shouldn't be. You did great! You danced all the steps. You've got it."

Carolyn's mother stroked her hair as a reservoir of silent tears continued to stream from Carolyn's eyes. "What is it, *mi niña?*"

Carolyn didn't know how to explain what had just happened inside her.

Lydia spoke, and Carolyn's mother voiced the wise woman's insight. "You have thrown away something that was poison to you, have you not?"

"Yes," Carolyn whispered.

Tikki reached for Carolyn's hand. "Mom, what did you throw away?"

Something inside her felt stilled. *Tranquila.*

"I was . . . I was angry. At God. I have been mad at him for a long time." A silent trickle of tears flowed down Carolyn's cheek. "When you're angry at someone, you think you have the right to ignore them. I chose to throw away that anger. I can't ignore God anymore."

Abuela Teresa took Carolyn's face in her hands and kissed her on both cheeks. Tikki put her arms around Carolyn and rested her head on her mother's shoulder. Lydia smiled softly.

The rest of the lesson was a blur. What had happened inside of Carolyn was in sharp focus. She felt different. New. Lighter inside as well as with her steps. The padding of sorrow, doubt, and pain that had been a hidden buffer in her life for so long seemed to have lifted.

As they said their good-byes, Carolyn was reluctant to leave this place of unexpected hope and healing. She wanted to align her life with the steady rhythm of the island and always live the way she felt right now, with her shoulders back and her stomach strong.

Lydia pressed her hand once again to Carolyn's stomach, as if Carolyn was now carrying new life within her and Lydia was feeling for movement. She had a few last words.

"Lydia says that you have been given one of the

best gifts this island has to give. For centuries sailors have come here for repairs and for supplies. They leave this island ready for the next part of their journey. Today you have been made ready for the next part of your life's journey. The wind has returned to your sails."

Carolyn immediately thought of the dream she had experienced weeks ago in which she and Jeff were sailing together off Angel Island. The wind filled the sails, and in her dream Jeff had laughed his best, free-spirited laugh. She almost felt as if she could hear the faint echo of his liberating laughter rolling from the courts of heaven as she left Lydia's home. Carolyn no longer blamed God for the tragedy that had so altered her life. She knew Jeff was with the Lord. He was free.

And now so was she.

20

"Al vivo la hogaza y al muerto, la mortaja."
"We must live by the living, not by the dead."

THE DECISION ABOUT what to do next after the dance lesson was an easy one. Lydia's house was four short blocks from the boardwalk at Las Canteras. The three women strolled arm-in-arm and found an open table in front of Al Macaroni under one of the shaggy beach umbrellas.

"You two have spoiled me, you know," Carolyn's mother said. "After you leave, I won't want to eat my own cooking. I think I would eat lunch here by the sea every day, if I could."

"I love it here, too, Abuela," Tikki said. "This time has been a treat for all of us, don't you think? I loved the dance lessons. Absolutely loved them. I wish I could go back for more."

"You can," Carolyn's mother said. "All you have to do is extend your visit. Or move here."

Carolyn looked up from her menu. She half-expected her mother to be looking at her with a visual nudge to let Carolyn know that that last comment was meant for her. But her mother wasn't looking at her. She was reaching into her purse for a tube of lipstick, which she expertly applied to her lips without the use of a mirror.

"I've never known how you could do that," Carolyn said. "You never miss either."

"Practice, *mi niña*. Many years of practice. Now, what should we have for lunch today?"

"Will you order for me, Mom?" Tikki asked. "Whatever you get is fine with me. Nothing with too many onions, though. I need to use the restroom."

When Tikki stepped away from the table, Carolyn asked her mother, "Are you happy here? Living here, I mean. Are you glad you moved here?"

Her mother looked surprised at the question. "Do I not seem happy to you?"

"You seem happy. You have your sisters and you live in a nice apartment. But don't you miss the life you had before this?"

"Of course. Every day I miss you, Marilyn, and your girls. Every day."

"Do you ever think you might come back to the States to live with us?"

She paused and looked out to sea. "I will tell you something. I did not know what I was doing when I moved here. That is the truth. I think I was in shock after your father died. I missed him so much. It was a big move across a big ocean. At the time, you and Marilyn had your husbands and your daughters. I know you will scold me if I say this, but I didn't think either of you would have time for me if I stayed living near you."

She put up her hand before Carolyn could protest. "It's what I thought. No one expected both of you to be without husbands so soon after I left. My feelings were . . . well, it was as you experienced in the release within your spirit at our dance lessons. I was angry, even though I didn't know that's what it was. I was angry that your father was gone and that I was left alone. Somehow I thought I would be less alone here."

"And have you been?"

"Most of the time. But as I said, I miss you, Marilyn, and your girls very much. Why do you ask these things, Carolyn?"

The moment had come for Carolyn to process

aloud Bryan's idea for how they could move forward now that their paths had brought them back together.

"Bryan is staying here, in Las Palmas. He realized it will take a long time to work through the settlement on his stepmother's house, and he's decided to stay during the process."

"What about his job?"

"He can work anywhere. Do you remember how he explained that he works from home with just his computer and his phone? He can do that here."

"This is interesting." Carolyn's mother pressed her lips together. "And how will this affect what has begun to blossom between the two of you?"

Carolyn looked down at her hands. She realized she had just folded her paper napkin, neatly matching the corners and smoothing the crease in the center. "He's asked me to consider staying here too."

"Staying here?"

"Yes, with you."

"How long?"

"I don't know."

"What about your job?"

"I'd take a leave of absence from now until school ends in June. That's eleven weeks. Then I'd have the summer off."

"You can do that?"

"I think so. One of the teachers took a similar

leave a few years ago, and he was able to come back to his position."

"And would you want to go back to your current position?"

"I don't know. That's the thing. There's so much I don't know. I don't know what I'd do with my house. Rent it, maybe. Or find someone to house-sit. I've even wondered if it's time to sell it since it's just me living there now. Some of the rooms are freshly painted; so I think it would show well, if I put it up for sale. But I've thought that if I rent it I'd at least have some income. Some houses in our area have sat vacant for a year or more before they've sold. I don't want that to happen to my place. I've put too much love and effort into keeping it up. That house is full of so many memories. And it's not that I'm saying I need to hold on to the house to preserve all those memories, it's just that . . ."

"Tranquila, mi niña." Carolyn's mother reached across the table and took her hand. "You do not need to answer any more of the questions about the house or your job right now. Those things will settle themselves. They always do. You have only one question you need to answer. What is your heart telling you about staying here to be close to Bryan?"

Carolyn hesitated. She had asked herself this question a hundred times in a dozen different ways.

"I take that back," her mother said. "I asked the

wrong question. Your face tells me that you would very much like the chance to linger here and see what might come of this relationship. Am I correct?"

"Yes."

"Then here is the right question for you. Are you willing to follow your heart, to trust your gut, as your daughter would say?" Carolyn's mother offered a soft smile as she added, "Because when you are willing to take a risk, even if the outcome is not as you hoped, then you will be ready to love again."

Carolyn thought about the risk of trusting her gut. She felt the same fear that had pressed in on her during the shadowed hours of her sleepless night. "I don't know, Mom. I just don't know."

"He's not in a rush, is he?"

"No. I don't feel as if he's trying to rush anything between us."

"What about you? Are you willing to trust your heart?" Carolyn's mother asked again.

"No." Carolyn did not pre-think her answer. She didn't even intend to answer her mother. But there it was. The truth that she had wrestled with most of the night.

"You never were good at hiding the truth," her mother said. "It shows on your face, and it tumbles out of your mouth. Every time."

"So I guess that's it. I'm not willing to give up so much to stay here."

"But you forget. Your face did not lie to me a moment ago when I asked what your heart is telling you. Your eyes told me you want to stay. You want to stay very much."

Carolyn nodded. "I do. I'd love to spend more time with you, and like Tikki said, I'd love to take another dance lesson. I'd love to go swimming every day and learn how to make your *ropa vieja*. And I'd very much like to see what might grow between Bryan and me. But what he is asking is so much. My house, my job . . ."

"You have a dilemma, then. Your heart is telling you to stay, but your mind is telling you to flee."

"So what do I do?"

"A donde el corazón se inclina, el pie camina."

"And what does that bit of wit mean?"

" 'To where the heart is inclined, the feet will follow.' "

The waiter arrived just then with his pad and pen ready. Carolyn's mother turned to him. She talked, he scribbled. She pointed to Carolyn, and he nodded. Then with a flash of a smile revealing a gold front tooth, he picked up the menus and left.

"Did you order for all of us?" Carolyn asked.

"Yes, I did." Abuela Teresa settled back in her chair and looked out toward the ocean. "I had no difficulty making the decision. I knew what would be best for all of us. I followed my heart."

Usually Carolyn found her mother's wit to be

winsome and endearing. At the moment, she felt she should be offended. What an overt message! Her mother's blood connection to Aunt Frieda certainly was showing.

Tikki bounced up to the table with a big grin. Her new short haircut certainly gave her an extra dose of charm.

"Guess who's going to go ride camels tomorrow? Us! I just settled it with Bryan."

"Bryan? Did you call him?"

"No, he's inside the restaurant."

"He is?" Carolyn tried to see inside the darkened interior of Al Macaroni, but the only diners she could see were the ones at the window seats.

"I think he's in a business meeting. They're at the back of the restaurant. He'll probably come out because I told him you were both here. He said he'll pick us up at nine in the morning for the camels."

Carolyn ate her salad when it arrived and listened to Tikki as she carried the conversation for most of the lunch. The entire time Carolyn's eye was on the restaurant's door, watching for Bryan. She felt the same way she had the morning she was hiding out in Aunt Isobel's kitchen while her mother was in the living room only a few yards away and yet she couldn't go to her.

The so-close-yet-so-far-away sensation made her wonder what it would be like if she didn't take the risk and arrange her life so she could be here for a longer period of time near Bryan. What if she didn't follow her heart to see if this relationship might work out? Would there be a repeat experience down the road in which Carolyn would be in the position Bryan was in when he rode his motorcycle to Cal State Hayward? Would she be the one who might stand back one day and watch as Bryan went to another woman and kissed her, unaware that Carolyn was looking on, regretting that she didn't act when she had the chance?

¡Tranquila! she shouted to herself. *Put all these crazy-making thoughts aside. For now. Be in the moment here with your mother and your daughter.*

The internal shaking did its work, and Carolyn reentered the conversation with her mom and Tikki. However, Bryan didn't exit the restaurant. As they were getting up to leave, she considered for a moment going inside, but what would she say? If he was in the middle of an important business meeting, as Tikki surmised, then Carolyn's appearance would be a disruption. She could wait. He would be at the apartment at nine in the morning. That would give Carolyn a chance to curl in just enough before then to ask herself all the essential questions and come up with an answer to the life-altering decision that was before her.

Not until Carolyn was watching her mother light her candle and offer her prayers that evening did her day of internal evaluating reap a key insight. Carolyn realized that, when you spend years having something inside that you are secretly angry about, it leaves an open space when that anger is resolved. That space within her was ready to be filled with love. She knew it. But oddly, all day fearful thoughts kept coming to her that it would be easier or at least more familiar if she now filled that opening once again with invisible white anger at something or someone else. Anger still felt familiar. Hope and love and joy did not.

Carolyn got ready for bed and wished she could go to the chapel where Columbus prayed. She would go there right now if she knew for sure she could get inside. She would pray, as Columbus did before he started his journey into unknown waters. Her prayers would be for blessing and protection and for the fear to go away.

Tikki was tucked into her cocoon on the sofa. Alma was covered in her cage. The night sounds through the half-opened window felt familiar. Carolyn double-checked with Tikki about the camel plans in the morning.

"Bryan said he would be here at nine, right?"

"Yes. I told him you and I would be ready. It wasn't a long conversation because the woman he was with didn't seem to speak much English, and she didn't have a very hospitable tone in her voice."

Carolyn was surprised when Tikki said Bryan was meeting with a woman. "Did he introduce you?"

"Yes, her name was Angelina something."

Angelina. That makes sense.

"As I said, I could tell I was interrupting. They had papers all over the table, and she was really putting on the body language that she didn't appreciate my being there; so I just said we would be ready at nine, and that was it."

"Okay. Well, nine o'clock tomorrow it is. Sleep well." Carolyn bent over and kissed Tikki on the forehead. She caught a whiff of peppermint.

"I hope you sleep well, too, Mom."

"Thanks. So do I." Carolyn slid into bed before her mother was finished with her night preparations. Rolling on her side, Carolyn pretended to be asleep. The imitation of slumber worked so well that she did fall asleep in a few minutes and avoided the anxious contemplation that she had experienced the night before.

She awoke feeling good. Really good. Her first thought, as she smiled at the way the morning breeze was ruffling the lacy bedroom curtains, was, "Good morning, Lord." Those had been Jeff's first words every morning. In the same way that Carolyn's mother lit a candle every morning, Jeff would open his eyes and say, "Good morning, Lord." Then he would turn to Carolyn, kiss her, and say, "Good morning, Love." He did that nearly every morning during their marriage that she could remember.

The first morning that she had awakened and he wasn't beside her had been the worst morning of her life.

That her thoughts turned on this new day immediately to a greeting of "Good morning, Lord" filled Carolyn with hope. She really had experienced a breakthrough in her heart yesterday during the flamenco dance lessons. This was what her mother probably would call "getting your heart back."

As she slid out of bed and tiptoed into the shower, Carolyn's second thought that morning was, "I'm going to see Bryan today." That prospect filled her with more hope and happiness. Stepping into the shower, Carolyn remembered the saying from the Columbus Museum next to the hourglass that was turned to mark each new beginning of a twenty-four-hour stretch: "The time spent has been good. The time to come will be better."

She thought of what a risk Columbus took to set sail without any assurance of what awaited him on the other side of the wide blue distance. But he took the risk. For better or worse, history was changed.

Then, just as effortlessly as the shower's water

poured over her, a peaceful conclusion settled in Carolyn's mind. *It's worth the risk.*

She couldn't stop smiling. Her heart and her head finally had blended on this decision.

Tikki was up and ready for the shower. Abuela Teresa was in the kitchen making what Carolyn was sure would be too much breakfast for just the three of them. Bryan would have to stay a little while that morning and have some coffee. And some toast. And some of her mother's delicious scrambled eggs with the small sausages Carolyn remembered seeing in the freezer and could now smell cooking.

She decided on wearing jeans and one of her new tops. She also decided that the first chance she had, she would buy a new pair of shoes. Something cute, stylish, and European-looking. After all, if she was going to be staying for an extended time, she wanted to blend in.

The phone rang. Carolyn was the first to reach for it. She answered with a lot of warmth in her voice, assuming it would be Bryan. To her surprise, it wasn't Bryan. It was Matthew.

"Is Tikki there?"

"She is, but she's in the shower, Matt. Do you want me to . . ." Carolyn wasn't sure what to say. Take a message? Tell her you called? Her mother's heart did a loop-de-loop.

Before Carolyn could finish her question, Matthew said, "Listen, don't tell her I called."

"Okay." Carolyn immediately wished she hadn't agreed to his request. This would be a terribly difficult secret to keep.

"I want to surprise her."

"Okay," Carolyn said, feeling her motherly heart take another revolution.

"I know this is going to sound ridiculous, and if you want to give me a lecture, that's fine. I'll take it. I love your daughter, and I don't know why it's taken me so long to finally admit that to myself."

"I'm not going to lecture you, Matt." Carolyn lowered her voice as she heard the water turn off in the bathroom. "When it comes to matters of the heart, it sometimes takes awhile for the heart and mind to come to the same conclusion."

"Exactly. That's exactly how it's been for me. And now that I've figured things out, and she's not here to talk to, it's torture. I guess it took her leaving to make me realize how much I care for her and how much I look forward to seeing her every day. There's so much I want to tell her."

Carolyn smiled. She understood completely. "I'm sure you can talk it through when she gets back to California."

"Well, actually, I want to talk it through sooner than that. I'm here. I'm in Las Palmas."

"What?"

"That's what I meant when I said I hope she isn't too upset at what I did. I cashed out all my savings and bought a ticket. Her roommate gave me the number for her aunt Marilyn. But when I finally got a hold of her, Marilyn said she knew that Tikki wasn't in the Canaries. I boarded the plane anyway. I didn't know what I was going to do if I got here and found out that Tikki was actually in the Bahamas or something."

"Don't worry, she's here. My sister didn't know she was coming."

Matt paused. "Well, to be honest, I'm not sure what to do next. Should I come there? I don't exactly have a plan. This is totally not like me."

"You did the right thing, Matt."

"So, can you give me the address? I rented a car here at the airport, and I thought if I could just see her and explain things, maybe she would forgive me, and we could take it from there."

"I have an idea. This is, of course, entirely up to you, but we're planning to leave in a little while to go ride camels."

"Did you say 'ride camels'?"

"Yes. What if you met us there?"

"Okay, that's probably better than going to her grandmother's house. That way, if she wants to kick me in the rear, at least it won't be in front of her relatives. Tell me the name of the place, and I'll meet you there."

The sound of the bathroom door opening prompted Carolyn to hurry and finish the call. She heard Tikki emerging as Carolyn quietly gave Matt the information. He thanked her, saying, "I owe you big time for this."

Carolyn hung up and tried without much success to subdue the smile on her face. Tikki walked in and said, "You sure look bright and cheery. Let me guess. You were just talking with Bryan. Is everything still set?"

"Yes," Carolyn said truthfully. "Everything is all set." She avoided giving any more information by turning the focus on Tikki. "Are you sure you want to wear shorts?"

"I'm sure the camels won't care."

"Do you have anything else you could wear?"

"Like what? I'm not wearing my new skirt."

"What about your khakis?"

"I don't think they got washed."

"We can do a quick load this morning while we eat."

Tikki looked at the clock. "Bryan's going to be here in ten minutes. We can't eat and wash and dry a load of clothes in ten minutes. Why does it matter what I wear?"

"I was just thinking you're going to be sitting in a saddle and . . ."

"Okay, I get it. Better to be ladylike and save the shorts for down at the pool. I'll see what I have that's halfway presentable."

Tikki went back to the spare room where she had stashed her suitcase, and Carolyn blasted into the kitchen. She grabbed her mother by the shoulders and gave her a big kiss on the back of her head. Carolyn's mother turned around with a spatula in her hand and a grand smile on her face.

"You've decided to say yes, haven't you? You're going to stay."

"No, I mean, yes. I have decided to stay. I haven't told Bryan yet. But that's not why I'm so excited." Carolyn lowered her voice and quickly told her mother about Matthew being here and meeting them in Maspalomas, and how he wanted to surprise Tikki.

Carolyn's mom's face turned rosy with delight. "I'll call Isobel while you're gone and make all the arrangements."

"Arrangements?"

"He'll need a place to stay, and I'm out of beds. He can stay at Isobel's. How long will he be here?"

"I don't know."

With her hands on her hips, Carolyn's mother said, "How is it that no one ever knows how long they will be staying? You buy a plane ticket in a day and are on the other side of the globe the next. I don't understand how everything got to be so quick. So much speed and technology. Yet no details for the *abuela*."

"I know. It is a fast world. But I plan to slow down now that I've decided to stay here, Mom. You can teach me the fine art of sauntering in the weeks ahead. Not today though. We need to eat quickly and leave as soon as Bryan shows up. And remember," Carolyn put her finger to her lips, "Tikki doesn't know."

"Tikki doesn't know what?" Carolyn's quiet-as-a-mouse daughter's entrance to the kitchen had been masked by the sizzling of the sausages in the frying pan and the fan over the stove.

Carolyn quickly said, "Nothing."

"Oh, but it is something, Carolyn," her mother said, pulling a quick save in the moment. "It's something wonderful, and I think you need to tell your daughter what you've decided about what you're going to do."

"Oh, yes, well . . ." Carolyn turned to face Tikki. "I've just come to the conclusion that I am going to stay here. With Grandma. I'm going to take a leave of absence from work so that I can be with her longer and . . ."

"And spend more time with Bryan," Tikki added with a twinkle. "He told me at the restaurant yesterday that he would be staying on until he settled his stepmother's estate. The woman at the table with him looked as if she really didn't like hearing that."

"It was his stepsister," Carolyn's mother said. "Of course she didn't like hearing that."

"Oh, I didn't realize that's who she was. This is starting to make more sense. But forget her. What's going on with you and this decision to stay?"

Carolyn stepped closer to Tikki and looked in her eyes. "I was going to talk with you about all this, Tikki, but I wanted to wait until you and I had a chance to sit down and . . ."

Tikki seated herself at the kitchen table. She crossed her arms, holding on to her elbows. "Okay. Sit down then. Let's talk."

Carolyn pulled out the chair across from her very mature-appearing daughter. "I've been thinking about this for the last day or so. Bryan asked if I'd consider staying so we would have a chance to see if there's anything that might grow between us."

"Mom, I think you and Abuela and I all know that something already is growing between the two of you. It's obvious."

"Well, yes, I agree. But I didn't want to stay if it would be too difficult for you if I lived so far away for a little while."

"How long is a little while?"

"I'm not sure. Possibly through the summer."

A hint of sadness brushed over Tikki's expression.

"What are you thinking, honey?"

"I'm thinking I'll miss you."

"I'll miss you too."

"But you know what? Mom, it's your turn to get a life."

Carolyn smiled.

"Do you remember when I first told you that I

wanted to go to college at Rancho Corona even though it was a nine-hour drive from home? You said to me, 'Teresa Katharine, you are a Woman of Options,' and then you let me make the decision, and you supported me. It was a memorable moment because you so rarely called me by my full name. I knew you were giving me your blessing to become an adult, live my life, and make my own disasters or triumphs."

"Yes, I remember that day."

Tikki became misty-eyed. "Obviously, I've had both the triumphs and the disasters. But I've never forgotten what you told me. I am a Woman of Options. And so are you. You're free, Mom. Totally free. It's your turn to live your own life and not to worry about me or Marilyn or anyone else."

Carolyn went over to Tikki, wrapping her arms around her daughter's neck and hugging her close. What a beautiful, selfless send-off her daughter had given her without any sense of awareness that love and hope and Matthew were waiting down the road for her. Tikki could have pouted and said what a difficult time she was going through with the job change and the breakup and how she needed to know that her mom was only a quick drive away when she needed her. But Tikki had said none of that.

"Thank you," Carolyn whispered into Tikki's short hair. "I love you."

"I know you do. And I love you, too, Mom."

They kissed each other on the cheek, and Carolyn tasted her daughter's salty tears.

"Besides," Tikki said, pulling back and shooting a smile at her *abuela,* who was loading up two plates with eggs and sausages, "I think it's Abuela's turn to keep an eye on you for a while. I've had to keep this wild child in line all these years. I think it's your turn now. Just watch out for her tendency to redecorate on a whim. She'll have you up at midnight painting your walls."

"Not here she won't. This is still my nest. If she wants to paint something, she'll have to go to Bryan's stepmother's home. She'll find plenty to fix up over there."

Carolyn's spirit did a little flutter thinking of fixing up that old house. She remembered it well. Oh, the things she could do with the place! It hadn't occurred to her that entering into the renovation project with Bryan might be one of the things she would do in the next few months. The possibility made her even more excited about the future.

The three of them sat down together to enjoy their lovingly prepared breakfast. Before any of them took a first bite, Carolyn said, "Wait. I'd like to pray first." They linked hands, and Carolyn prayed simply and sincerely, from her heart, thanking God for her mother, her daughter, and the food.

After Carolyn said, "Amen," Tikki added a willowy, "And God bless Bryan and keep him safe." Tikki caught her mom's eye and gave her a wink.

Carolyn countered with, "And God bless Matthew and keep him safe too." She immediately saw the shadow of sadness pass in front of Tikki's eyes and regretted the small tease. She didn't intend to hurt Tikki.

Keep your mouth closed, Carolyn. Don't blow this surprise for Matt. Don't mess with your poor daughter's emotions. Just hold it together for a little longer.

Tikki reached for her napkin and dotted the tears in the corner of her eyes. "I can't believe I'm still crying over him."

Both Carolyn and her mother gave Tikki sympathetic glances. But Carolyn could see in her mother's eyes the same glimmer of secret hope that Carolyn was trying hard to conceal.

Tikki bravely gave them both a smile. "Why am I so emotional every time I think about Matthew? How much longer will it take before I can just be here with you both and not feel so sad and lonely when his name comes up?"

Carolyn pressed her lips together. She didn't dare open her mouth. She knew she could not be trusted with what might pop out.

Her mother looked at Tikki with deep kindness. "Not much longer, *mi niña*. Not much longer."

21

"Más vale tarde que nunca."
"Better late than never."

BRYAN ARRIVED WITH a ready appetite for Abuela's plate of eggs and sausages and joined them at the table. Suddenly the kitchen felt full. Just like Carolyn's heart.

"How did the dance lessons go yesterday?" Bryan asked.

"Great," Tikki said.

"Really amazing," Carolyn said.

"Perfecto," was the response from Carolyn's mother.

"And how was your lunch at Al Macaroni?"

"Perfecto," Carolyn's mother replied again. This time her answer sufficed for all of them. Carolyn suspected they all were a bit enamored of Bryan as they sat in a cluster and watched him eat.

Tikki asked him, "How did your meeting go yesterday? I thought we might see you when you left the restaurant, but I think we left before you did."

He nodded. "I think you did," he said before taking a gulp of coffee.

"Let the poor man eat," Carolyn's mother said.

"My meeting went about as well as I hoped. My stepsister isn't very happy that I've turned down her original offer for the house, and she doesn't like the attorney I've hired, but I think we'll be able to work it all out in a way that's fair to everyone."

"And how is her husband?" Carolyn's mother raised an eyebrow in such a way that only Bryan and Carolyn would catch the underlying meaning to her question. Bryan said before that he hadn't told anyone in his family about his stepsister's affair. The Casanova appraiser who practically kicked Bryan out of his office apparently assumed that Bryan would divulge the man's secret or try to blackmail him. Carolyn's mom wasn't the only one curious about the status of the fuse on this potential powder keg.

"They're still happily married, as far as I know." Bryan scooped up another forkful of eggs, and the topic seemed to be closed.

Carolyn and her mom exchanged small glances that said, "Well, isn't that interesting?"

Rising from the table, Carolyn said, "I'm going to get my purse."

"What's the rush, Mom? Let Bryan finish eating like Grandma said."

Tikki had changed into a pair of jeans and a crumpled shirt. Carolyn gave her a closer look. "Are you ready to go?"

"Yes, why?"

"I just wondered if you were thinking of changing."

"No, I already changed. This is my final selection. Why? Is there something wrong with it?"

Carolyn backed down. "No, you're fine. You look great. Your new haircut looks really cute. You're fine just the way you are." She was so caught up in trying not to give any hint that Matthew would be waiting for them that she fumbled through the most basic comment. She slipped out of the kitchen and went to the bathroom to brush her teeth. Better to put a toothbrush in her mouth than her foot.

Part of it, she knew, was also her nerves about being around Bryan. They were the best kind of nerves. The butterfly kind of nerves. Carolyn tried to calm down and told herself that she needed to pull back and let this day be about Tikki and Matthew. She could tell Bryan later that she had decided to stay.

A tap sounded on the bathroom door, and Tikki let herself in. "Mom, I think I'm going to pass."

"What do you mean pass?"

"I think I'll stay home."

"No!" The word leaped from Carolyn's throat and startled Tikki. "I mean, why would you want to miss the camel rides? This was on your list. You've been looking forward to it."

"I know, but I think it might be better if just you and Bryan went. You need to tell him your big decision to stay here, and you'll have lots to talk about after that. I'll just be in the way."

"No, you won't. You absolutely will not be in the way. You have to come, Tikki. This is a once-in-a-lifetime chance. It's really important to me that you be there. Besides, I was just thinking that I want to wait and talk to Bryan about my decision after everything anyway."

"What do you mean by 'everything'?"

"After the camel rides."

Tikki squirted toothpaste on her toothbrush. "You and Abuela are both making such a big deal of this. She convinced me to change my shirt. For the photos, she said. I hope this big buildup doesn't turn into a big letdown like that movie was that we went to for my tenth birthday. Do you remember?"

Carolyn wasn't sure she remembered, but she said she did, just to leave the bathroom and speed things along. The sooner they reached the camels and Matthew, the better. Grabbing her purse and a sweater, Carolyn dipped back into the kitchen where Bryan stood by the sink, wiping dishes for Abuela. He was all smiles.

"Your mother told me," he said. "That's really great news."

Carolyn gave her mom a scowl. Why would she steal Carolyn's thunder and tell Bryan that she had decided to stay? That should be her decision and her announcement.

Bryan lowered his voice and leaned closer. "Tikki has no idea he's going to be there, does she?"

Carolyn's posture relaxed. Her mother hadn't spilled the happy beans. Bryan was referring to Tikki's good news. Not hers.

"No, she doesn't know. But we need to get going. I'm really bad at keeping secrets."

Bryan gave her a closer look, as if trying to read for hints on her decision about staying. Carolyn gave him a winsome hint of a smile, and he gave her a half smile back.

In her heart, right then and there, if Carolyn hadn't already decided, she would have willingly stepped out of the safe cocoon of her life and into the risk of exploring a relationship with Bryan based simply on the closeness she felt during their exchange of small smiles.

And the man had a kitchen towel in his hand. He knew how to score points with her in all the right areas.

The drive to Maspalomas was redeemed by Bryan's ability to keep Tikki talking. If it had been up to Carolyn to carry the conversation between just her and Tikki, she would have cracked. The way it was, she could keep her gaze fixed out the window while Bryan heard thorough descriptions of Tikki's previous job and her roommate, but then it leaked out—her "old boyfriend" who liked to play softball.

"Where did you meet him?"

"In college. He went out a couple of times with my roommate Jenna, and we all started hanging out together. Matt and I took the same class the next semester, and we started studying together and . . ."

"So you stole your roommate's boyfriend," Bryan teased.

"No, it wasn't like that at all. They went out only twice. We're all still good friends."

"Where did you go to school?"

"It's a small Christian college in southern California you probably never heard of. Rancho Corona University."

Bryan shot her a glance in the rearview mirror. "My son went there his senior year. So did his wife, Christy. Did you ever run into Todd Spencer?"

"No way! Are you kidding me?" Tikki *fwapped* Bryan on the shoulder. "Of course I know Todd and Christy! I went to their wedding. It was so beautiful."

"It was," Bryan said with a grin. "I was my son's best man."

"Yes! That must be why you looked familiar at the airport. I thought you were one of my uncles that I'd seen only in photos. I can't believe this! You're Todd's dad? That's crazy. I kind of see the resemblance, though. Wow!"

Carolyn didn't recognize the people Tikki was talking about, but she was glad the two of them had struck upon another topic that would keep Tikki distracted until they arrived in Maspalomas.

"And did you know that Christy was from Wisconsin?" Tikki asked.

"Yes, I did know that."

"Well, my boyfriend was from the same town. He and Christy actually went to elementary school together, and I think she's a big part of the reason he looked into going to Rancho. I suspect he had a crush on her for a while back in the day."

"So now you're telling me you stole my daughter-in-law's old boyfriend too. Is that it?"

Tikki laughed, and the lightness sounded good to Carolyn.

"No, no. Nothing like that. You of all people should know that with your son and his wife it was Todd and Christy forever. Matthew Kingsley never messed with that equation. I doubt any other guy or girl ever came between the two of them. As a matter of fact, I heard Todd talk at church one night about how he was a 'one-woman man,' and how he had set his affection on Christy from the day he met her. Your son is quite a romantic."

Tikki leaned back and let out a melancholy sigh. "But he is one in a million. Not all of us end up with the person we think we're going to end up with."

Carolyn was biting her lower lip so much she had nibbled a row of tiny blisters. It was killing her to keep a straight face as she listened to Tikki. She wanted to tell Bryan to drive faster.

"And some of us do," Bryan said calmly. "Eventually."

Carolyn wanted to glance at Bryan, but she kept her gaze straight ahead. His words were piercing. It seemed he was talking to Carolyn as much as he was talking to Tikki. The tenderness in his voice captivated her. The way he was interacting with her daughter filled up a place in Carolyn's heart that had been empty for a long time.

"Tikki, with some men it takes awhile," Bryan said. "It's not you; it's him. He needs to learn the hard way what a gift you are. He needs to make it clear that he wants to be with you, and nothing or no one will get in his way this time."

Again, Carolyn felt Bryan's words were meant for her as much as they were for Tikki. Her heart beat faster. She wanted to reach over and give his arm a squeeze. But she didn't. She looked out the window and kept pressing her lips together.

Tikki had grown quiet in the backseat. Carolyn was sure that somewhere in the middle of Bryan's last statement Tikki also had picked up the deeper message Bryan was broadcasting from the driver's seat. The hesitancy Tikki had expressed about coming with them was being validated. If she wasn't with them, they would be discussing their future at this very moment.

But Tikki was here, and they were almost at Maspalomas. Now, if only they could find a new topic. Something less loaded with emotion.

"It sure is a beautiful day." Carolyn inwardly cringed over her wimpy choice of topics.

Neither Bryan nor Tikki took the bait. Thankfully, they were pulling into a parking area that had a sign in Spanish and German with a picture of a camel.

"Is this it?" Carolyn asked.

"I think it is. We have to walk toward the dunes." Bryan turned off the car's engine.

As soon as Tikki was out her door, she took Carolyn by the arm and whispered, "I shouldn't have come. This should have been your day, Mom."

With a slightly swollen-lipped smile, Carolyn whispered back, "It's your day too. It's both our days. We'll share, okay?"

Tikki gave her a puzzled look, and Carolyn knew she would fumble things if she said anything else. Strapping her purse over her shoulder, she pulled out her sunglasses and looked around as inconspicuously as she could for any trace of Matthew. Their only plan had been for him to show up at the camel ride.

"Ready?" Bryan asked.

Carolyn nodded. The three of them walked toward the enclosed area in the sand where the pointed top of a large, Arabian-style tent poked up from the center of the compound. Carolyn could smell the camels before she saw them. When she observed the several dozen beasts of burden all linked together in a train and in a seated position in the shade, she felt both sorry for them and amazed at them.

"They have such gentle faces. Like giraffes." Tikki headed toward the first gathering of six camels without hesitation.

"Do you see him anywhere?" Bryan whispered.

Carolyn scanned the area. The big tent's two front flaps were open, and she guessed that was where they bought tickets for the rides. A group of tourists was just arriving and following a leader to the small building on the other side of the tent. Two men in Moroccan-style flowing robes stood near the camels, talking with each other in a language Carolyn didn't recognize.

"No, I don't see him. Maybe he's in the tent. Or over by the building where the tour group went."

Bryan called to Tikki and said they were going to buy tickets. She left the camels and joined them. In the fifteen minutes it took to arrange everything for their excursion, Matthew was nowhere to be seen. All the while Carolyn and Bryan kept exchanging small glances, communicating with their eyes, a tilt of their heads, or a twitch of their lips.

When they and the tour group were ready to climb onto the camels, Bryan stalled, saying he had forgotten his phone in the car and needed to retrieve it. As soon as he was far enough away not to hear, Tikki asked, "Okay, what's going on? Seriously, Mom."

"What do you mean?" Carolyn stepped into the shade under the vivid canopy of a wide-spreading, deep magenta-colored bougainvillea bush. She positioned herself so that she could watch the opening to the compound while Tikki stood where she couldn't see who was entering or exiting.

"You can't play dumb with me, Mom. This isn't like pretending that you're sleeping."

Carolyn looked down. "I'd tell you if I could, Tikki, but I can't. I can't tell you."

"Oh, you don't have to tell me. It's all over your face. Even with your sunglasses on, I can see it in your eyes. You and Bryan have your own little silent love language going on. And I know you don't need me to translate it for you the way Abuela translates for us. Mother, the man is completely taken with you. He's crazy about you!"

Carolyn felt like saying, "Oh, that!" She felt relieved that Tikki hadn't caught on to the surprise of Matthew's arrival.

"So tell me what's going on. Has he told you how he feels about you?"

"Not really. Things are just beginning for us."

"More like restarting."

"Okay, restarting. But you know, relationships take time, honey. I'm not going to rush into anything. I'm staying here so that I can give myself the opportunity to see what might be there for us long-term."

Tikki put both her hands on her hips as they had done in their dance lessons, fisherman's wife style. Just before she delivered some well-chosen words to her mother, Carolyn looked over Tikki's shoulder and there, entering the compound, was Matthew.

He looked as if he had run all the way. He glanced at the camels, glanced at the tent, and then, noticing Carolyn and Tikki, he plowed forward toward where they stood.

With conviction Tikki said, "Mom, don't let fear make any of the decisions for you or slow down your relationship until it trickles away to nothing and dies. If you love him and he loves you and you know it, then tell each other openly, get married, and get on with your lives together."

Matthew was just behind them and obviously had heard what Tikki was saying. Before she had any idea that he was standing there, Tikki concluded her lecture to her mother by saying, "Finding someone you love and who loves you is far too rare a gift in this world to let it slip away from you."

In a clear voice Matthew said, "I agree."

For a microsecond Tikki didn't turn around, as if the voice had been an echo in her heart and she couldn't bear the pain of turning to find that Matthew wasn't there after all.

But he was.

He scooped her into his arms and whispered in her ear all the things he should have said long ago.

Carolyn stepped away, giving freedom to the tears that spilled from her motherly heart. She could hear Tikki laughing and crying in the same breath, and Carolyn began doing the same. By the time Bryan returned, Carolyn had pulled herself together. He entered the compound and gave her a questioning look from across the sandy ground. She nodded, dipping her chin in the direction of Matt and Tikki, who still were locked in an inseparable hug under the vibrant bougainvillea. Less than ten feet away from them, one of the kneeling camels looked on with big brown eyes, chewing on a long piece of dried beach grass.

Pulling out his phone, Bryan took a picture, and with a big smile he walked across the grounds to where Carolyn stood, holding her elbows and hugging her stomach. They smiled at each other, as if they were two undercover agents who had just successfully completed a mission they couldn't discuss in public.

"Do you remember?" Bryan asked, nodding at the canopy of bougainvillea.

"Yes." She knew he was recalling the same memory she had the moment they walked into this area—their first kiss under the umbrella of delicate purple flowers.

He leaned close and brushed a kiss across her cheek.

Carolyn felt all the butterflies rise in her stomach. Clearly, Bryan remembered the sweet and innocent times they had shared that summer so long ago. He was taking his time, restoring those memories and adding new moments. Each careful, deliberate act on his part renewed her trust as well as her hope. They really had forgiven each other. They could go on from here.

With a light spirit, Carolyn leaned over and kissed him back on his shaved cheek. Then, uncrossing her arms, she let her hand fall into the short space between them. And just as he had done the first time they came here to ride the camels, Bryan took her hand in his and held it tight.

Matthew and Tikki came toward them, hand in hand, beaming.

"I can't believe you kept this a secret from me, Mom!"

"I can keep a secret when I need to. Aren't you glad I did?"

"Yes. All your little hints and suggestions that I change into something nicer to wear . . . Oh, Bryan, I didn't introduce you yet. This is Matthew Kingsley. Matt, this is Todd's dad."

The two men talked for a few minutes, discussing where they had met before and deciding that it had been at the wedding of

Bryan's son. The three of them made comments about the song that Todd had sung as his bride came down the runner in the meadow where the wedding was held.

"That must have been quite a wedding," Carolyn said.

"It was." Tikki looked at Matthew, and the happiness seemed to leak out Tikki's every pore.

One of the men who had been tending the camels came over to them and let them know it was their turn. Bryan nodded and pulled out some money for him. He motioned to Carolyn.

The chummy quartet followed their guide to where the kneeling camels awaited them. The tour group had gone ahead in a separate caravan, so now it was just the four of them. Their guide was wearing the sort of garments seen in a movie about life in the Sahara Desert five hundred years ago. The modern twist to the ancient garb was his wraparound sunglasses and surfer-style sandals.

A muzzled camel was in a seated position, with its long, spindly legs folded underneath its fly-attracting body. The two side-by-side saddle chairs looked like the same saddles they had clambered into twenty-five years ago. Each saddle was designed with a narrow seat, a wooden side railing, and a roughly hewn backrest—one on either side of the great beast's broad back. As the camel waited in its lowest possible position, Carolyn planted her foot on the step provided and climbed into the chair by grabbing the sides and pushing up into it backward. She managed the maneuver on her first attempt and held her arms back as the attendant cinched a leather strap around her waist.

Bryan repeated the maneuver on his side, and as soon as Bryan and Carolyn were both strapped into the fragile saddle seats, the caravan driver gave a command. The camel leaned far forward. Carolyn let out a quiet "Eeee!" and tried to quell the sensation that she was going to fall forward and tumble out of the chair. She reached for the center of the animal to steady herself, and when she did, she found Bryan's hand there waiting for hers. It was just as their ride had been all those years ago.

She glanced at him and made a face as the camel rose by rocking them backward until it came to a firm stance on all four feet. The force of the camel's rise was slow and even. They were up! And what a view. The sand dunes stretched out before them, and beyond the dunes lay the sea. The vista made it easy to believe that only fifty miles to the east was the coast of West Africa and the Sahara Desert.

Tikki and Matthew boarded their camel at the same time and made the same muffled "Whoa!" sounds, as their camel rose with its off-kilter grace. Their camel was led to line up behind Bryan and Carolyn's camel, and the two beasts were hooked together.

Carolyn turned around to wave at their caravan partners. Tikki lifted her hand, which was clasping Matthew's in the same way Carolyn and Bryan were holding hands. The gesture reminded Carolyn of the final triumphant lift of the arm in the flamenco steps they had learned. It had to it the air of a prizefighter lifting a gloved paw at the final bell.

With an easy tilt and a steady lilt, the journey into the sand dunes began. Carolyn felt her shoulders relax. She remembered this unhurried pace as one of her treasured memories of the Canary Islands. They seemed to have been transported through time to a place where only the basic elements of life existed. In such an uncomplicated place, she could readily distill her thoughts to only the ones that mattered.

Closing her eyes, Carolyn listened to the plodding hooves in the sand and felt the persistent heat from the sun on her head and shoulders. She was keenly aware of Bryan's strong hand covering hers, protecting her.

Carolyn turned to look at Bryan and gave him a contented smile. He had pulled out his cell phone, and with his free hand he snapped a photo of Carolyn. He turned and took a shot of Matt and Tikki. He then held it out in front of him and Carolyn and said, "Do me a favor. Take off your sunglasses."

She flipped them up on top of her head so that

they served as a headband, pulling back her hair from her face.

"You've decided, haven't you?" He still held the phone but hadn't snapped the shot yet.

Carolyn maintained her posed smile and glanced at him out of the corner of her eye.

"You're going to stay on here. You're going to give us a chance, aren't you, Carol Linda?"

As soon as he spoke the nickname he had given her that summer long ago, Bryan snapped the picture. She thought he had forgotten. He had dubbed her Carol Linda the last time they rode the camels. He told her the name meant "beautiful song," and that's what she was to him: a beautiful, Canary Island song.

Bryan held the phone close so he could review the shot and then showed it to Carolyn, as the camel sauntered down the ancient trail. "Tell me what you see," he said.

She saw Bryan smiling a fantastic smile a little too close to the camera to be entirely attractive. And she saw herself grinning ridiculously wide with glimmers of happy tears making her eyes misty.

"I see us," she said. "You and me. What do you see?"

"The future."

22

*"Lo que en los libros no está,
la vida te enseñará."*
"That which isn't in books, life will teach you."

FIVE MONTHS AFTER Bryan snapped the photo of their "future," Carolyn stood outside the open wooden doors of the Colon chapel. Inside, the pews were filled with people she loved.

The simple words on the plaque beside the ancient door brought Carolyn a familiar comfort.

EN ESTE SANTO LUGAR
ORO
COLÓN
1492

She, too, had come to this holy place to pray, as Columbus had before setting off on his journey to new worlds. However, her new world was here. And in a few minutes, one of her prayers was about to be answered.

The rest of the wedding party stood reverently waiting their moment to enter the shadowed chapel, where the fragrance of beeswax candles beckoned them to bow their hearts and offer up prayers of thanks.

Carolyn fingered the nape of her neck, making

sure all the strands of her coffee-colored hair were staying tucked up in the loosely pinned French twist. A few stray tendrils curled close to her face. Her fingers wrapped around the long stem of the single white calla lily, and she noted the shade of soft sunset pink her hugging manicurist had painted her nails. But she wore no rings on any of her fingers. Not yet.

This was Tikki's day.

Soon her daughter would walk down the aisle of this historic chapel and vow to love, honor, and cherish Matthew for as long as they both shall live.

Her motherly heart was filled as she tucked her chin and glanced over her shoulder one more time at her beautiful baby girl, adorned in white. Carolyn's thoughts couldn't help but tiptoe across the joy-strewn memories of the past five months and the two trips she had made back to California to list her house for sale and to help Tikki with wedding plans. Those were good days. As Columbus had said to his crew, "The time spent has been good. The time to come will be better."

She felt a wistful sadness when her house sold quickly and then again when her coworkers hosted a going-away party for her at the elementary school.

"You know, don't you," the principal had told her, "the rest of us are wishing we had an exotic place to run off to like you."

Carolyn hadn't told them about Bryan. It wasn't that she didn't want any of them to know. When she had returned to California the first time, their relationship had just begun to bud. Her commitment to Bryan was settled in her heart, but she wanted to give the new beginning a chance to blossom and open to a full-flowering bloom. They had time. And by the second trip, in the way all things should be in the islands, her heart was *tranquila,* and she didn't feel the need to announce any future plans. Their engagement would come at the right time.

Now Carolyn glanced up to the small bell chamber at the top of the chapel. Beyond the cross affixed to the very top, the blue autumn sky stretched across the heavens like an unending sea. On that placid blue a gathering of luxuriously floating clouds gazed down and bobbed along as if nodding their approval.

Then she heard it: the music began, and Carolyn knew.

This was her song. At last! It wasn't her wedding yet, but it was her song. She and Tikki had chosen it for the processional of the grandmothers and the mothers: "Ode to Joy."

Joyful, joyful, we adore Thee,
God of glory, Lord of love;
Hearts unfold like flow'rs before Thee,
Op'ning to the sun above.

Melt the clouds of sin and sadness;
Drive the dark of doubt away;
Giver of immortal gladness,
Fill us with the light of day!

Carolyn's mother went first, resting her arm gracefully on Matthew's tuxedoed arm. As the family's matriarch, she marched down the aisle with her lace shawl fluttering and her head held high.

In that moment of watching her mother move with such Canary Woman fortitude and elegance, Carolyn regretted that Marilyn hadn't come to the wedding. She had begged her sister to come, but she couldn't be persuaded. Bryan's stepsister, Angelina, declined her invitation as well.

None of those family conflicts mattered today. The people who waited inside the chapel formed the circle of her life in the Canaries.

Matt returned up the aisle, looking determined and glad. Carolyn slid her hand through his arm and made the journey down the runner, trying her best to emulate her mother's panache. She thought of Jeff for a fleeting, unsorrowful moment. He would have loved this. All of this. He would have loved walking his daughter down the aisle to marry this man.

When her moment came to fulfill her role as mother of the bride, Carolyn rose from the pew like a woman about to dance the flamenco—from the stomach up—and turned to face the back of the chapel. The guests all followed her lead. She felt as if her heart might burst with the joy and beauty of this moment. Down the aisle came Tikki, her arm linked through Bryan's.

Bryan gave Tikki's hand to Matthew and then took his place between Carolyn and her mother in the front pew. Carolyn slipped her left arm through Bryan's arm and placed her hand in his familiar hand.

As the young couple took their steps together toward the altar, the guests were asked to bow their heads as an opening prayer of dedication for the couple was offered. Carolyn closed her eyes, and her heart stepped into the place of mystery that no longer frightened her. She had once again found childlike delight in being open and vulnerable with God. She felt safe inside the enormity of God and his inexplicable ways.

The ceremony was simple, elegant, and God-honoring, just as Tikki and Matt had wanted it to be. They kissed each other with eagerness and innocence, the two best ingredients for love, and the two top ingredients they would take with them to their wedding bed that night. Carolyn and Bryan also had held on to those two ingredients as they mixed the recipe for their relationship. She gave his hand a squeeze and made a silent wish for a short engagement.

As soon as they were outside the chapel and

standing in the plaza in the bright autumn sunlight, Bryan leaned close and whispered to Carolyn, "Let's go to the fountain."

"Now? What about the reception and all the guests?"

Bryan took her by the hand. "No one will miss us if we're gone for five minutes."

Carolyn looked around. She knew he was right. The photographer was busy posing Tikki and Matthew and capturing the joyful expressions on their faces. Her mother was content to watch the photo shoot, and the guests were being treated to a final song before the ushers returned to dismiss them by rows.

The reception was going to be held in the private inner courtyard of Carolyn and Bryan's favorite renovated restaurant around the corner. They could leave for a while, and no one would miss them.

She gave him a whimsical grin. Bryan looked so handsome in his tux. Hints of summer's golden highlights remained in his short blond hair, and a youthful mischief shone in his blue-gray eyes.

"Come on," he coaxed.

For the second time in her life, Carolyn left her family to sneak off with Bryan Spencer. But this time everything was different because both of them were different. It wasn't just because they were older and wiser. It was because they were both familiar with the sort of transformation that takes place when a life is renovated by God's extravagant grace.

Bryan held Carolyn's hand close to his chest as they stole across the cobblestones and ducked around the corner. He led her to the fountain that had captured her glee the first time he had brought her here and she had watched two birds sip from the fountain and fly off toward the chapel.

Now she and Bryan were the two birds flitting from the chapel and finding refuge in the glistening spray of the free-flowing water. No one else was around as they approached. They perched on the edge and leaned in for a mutually initiated kiss.

"I have something to read to you," Bryan said. He slid his hand into the inside pocket of his tux jacket.

"Read to me? Now?"

"I think you'll like this." He pulled out a small book and opened to a page he had marked with a business card. "It's a book of Spanish quotes like the ones your mom and aunts are always saying."

Carolyn tried to hide her grin. "Did you find a good quote?"

"I think so. Have you heard this one? *'Aunque la mona se vista de seda, mona siempre queda.'*"

"No, I've never heard that one. What does it mean?"

"Although the monkey dresses in silk, she is still a monkey."

Carolyn gave his arm a swat. "That's why you brought me here? To read me insulting quotes? Are you saying I'm the monkey?"

"No, no, of course not! I just thought that one was funny. Here's the one I really wanted to read to you. *'No dejes para mañana lo que puedas hacer hoy.'* It means, 'Don't wait for tomorrow to do something you can do today.'"

He looked at her, as if she was supposed to see a hidden meaning.

"And this one is good, too," he said. *"'Cuando toca, toca.'"*

"I have heard that one." Carolyn remembered when her Aunt Frieda had quoted it to her at Marilyn's wedding. "It means, 'When it's your time, it's your time.'"

"Exactly." Bryan closed the book. He looked at Carolyn. "It's our time, Carolyn. I don't want to put off until tomorrow or any other day what I can do today, right now."

With unrushed and purposeful motions he slipped his hand back into the inside pocket of his tux coat, all the while keeping his eyes fixed on Carolyn.

Her heart pounded. A scattering of butterflies ruffled furiously in her stomach. She felt Bryan's strong grasp, as he reached for her hand and slipped the ring on her finger effortlessly. Their eyes were still locked as he silently asked the question her heart already had answered a hundred times since the moment Bryan took a picture of their future on the back of the camel.

His voice, resonating and rich, spoke to her over the sound of the fountain, as if deep were calling to deep. "I love you, Carolyn. I want to marry you and spend the rest of our lives together, loving God and serving each other. Will you be my wife? Will you give me the privilege of being your husband?"

Her answer was right on the surface and easily spilled over. "Yes. Yes, I will."

The kiss they shared was deep and unhurried, like their love.

As he pulled away, she looked down at her hand and gave a tiny gasp. The blue sapphire ring was exactly what she had wanted. "You remembered." She looked at him, scanning his expression.

"Yes, I remembered how much you liked it."

Carolyn admired close-up the ring that had caught her eye when they were at the jeweler's a few months ago shopping for a new battery for Bryan's watch. She had leaned over the case, watching the blue stone as it caught the light like the ocean on a summer day. Bryan had been watching. He remembered.

"I love this ring!" She kissed him again and whispered, "And I love you."

"I love you, too, Carolyn. You know that. It's time for us. Time to make our life together. The sooner the better."

"I agree. Oh, I love you, Bryan."

They kissed again.

Bryan drew Carolyn to her feet. He slid his arm around her waist, pulled her close, and for a brief moment the two of them swayed together, dancing in the sunlight as the spray from the fountain sprinkled them with its translucent, quickly evaporating confetti.

He lifted her ring-adorned hand up in the air, inviting Carolyn to take a spin the way he had learned to twirl her in the dance lessons they had been taking together from Lydia.

"Come on," he said. "I'll walk you to the party. We'll do the rest of our dancing with the others."

Hand in hand, Bryan and Carolyn headed for the inner courtyard where the guests would be gathering. As they walked, they discussed which one of the Women of the Canaries would be the first to discover the ring on Carolyn's finger. Carolyn said she guessed it would be Aunt Frieda; she was gifted at such observations.

"When she does, how about if I stand up and read one of the wise and witty sayings from my new book? The one about the monkey, perhaps?"

Carolyn laughed. There was still just enough bad boy concealed in Bryan to make him mischievous.

They spontaneously paused before entering the reception. With more whispered "I love you's," they exchanged a long, lingering shared smile, enjoying the final moment when their secret, this wonderful secret, was just between the two of them. Bryan kissed her warmly, and she responded with a soft kiss on the side of his smiling face.

The two of them had just stepped inside the restaurant's courtyard when Aunt Frieda appeared. "Why, there you two are! I was wondering where you went." She reached unsuspectingly for Carolyn's hand to draw her over to the designated table, and the busy aunt was rewarded with the find of the decade waiting on Carolyn's finger.

Aunt Frieda lifted Carolyn's hand and drew in a gasp.

Even before Bryan could pull out his book, Aunt Frieda trumped them with an Old World declaration:

*"Vivieron felices y comieron perdices
(y a mí no me dieron)."*

"They lived happily and ate partridge
(and didn't give me any)."

From the Author's Notes

I've made three trips to the Canary Islands. Each time it was at the invitation of my friend and fellow writer Anne. Just like Columbus, I discovered something different and wonderful on every visit.

Going for a camel ride was at the top of the "must do" list on my third visit to the island of Gran Canaria. Like Carolyn, I found the experience to be unforgettable and surprisingly relaxing.

Do you remember the scene in the story where the fisherman comes to the restaurant with fresh fish in a bucket and presents it to the owner as the catch of the day? I actually watched that happen when we were in Maspalomas and quickly shot this photo.

You may have noticed that I ended up describing a lot of food in this story. That's because Anne and I made it our little hobby to try all kinds of delicious meals while we were in Las Palmas. When this luncheon plate was delivered to me one afternoon I just had to take a picture. So fresh. So scrumptious.

My bravest food adventure was the sardines. Enough said.

Our absolute favorite food-find was the panna cotta at Al Macaroni. Melt-in-your-mouth deliciousness! Can you tell how much I'm enjoying this? I think this picture was taken on our third time back to the same café that week. The waiter told us in Spanish that he gave us extra chocolate this time because we told him a few days earlier how fantastic it was. On our last day we returned to Al Macaroni and got a different waiter who didn't know about our strong affection for the panna cotta. When we ordered it he said they were all out. We asked how that was possible, and he said some tourists had made so much noise about it everyone was trying it and now it was all gone. Tourists!

Anne's friend Christiana arranged for the three of us to take flamenco lessons. Our instructor was amazing, and after three lessons we were all feeling ourselves getting stronger and dancing "from the stomach up."

As I was writing the section about the camel ride, I pulled up this picture of Anne. I wanted to remember how it felt right after the camel rose and we began our uneven journey through the sand. You might notice something else in the photo that ended up in the story. Yes. The umbrella-shaped bougainvillea turned out to provide great inspiration.

The fountain where Carolyn and Bryan sat is a real fountain. It was easy to write about the way the sunlight illuminated the shimmering beads of water.

The chapel where—according to tradition—Columbus prayed is a real place. As Carolyn saw in the story, the sign by the door declares "Here prayed Columbus." The restaurant in the renovated house is also real, and the discovery of the tunnels to this chapel was quite a find. It is believed that those in need of sanctuary and protection would be quietly delivered to the house. They would escape through the secret tunnels and end up here where they would be safe.

Anne and I were both working on book projects while we were in the Canary Islands. When it came time to take a break, we would tell each other, "He makes me lie down in blue beach chairs," and then we'd head off here to the beach at Las Canteras.

Canary Island Song
Reading Group Guide

1. In the first chapter, Tikki tells Carolyn that she needs to get her own life. In what ways has Carolyn given up her life? How has each of these been resolved by the end of the story?

2. How does Carolyn's experience with Ellis affect her budding relationship with Bryan Spencer? How does emotional baggage affect your relationships? Read these verses and reflect: 1 Peter 5:7 and Romans 8:28.

3. What does Bryan's reaction to his stepsister's issues show about his character? What specifically has changed from the time he was a teenager?

4. Mother-daughter relationships are prominent in this story. What are the areas of strength in the relationships? What could the mothers and daughters work on to improve the relationships? Do you see any of these areas of strength or weakness in your mother-daughter relationships?

5. When Carolyn pampers herself with a manicure and pedicure she's congratulated for treating herself well. If congratulating others for

showing themselves kindness was a customary practice everywhere, how do you think our lives would be affected?

6. How does the adage "Live by the living and not by the dead" relate to Bryan's life? How does it tie into Carolyn's life? For Bryan, read Romans 6:4. For Carolyn, read Lamentations 3:31–33.

7. When Carolyn is learning flamenco, she tosses away a "bad apple" of anger from her life. This freed her to reconnect with God. Is there a poison in your life that God would have you toss away so that you can draw closer to him?

8. How do you think Tikki's trip to the Canary Islands affected this new step in her relationship with Matthew?

A Conversation with Robin Gunn

1. You chose a specific scripture quotation from Deuteronomy 4:9 to open your novel. What is it about this verse that caused you to select it for *Canary Island Song?*

I love the direction given in Deuteronomy for us to teach to our children what we have seen and heard in our lifetime. That's what happens between these three generations of women. Opening up our hearts and being truthful to the closest women in our lives allows space for healing to begin. That open, healed space provides room for love to grow. This is what happened to Carolyn when she finally told her mother the truth.

2. In the "From the Author's Notes," you mention that you've made three trips to the Canary Islands. Other than these trips, did you do much research on the Canary Islands and their culture while writing this book?

Yes. It's amazing what you can find on the internet! I also skimmed several travel books about the Canary Islands and while I was there I bought books in English about Christopher Columbus and one with local recipes. I think that's why food became such a big part of this story, because I had all the pictures and recipes to keep reminding me of the fabulous meals I enjoyed on each of my visits.

3. You also mention in "From the Author's Notes" that you and your friend Anne were both working on book projects while you were in the Canary Islands. Do you find the experience of writing in the company of a good friend to be different from writing alone? Which do you prefer?

I'd have to quote Winnie the Pooh on this one and say, "It's so much friendlier with two." Different books require different levels of concentration. I've been writing for so many years that to have the opportunity to be around a true Sisterchick while creating a new story was an exquisite treat. My favorite part of the process was when we would gather in the evening after a day of moving words around and read to each other what we'd composed that day. It's a much more fulfilling way for a writer to pull the curtain on that corner of the imagination than to simply turn off the computer and go to bed.

4. Where did you learn of the custom among the women of the Canaries to congratulate their sister when she "shows herself a kindness"? Were you ever congratulated for showing yourself a kindness on your trips to the islands?

This scene in the book is just about exactly what happened to Anne and me. We were on our way to the grocery store and decided to step inside a salon. We both had manicures and when we left the two young women in the salon "congratulated" us for showing ourselves a kindness. We loved the way that made us feel! For the rest of our visit we continued to show ourselves simple kindnesses and got in the habit of congratulating each other. It was amazing to meet so many women in the Canary Islands who all seemed to look out for us and for one another in this way.

5. Strong mother-daughter relationships are featured prominently in this novel. Why did you choose to explore these types of relationships? What about them is so important to you? Do you have a daughter? If so, were you influenced by your own relationship or experiences as a mother?

My daughter is twenty-five years old. She is an amazing, strong woman and she and I are very close. Over the past few years our conversations have deepened in many ways. I'm sure our relationship influenced me a lot as I was writing, even though I didn't intentionally set out to write a generational story. As a matter of fact, in the original draft of the first few chapters I don't think Tikki existed. Once I got into the story I realized Carolyn needed to have a daughter in her twenties and because of my daughter I had lots of relational ideas to draw from. My mother and my daughter both live more than twenty-five hundred miles away. I dearly value our visits.

6. Is there a particular character in *Canary Island Song* to whom you feel the most connected? If so, which character and why?

This might sound funny but the first character that came to mind when I read this question was Abuela Teresa. I think I feel connected to her because she reminds me of my grandmother who passed away seven years ago. My grandmother lived in Louisiana and always delighted in visits from our family. Those visits were infrequent because we all lived on the West Coast. My sister and I made several trips to see her together and we have great memories of those times. Now that I live on an island I feel the vast space of all those miles and I really treasure visits from my family.

7. Even though Carolyn's mom has no experience with dance, she is still excited to take flamenco lessons. You wrote the dance section with such vivid detail. Did you take lessons while you were in the Canary Islands?

Yes! As I mentioned in the photo section, Anne's friend set up a series of lessons for us. The experience was powerful and emotional because neither Anne nor I have ever felt coordinated at such things. But we tried and we learned and our instructor infused us with the thought that we were strong women and should carry ourselves in a way that demonstrated that strength. We took only three lessons and we know that it takes years to truly learn to dance flamenco. Just having a tiny taste of that world was a wonderful experience. On one of our last nights on the islands we went to see a world-class flamenco group from Madrid. The performance was astounding. You could feel the explosive power of the dance with each stomp and click of the heels. Amazing!

8. As you were writing this novel, was there ever any doubt in your mind that Carolyn and Bryan would end up together? How about Tikki and Matthew?

This was one of those stories when I knew how it was going to end before I knew how it was going to begin. At least I partly knew. I knew Carolyn was going to end up with Bryan because Bryan has been a character from the Christy Miller series that has stayed in my thoughts for years. I always wondered why he never remarried. It intrigued me to know Bryan's background and how he got to be where he is now. I knew I wanted to write about him in order to let my imagination tell me Bryan's story. I didn't know Tikki and

Matthew would end up together. Those two surprised me. I do think they are a terrific match, though. Matthew is another one of the Forever Friends in the Christy Miller books and I did want him to end up with someone extra special. I'm glad it was Tikki.

9. On your website (www.robingunn.com), you mention that you had not originally planned on becoming an author. What first inspired you to begin writing?

The inspiration came from a group of young teens who were reading a bunch of books on a church camping trip. I read a few of the books they'd brought with them and was concerned about the content of what they were putting into their thirteen-year-old hearts. I encouraged them to read books more suited for their age and they challenged me and said I should write a book for them. As a matter of fact, they'd help by telling me what to write. And they did. It took two years to finish the first Christy Miller book and I wanted to give up after the first ten rejection letters from publishers. But those girls kept pressing me onward and once that first book was accepted for publication we had a big party to celebrate. That was in 1988 and I haven't stopped writing.

10. More specifically, what was your inspiration for writing *Canary Island Song*?

My inspiration was similar to what prompted me to write Under a Maui Moon. *I wanted to write about a woman in midlife who needed to get her heart back. The older I get the more women I meet who have been through really difficult life situations. I've watched many of them curl up and let their lives become small. It's tragic, really, because as long as they are alive there is life to be lived and daily adventures to experience.*

In writing this story I wanted to explore what might happen with an average woman who is dealt a blow but finds that God is drawing her out of hiding and into a new, restorative season of life. I think it's a beautiful thing to be around a woman who has been through a terrible battle and managed to come out of it scarred but undefeated. She is strong and confident and exudes an unmistakable sense of joy as if she and Jesus have a secret. That sort of beauty is irresistible to those who are in the midst of the battle. We all need that picture of hope. That's been my prayer as I was writing this book—that the women who read this book might find the courage to ask God to give them their heart back. He still has dreams for you, you know. As Aunt Frieda would say, "A donde el corazón se inclina, el pie camina." *To where the heart is inclined the feet will follow.*

Center Point Publishing
600 Brooks Road ● PO Box 1
Thorndike ME 04986-0001 USA

(207) 568-3717

US & Canada:
1 800 929-9108
www.centerpointlargeprint.com